RETROGRADE

A Post-Apocalyptic Thriller

Part Three of The SpaceMan Chronicles

Tom Abrahams

A PITON PRESS BOOK

RETROGRADE

Cover Design by Hristo Kovatliev
Edited by Felicia A. Sullivan
Proofread by Pauline Nolet
Proofread by Patricia Wilson
Interior design by Stef McDaid at WriteIntoPrint.com

tomabrahamsbooks.com

FREE PREFERRED READERS CLUB: Sign up
for information on discounts, events, and release dates:

eepurl.com/bWCRQ5

WORKS BY TOM ABRAHAMS

THE SPACEMAN CHRONICLES
SPACEMAN: A POST-APOCALYPTIC THRILLER
DESCENT: A POST-APOCALYPTIC THRILLER
RETROGRADE: A POST-APOCALYPTIC THRILLER

THE TRAVELER POST-APOCALYPTIC/DYSTOPIAN SERIES
HOME
CANYON
WALL
RISING (FALL 2017)

POLITICAL CONSPIRACIES
SEDITION
INTENTION

JACKSON QUICK ADVENTURES
ALLEGIANCE
ALLEGIANCE BURNED
HIDDEN ALLEGIANCE

PERSEID COLLAPSE: PILGRIMAGE SERIES NOVELLAS
CROSSING
REFUGE
ADVENT

RED LINE: AN EXTINCTION CYCLE STORY

For Courtney, Sam, & Luke:
The stars at the center of my universe.

"The family is one of nature's masterpieces."

—George Santyana

CHAPTER 1

MISSION ELAPSED TIME
74 DAYS, 22 HOURS, 22 MINUTES, 12 SECONDS
DENVER, COLORADO

Clayton Shepard would have thought he was dreaming if the pain coursing through his body weren't so acute. Dreams, even nightmares, didn't hurt.

His quick but faltering pace toward the airport had slowed considerably since he'd begun, his path less than direct. His only assurance he was still headed in the right direction was the collection of artificial white peaks directly ahead. The sun was dropping fast and the cold air was harder to breathe. He pulled short, shallow breaths to lessen the sting.

"The glacier was easier," he slurred the moment before someone yelled at him.

The call echoed around him, but Clayton dismissed it. He thought he was hearing things.

He scanned the ground around him and then searched the horizon, working to focus on the grassy, rolling field between him and his destination. He kept walking until he heard the muffled, unintelligible command again. He didn't obey until a shot from an M4 zipped past his aching head.

"Stop right there!" the man barked. "Don't move. Raise your hands above your head."

1

Clayton stopped, his boots cementing themselves in the soft mud. He looked down at his chest and saw a half-dozen crimson dots dancing at what shooters called center mass. He touched his chest, the laser beams painting his hand. Through the throbbing in his head, the exhaustion, and the searing heat radiating from his injured leg, he couldn't tell what was real and what wasn't.

The ringing in his ears was getting worse. He mumbled, "Why are—"

The man repeated his order with less patience. "Raise your hands above your head!"

Clayton blinked, trying to find the source of the commands. He raised his hands but couldn't get them much past his shoulders. The stitch in his side wouldn't allow it.

"I'm trying," he said. "I think I've got broken ribs."

"Keep them as high as you can," said the man. "Do not react when my men approach you. They *will* shoot you."

Clayton winced against the sharp pain in his side, but he kept his hands as high as he could. Five men covered in shaggy green and brown camouflage ghillie suits materialized from the ground. With their weapons pulled to their shoulders and eyes they crouch-walked toward him. They stopped a few feet from him, weapons trained on his chest, forming a semicircle around him. The leader of the group rose from the ground and marched to join them. He halved the distance between Clayton and his men and lowered his weapon.

The man's face was painted with alternating stripes of green, tan, and brown. Only the whites of his eyes and teeth made him distinguishable from his outfit. Clayton still wasn't certain he was real.

"I'm going to pull the pack from your shoulders," he said. "Don't resist. Just relax and let me remove it. Is that understood?"

Clayton nodded.

The man walked around Clayton, circling him like an animal about to pounce, and grabbed the pack from behind. He wasn't gentle.

He grunted and walked around to face Clayton, holding up the pack. "What's this?"

The ringing softened for a moment and Clayton glanced past the alpha male and his team to the row of white peaks stretching skyward from the Denver International Airport Jeppesen Terminal. He couldn't be more than two hundred yards from it. He was so close. At least he thought he was. Was it a mirage? Was all of this a dream? His eyes strained to focus and look the soldier in the eyes.

"Survival gear."

The soldier's breath smelled like licorice. Strong black licorice. "For what?"

The ringing was worse. Clayton could barely hear himself speak. "Surviving."

The soldier leaned in, his face inches from Clayton. He shook the pack. "This is Russian. What are you doing with Russian survival gear?"

Clayton looked at the Cyrillic lettering on the pack. "I'm an astronaut," he said. "Do I smell licorice?"

The man narrowed his gaze before stepping back. A smile spread across his face. He tossed the heavy pack to one of his men.

"All right," he said. "You want to be coy. That's your prerogative. We'll let them handle you."

Clayton coughed and clenched his teeth against the bolt of pain in his side. He bent over and grabbed at his rib cage before dropping onto his knees. Each successive breath stung more than the last. The cold, dry mountain air didn't help. He squeezed his eyes shut.

The leader snapped another order. "Leigh, Turner, go check the aircraft. See if there are any survivors. Pull anything of value. They'll want to see it."

"Roger that," one of the men said. They marched past Clayton in the direction of the downed RV-8 he'd crashed.

"Who are you?" Clayton asked. "Who are *they*?"

The leader grabbed Clayton's elbow and forced him to his feet. "The real question here," he said, "is who you are."

Clayton leaned on the man and gripped a handful of the fabric strips at his shoulder. He leaned on his good leg and tried opening his eyes. A wave of nausea crashed through his body and he retched. The man let go and Clayton dropped to the ground on all fours.

"Sergeant," said the man holding the pack, "I think he's got a concussion."

"Could be," said the sergeant. "Looks like his leg is injured too. He's bleeding."

Clayton wiped the vomit from his chin with the back of his wrist. All of this seemed surreal. He tried to concentrate, tried to focus on what was happening, but couldn't. All that filtered through the sticky web of confusion was the realization that he couldn't concentrate or focus.

The world was spinning. Its gravity weighed heavy. Clayton choked back the sour bile that coated his tongue and throat and took as deep a breath as his lungs would allow. He leaned forward on his palms and grabbed at the grass.

"My name," he sputtered, "my name is Clayton Shepard. I'm an astronaut. I'm an astronaut."

Through the dog-whistle tone in his ears, he heard the men talking. He couldn't make out what they were saying. Everything was muddied. Only occasional words poked through.

"Gasoline."

"Maps."

"Russia."

"Transfer corral."

"Building four."

Building four? Transfer corral?

As Clayton slipped from consciousness someone lifted him from the ground and he felt the toes of his boots dragging in the mud. The men were taking him somewhere. Clayton tried protesting. He knew he needed to be somewhere else. He was late. He was running behind schedule. That much he remembered.

***

MISSION ELAPSED TIME
75 DAYS, 0 HOURS, 04 MINUTES, 45 SECONDS
DENVER, COLORADO

Clayton could see the bright artificial light before he blinked open his eyes. It was piercingly white and aggravated the thick ache in the back of his head and at his temples. He was so focused on adjusting his vision to the blinding glow it wasn't until he tried blocking it with his hands that he realized he was bound at the wrists and ankles.

He tugged at the nylon straps holding him flat against a bed. As his vision gradually returned, he noticed the plastic tubing running from an infusion pole into an intravenous catheter taped to his forearm just above the nylon bind.

The soft, rhythmic beep of a heart monitor was nearby. Clayton scanned the sterile room. To one side of the bed was a surgical tray littered with instruments, bandage packages, and bloodied gauze. On the other was an array of monitors and scopes. There was a sink and a fire-engine-red sharps disposal container mounted to the wall above it.

It looked like any number of ordinary doctor's offices or hospital rooms he'd seen. But it clearly wasn't ordinary. The cinder-block walls were barren except for a spray-painted stencil that read C4L4 STALL 8 and a camera perched high in one corner. A red light above the lens was blinking. It was aimed at the bed. Clayton tugged again against the binds and the heartrate monitor kept pace with his elevated pulse. All that was missing was the proverbial alien probe, but the usual placement for that instrument was the only place on his body that didn't ache.

"Hey!" he tried calling for help. His voice was little more than a scratchy rasp. Nobody would hear him. He looked directly into the camera and tried speaking again.

"Help," he squeaked.

From behind him and out of his field of vision came a pneumatic hiss followed by the shuffling of feet. He tried craning his neck to look over his shoulder, but it wasn't until a trio of people arrived at his bedside he could see who'd entered his room.

Clayton knew one of them as the ghillie-suited sergeant from the field. Although his face was clean of war paint, Clayton recognized the man's eyes and the way his mouth curled downward into a frown at both ends. The others were also in uniform.

"My name is Van Cleaf," said one of them. She was a tall woman who carried herself with her shoulders pulled back. "This is Sergeant Vega. I believe you've met."

Clayton eyed the sergeant and offered a subtle nod of recognition before returning his attention to Van Cleaf. She motioned to a burly, bearded man standing at her other shoulder. "This is Perkins. He will be handling the debrief."

Clayton's brow furrowed. "What debrief?"

Van Cleaf stepped back from the bed. She nodded at Perkins and disappeared from Clayton's field of view.

"What debrief?" he asked again, his voice little more than a sandpaper whisper. "Why am I restrained?"

Perkins edged to the bed, his thighs pressing against its edge. His voice resembled the low rumble of a motorcycle exhaust pipe.

"We've stitched you up," he said. "We've pumped you full of meds. You were pretty banged up from the crash, but you'll be good. You'll recover."

Clayton studied Perkins's leathery face. The beard covered barely visible scars along his cheek and neck. There wasn't much benevolence there and he sensed there was a "but" coming.

Perkins sniffed, contorting his offset nose. "But," he said as if on cue, "our kindness comes with a price."

"I have insurance," Clayton muttered.

Perkins chuckled, patted Clayton on the leg, and nudged Sergeant Vega. "Funny guy here, right?"

Vega's blank expression was unmoved. He didn't even blink. His eyes stayed focused on Clayton like a dog seeking dominance.

The smile evaporated from Perkins's face. He scratched his beard. "Look, this is a give and take. You give; we don't take. We ask questions; you answer. I'd prefer not to escalate this to a typical interrogation. That's up to you though."

Clayton exhaled and pushed his voice. "I'll answer questions when you tell me who you are and where I am."

Vega leaned in, his lip curling in a snarl. "You entered restricted space with an unauthorized aircraft. You were armed. You were carrying gear supplied by the Russian government. We are the ones charged with finding out what exactly your intentions are."

Perkins shrugged. "You now know where you are and who we are."

Clayton tensed against the binds and tried to sit up. He clenched his jaw, gnashing his teeth against the ache in his side.

"You have two fractured ribs," Perkins said.

Clayton relaxed and sank into the bed. He looked into the bright light directly above his head before closing his eyes.

Perkins jabbed at his hip with a knotty finger. "Who are you?"

"My name is Clayton Shepard," he replied, answering as clearly as he could. "I'm an American astronaut."

Perkins sighed. "Vega told me you said that. Said you claimed to fall from orbit. Said you babbled about a dead cosmonaut and somebody named Ben."

Clayton snapped open his eyes. He didn't remember having divulged that. His expression must have betrayed his surprise.

"You were out of it when you talked," said Perkins. "You didn't say how you got off the space station or how you managed to get a plane with a Canadian tail number."

"Complicated," said Clayton. "Basically used Soyuz. Other two crewmates died from CME. I brought them back."

"Where are they?"

"Canada," said Clayton. "I landed in Canada."

"That's where you got the plane?"

Clayton nodded. His throat was on fire. "Where am I?" he whispered.

Perkins's chest expanded as he took a deep, contemplative breath. He flexed his hands, cracking his distended knuckles before patting Clayton on his leg.

"Tell me more about the Russian gear," he said.

Clayton shook his head. "Nothing to tell. It's from the Soyuz."

"Why were you coming here?"

Clayton tugged at the wrist restraints. "Can you let me out of these?"

"Why did you come here?"

"Could you please—"

Perkins voice deepened. "Answer the question."

"But—"

Perkins growled. "Answer the—"

"Stop." It was a new voice, one Clayton hadn't heard before. It was coming from the door behind him and moving closer. "Perkins, is it?"

"Who are you?" Perkins said, looking toward the new visitor.

The man appeared at Clayton's side and offered the wounded astronaut a sympathetic, if not pitying, smile. He edged himself next to Perkins and gripped the nylon cuff.

Perkins's eyes widened and his face reddened. "What are you doing?" he snarled. "Who are you?"

The man wasn't in uniform. His hair was cropped short and graying at the temples. His lips were squeezed into a permanent smirk, as if he knew something nobody else did. He unbuckled the strap and freed Clayton's wrist and motioned to the other one with his chin. "You can do the other one yourself."

"Thank you." Clayton carefully reached across his body and started manipulating the strap's buckle. It was difficult. His stiff fingers were thick and swollen, but he managed and freed his other hand.

At the same time, Perkins was jawing with the stranger who'd yet to identify himself. He was yelling at him, calling him names, poking his finger in the man's chest. The sergeant had stepped closer and had the man bracketed. Apparently his job was to keep the intruder in his spot. When Perkins took a breath, the man folded his arms across his chest. The smirk on his face hadn't changed. Clayton noticed all three of them were wearing identical watches.

"You finished yet?" he asked. "You done with your little tirade? If so, I'll be happy to answer your myriad of questions."

Perkins eyed the sergeant and grunted.

"My name is Chip Treadgold," he said. "I presume by your facial hair and overly developed musculature that you and I work for the same people but in far different capacities."

Perkins looked the stranger up and down and chuckled. "I doubt that. You're wearing the same thing as the rest of the herd."

Treadgold looked down at his shirt and pants. He tugged at the shirttail, straightening out the wrinkles. "I'm blending in," he said. "I came on the buses with the 'herd' so I could observe."

Clayton rubbed the soreness from his wrists and listened intently to a conversation he didn't understand. *Herd? Blending in?*

"You don't have any authority here," stressed Perkins. "This is my interrogation. He is a perceived threat. I handle all—"

Treadgold held up a finger and then pulled a device from his back pocket. It looked to Clayton like an iPhone, but different. He pressed the screen and used his thumbs to type. The device clicked with each tap.

"Let's get Van Cleaf in here," Treadgold said. "You ask her what authority I have." He looked over at Clayton with the same omniscient smirk he'd carried since walking into the room. He walked to the end of the bed and, one at a time, unbuckled the ankle straps. A smile spread across his face, momentarily replacing the smirk. He played with a ring on his finger, spinning it in circles.

"That should feel better," said Treadgold. "No need to have you restrained. It's not as though you're in good enough shape to run anywhere."

The door hissed and someone entered the room. "What's the issue here?" It was Van Cleaf, the woman to whom Treadgold had referred. She joined the others at the side of Clayton's bed.

"Why is he unrestrained?" she asked. "We don't know—"

Treadgold stepped toward Van Cleaf with a raised hand. "We know he's not a threat in his current condition. Why complicate matters by making him feel like more of a prisoner than he already is?

9

That makes no sense."

Perkins scowled. "I was in the middle of asking questions when he shows up. He says he has authority to be here."

Van Cleaf frowned. "He does," she said. "He's got the highest-level clearance, but he's embedded with the others so we have eyes on the herd. He's not the only one. There are a couple in every building."

"Excuse me," Clayton squeaked. "Where am I? What *is* this place?"

Van Cleaf, Treadgold, and Perkins exchanged glances. The sergeant stood in the corner of the room. His arms were folded at his chest and his upper lip was curled as if he'd smelled something rotten.

"This is a secure facility," said Van Cleaf. "We're preserving civilization here."

Perkins sneered. "You got lucky, 'astronaut'. You found one of the few safe places left on Earth."

Clayton pushed himself onto his elbows. "What does that mean?"

Treadgold played with his ring. "It means the world is dark. Two coronal mass ejections have seen to that. Soon enough, we believe the world will devolve into chaos. The herd up there will thin. The herd down here will multiply. Eventually, we'll resurface and begin anew."

Clayton studied their faces. They were serious. "We're underground?"

"Yes," said Van Cleaf.

Clayton's pulse quickened. His palms were suddenly damp with perspiration. His mind raced with this newfound problem to solve. He had to get out. He had to find his family. He had to protect them.

"I can't stay here," he said. "I need to get home to my wife and kids in Texas. I can't stay."

Van Cleaf's eyes narrowed with confusion. She tilted her head to one side. "You don't understand, do you?" she asked Clayton. "You can't leave."

CHAPTER 2

Vihaan Chandra had his hands stuffed in his pockets and was walking the corridor back to his room when he passed a group of men talking amongst themselves. He heard the words *captured* and *intruder* and slowed his pace.

"They've got him in building four is what I heard," said one of them.

"He's a Russian spy," said another. He kept talking but had moved too far from Chandra for the scientist to hear the rest of the conversation.

Russian spy?

He picked up his pace, found his way to his room, and immediately reached into his pocket for the DiaTab and keyed on the Telenet screen on the wall in front of his bed. The screen came to life; Chandra pressed the glass screen on his DiaTab and spoke into it.

"How many buildings are there in this complex?"

The icon at the bottom of the screen spun and flipped as the machine's algorithms worked to find an answer. Van Cleaf's image, the one he'd seen from the welcome message, appeared on the display.

"There are five buildings here. Buildings one, two, and three are virtually

11

identical. They contain three levels of housing units like yours, a dining level, and a transfer level."

He pushed the DiaTab's glass. "What is in building four?"

Van Cleaf's image froze as the computer found the answer. Then she jerked to life, *"Building four has a command level and a transfer level."*

"That's only two levels," said Chandra. "There should be five. What else is in building four?"

"Building four," said the avatar, *"has a command level and a transfer level."*

Chandra paced the tiny room. The rabbit hole, it seemed, was bottomless. The deeper he dug, the deeper it went. These people, his boss Treadgold included, were hiding things.

"What is in building five?" he asked. The response was almost immediate.

"I'm sorry. I don't understand your question. Could you rephrase it, please?"

Chandra stepped closer to the Telenet. He spoke into the DiaTab. "How many buildings are there in this complex?"

"There are five buildings here," the system reiterated. *"Buildings one, two, and three are virtually identical. They contain three levels of housing units like yours, a dining level, and a transfer level."*

Chandra curled his free hand into a fist and clenched his jaw. He thumbed the glass DiaTab screen with force and said through his teeth, "If there are five buildings, why can't you tell me what's in buildings four and five?"

The icon swirled in the corner and the Van Cleaf avatar reset before the machine spit out its preprogrammed algorithmic response.

"I'm sorry. I don't understand your question. Could you rephrase it, please?"

Chandra tossed the DiaTab onto the bed and ran his hands through his hair before plopping onto the bed himself. He leaned against the wall, pulled his knees up to his chest, and leaned his head back, resting it on the cement wall. He'd just closed his eyes to focus on the myriad of thoughts running through his head when the Telenet beeped an alert with a series of tones that resembled an incoming call on a smartphone.

Chandra turned to look at the monitor. It was black with a

message displayed in green lettering.

YOU HAVE A NEW INCOMING MESSAGE
PRESS ACCEPT ON DIATAB TO VIEW

He reached onto the bed and found the DiaTab. Holding it with one hand, he thumbed the ACCEPT button. The screen dissolved to black and transitioned to an image of a man he'd not seen before. His eyes were hidden behind large black-framed glasses. His mustache was wiry and complemented by what Chandra imagined was several days of scruff on his face and jawline. His head was bald save the few strands of hair he carried from one side to the other of his tanned scalp. He was alternately looking at the camera and a DiaTab in his hand.

"Hello, Dr. Chandra. My name is Henry Rector," he said. *"I'm the lead for our meteorological division in building four and you are assigned to work with me. We have a lot of work to do in the next few days. I'll need you to come over here and get acquainted with our setup."*

Chandra turned his body from the wall and dropped his feet to the floor. He slid the volume scale on the DiaTab and turned up the volume. Then he keyed the microphone. "Is this message live?" he asked. "Are you talking to me right now, Mr. Rector?"

There was a momentary pause before Rector pushed his glasses up the bridge of his nose and nodded. *"Yes,"* he said. *"I am speaking with you in real time through our video-conferencing network. Do you have any questions?"*

Chandra chuckled. "Too many to count," he said. "You're able to see me?"

"Yes," said Rector. *"There's a small camera embedded in the bezel of your Telenet display. I can see you're sitting on your bed. Your eyes have shifted from looking at me on your display to the camera in the bezel. Now you're getting up and walking toward the camera."*

Chandra stepped to the monitor and squinted at the small circular lens in the center of the top edge bezel. "I hadn't noticed it before," he said. "That's creepy."

Rector pushed his glasses again. *"Why? It's no different from a webcam atop a standard computer."*

"Yeah," said Chandra, "but I know that's there."

"Now you know it's there," Rector said flatly. *"Any other questions, or can you come to building four?"*

Chandra shrugged, still eyeing the almost imperceptible camera lens. "Sure," he said. "Do I need to bring anything?"

"Just your DiaTab, please," said Rector. *"Take the elevator to the transfer level. You'll be guided to the tram for building four. I'll be waiting for you there. You'll see me when you step off the tram."*

Chandra acknowledged the instructions and turned off the Telenet. He crossed his small room, letting his fingers trail on the edge of his desk and he passed it, and walked into the bathroom. He flipped the faucet and let the water run, pulling a white cotton towel from the rack next to the mirror.

While the water heated, he studied his reflection and almost didn't recognize himself. His eyes carried heavy bags underneath them. His cheekbones appeared more pronounced. His brown skin was dry and his hair was a mess. He tugged at his eyelids, leaning into the mirror to get a closer look at the red web of capillaries that shot across his eyes. The last time he remembered looking this fatigued was in graduate school. Then he'd had access to unlimited amounts of cheap, syrupy coffee. That had made the forced insomnia palatable. He hadn't had any coffee, or caffeine for that matter, since he'd left the Space Weather Prediction Center.

Steam formed at the bottom of the mirror and Chandra dipped his hands into the hot water. It stung at first, but his skin adapted and he bent over to splash handfuls of the water on his face. With his eyes closed, he fumbled for the soap dispenser and pumped out a handful. He massaged the dollop onto his skin, feeling his pores tighten. He washed off the residue and flipped the faucet to cold. He splashed his face again, almost losing his breath from the icy water. He lifted his head and turned off the faucet. He looked at the water dripping down his face. He licked his lips with a renewed energy and dried his face with the plush towel.

Something as simple as washing his face hadn't ever felt so cleansing, so purposeful. He wondered how many of life's mundane rituals would become more substantial, more life-affirming, the longer he lived in the post-CME world. He sucked in a deep breath of filtered air, filling his lungs before exhaling.

"Time to go," he said to himself and faked a smile in the mirror. He grabbed the DiaTab off the bed, left his room, and trudged along the long hallway back to the elevators. Others dressed in the same drab clothing as he passed him on their way back to their rooms. All of them were men, which was unsettling. He still didn't understand the separation of sexes or the naming of the different areas.

He walked from the INTACT section of level five, following the stencil-painted arrows on the walls. As he neared the corridor that led to the elevators, he saw women walking from the OPEN area of the level. One woman glanced up from her DiaTab and offered a demure smile.

Chandra, overriding his timidity with his curiosity, caught the woman's attention. "Excuse me," he said. "You are assigned to the OPEN area?"

The woman looked at him, glanced over her shoulder, and then nodded. "Yes," she said softly. "Why?"

Chandra kept walking toward the elevator and kept pace with the woman. "Just wondering," he said. "Is it all women over there?"

The woman's eyes narrowed as if she hadn't considered the segregation. "I guess it is," she said. "I hadn't thought about it. I've been too preoccupied with all of this technology."

She held up her DiaTab, tightly gripping the sides of the glass device. "I was just getting settled when they called me to go to my job. I had no idea I'd have a job."

"Me too," said Chandra. "Where are you working?"

"I'm a software engineer," she said. "They have me in systems and operations."

Chandra stopped walking and offered his hand. "I'm Vihaan," he said. "I'll be working in meteorology."

"I'm Sally," she said, stopping beside him. "A scientist, huh?"

"Yes," he said. "You said you were struggling with the technology, but you're a software engineer?"

"I didn't suggest I was struggling. I said I was preoccupied. I'm fascinated by its intuitive capacity."

Chandra's cheeks flushed. "My apologies," he said, looking at his feet. "I didn't mean—"

Sally laughed as they reached the elevator. "It's fine, Vihaan. I'm not some snowflake who's offended by everything. Are you headed up now?"

He punched the call button. "Yes. Building four. You?"

"Same," she said. She stretched her hands above her head, revealing a shiny object tucked at her waist.

Chandra pointed at it. "What's that?"

Sally felt at her waist and touched the object. She chuckled. "Oh, that's my pocketknife. I keep it with me all the time. You can't trust anybody these days."

"Good idea," said Chandra.

The doors to the elevator whooshed open and the familiar uniformed guard greeted the pair. Another man rushed into the car before the doors closed. The guard surveyed the three before asking their destinations.

"Feed," said the new passenger. "Level two."

"We're both level one," said Sally. "Transfer, please."

The guard pressed the corresponding buttons. The elevator surged upward and Chandra felt the gravity push him into his shoes. He grabbed onto a stainless steel waist-high railing and kept his balance as the car rushed upward. It slowed almost as fast and the doors opened for the man to exit at the feed level. The doors closed and in an instant Chandra and his new acquaintance were at the transfer level.

They followed the directions to the main tram, the one that had carried them from underneath the Jeppesen Terminal to this new subterranean world. A lighted sign above the track indicated they had two minutes to wait.

Chandra broke the awkward silence. "Software engineer?"

"Yes," she said. "I helped design weapons systems for a prominent defense contractor in Colorado Springs. Guidance and telemetry mostly. You? You're a weatherman?"

Chandra smirked. "In a manner of speaking," he said. "My expertise is in high-altitude and space weather."

Sally raised her eyebrows and ran her long, thin fingers through her strawberry blond bob, whisking stray strands away from her eyes. "Like the solar flares that hit Earth?"

He hesitated. Solar flares weren't the same thing as coronal mass ejections. A lot of people got them confused. Both flares and CMEs were rapid, dramatic releases of energy and both disrupted the solar corona, but they were distinctly different phenomena. Normally, he'd bristle at someone making that common mistake. It was like nails on a chalkboard. But here, in this place, with this woman, Chandra bit his lip.

He nodded. "Exactly," he said. "Just like that."

She smiled. "That's fascinating," she said as the train whooshed into the terminal. "I'd love to learn more about that."

Chandra felt a fluttering in his tightened chest that momentarily made it difficult to breathe. He nodded. "Sure."

The doors slid open and he motioned for Sally to enter the cabin first. She stepped across the threshold and grabbed onto a pole planted in the middle of the car. Chandra followed her and gripped the same pole just beneath her hands.

A sterile voice announced the train's departure for building two, the doors closed, and the train accelerated along the tracks. Chandra felt the inertia pulling his body slightly outward. The tracks were curved, something he hadn't noticed on his arrival.

They made brief stops at buildings two and three, with their identical "transfer corral" terminals, and then headed for their destination. Neither of them spoke during the short trip and both exited the train to find supervisors awaiting them in the building four corral.

Sally ran her fingers through her hair, pulling it from her face. "I'll see you later?" she asked. "Breakfast tomorrow?"

Chandra glanced at the lab-coated Rector just ahead of him and self-consciously nodded at Sally. "I'd like that," he said and then turned his attention to his new boss, extending his hand.

Rector was much shorter than he'd appeared on the monitor. He couldn't have been more than five feet tall. He reached up and took Chandra's hand, shaking it vigorously before abruptly letting go. He pushed his glasses up the bridge of his nose and sniffed.

"It's nice to meet you, Dr. Chandra," he said. "I trust you got here without any issues?"

Chandra motioned toward the painted stencil on the wall marking the BUILDING 4 TRANSFER CORRAL. "Yes," he said. "It's hard to get lost with directions posted everywhere. I feel like I'm in a factory or a processing plant."

Rector's left eye twitched, but he otherwise didn't react. "Follow me," he said, dipping his hands into his lab coat's wide pockets. He marched with short, quick steps to the elevator at the far left end of the corral. The doors opened and he stepped into the car, directing the uniformed guard to level four. He offered his DiaTab to the guard, who held it up to a wall-mounted scanner before pressing the button on the elevator's number bank. He handed the device back to Rector, who turned to Chandra with a raised eyebrow.

"Do you have your DiaTab?" he asked. "You'll need it. We'll get it updated with the appropriate Quick Response Access Code once we reach the lab. You won't be able to get into the building without it."

Chandra patted his back pocket. "I have it," he said. "So what is level four?"

Rector's eye twitched. He sniffed, crinkling his nose. "Meteorology, Climatology, and Environmental Engineering."

Environmental Engineering?

Chandra watched the floor indicator change from two to three to four. The elevator eased to a stop and the doors opened to a resonant, ambient hum, revealing a space straight out of a science fiction novel.

The flooring, unlike the other levels he'd visited, was made of large lacquered black square tiles that Chandra recognized as those used to cover electronic cabling. When he stepped across it into the lobby awash in the blue glow of wall-to-wall Telenet monitors, it clicked with the hollow sound of a false floor. The flooring reflected the variety of LED colors flashing across the displays. There were no spray-painted labels marking the direction of various "corrals" or "levels". Everyone appeared to know exactly where they were headed without guidance. It was as if they had a familiarity with the space acquired after having worked there for weeks or months.

Men and women, all of them wearing identical white lab coats and carrying DiaTabs, hurriedly moved across the lobby area. All of them appeared deep in their work, preoccupied by whatever was on the screens of the handheld glass devices. Their shoes squeaked and clicked across the floor. It was as impressive as it was unsettling.

"You can gawk later," said Rector. "We have work to do, Dr. Chandra. Please follow me."

When they walked past the monitors, Chandra noticed they displayed video from outdoors. The monitors individually cycled through what appeared to be a series of cameras. Some of them, however, didn't appear to be at their facility. It was nighttime in Colorado, but some of the displays showed daylight. A couple of them were trained on a coastal region, another in the middle of an empty metropolitan street.

Rector huffed. "This way," he said and led Chandra into a darkened corridor. As they moved into the hallway, overhead lights flickered to life, their steps triggering the illumination. Chandra expected a Xenomorph from the *Alien* movie franchise to burst from the darkness, slime him, and rip him to shreds.

Rector plodded forward, his feet clicking on the hollow flooring until he stopped at a door at the end of the hallway. The door was marked only with the number 29 at its center. Next to it was a display slightly larger than the DiaTab.

Rector waved his wrist and DiaWatch over the display. A voice prompted his next move.

"Hello, Henry Rector," it said. *"Please state your full name and place your face directly in front of the screen."*

Rector angled his body to comply and said his full name. The voice directed him to stand still while a laser scanned his eye.

"Thank you, Henry Rector. Admission granted."

The screen went black and the door slid open with a metallic click. Rector walked through the door, ushering Chandra into the room beyond the threshold, and the door clicked again, sliding shut behind them.

Rector offered Chandra a hint of a smile. "This is our work space," he said. "You'll be here several hours a day on most days. We have a good team, I think. It's still coming together, of course, given the recency of the activation."

Chandra planted his hands on his hips and looked around the room. There were a dozen workstations, each of them with a sextet of curved monitors. Three were occupied. At the maple-colored desks were three men, each of them wearing lab coats identical to Rector's. They each wore a microphone-equipped headset and palmed a large mouse, which they slid across the desks. Chandra recognized the predictive modeling software on some of the monitors. Others appeared to be satellite imagery, which was odd, because Chandra was under the impression all satellites were down.

Rector referenced one of the empty workstations. "You'll be over here," he said. "You've got a Kameleon suite of software working on this display. The SWX2 Java 3-D model is accessible here."

Chandra was familiar with both of the space weather data models. He'd used them at NOAA.

Rector puffed his chest. "What's fantastic about the SWX2 we've got running here is the proprietary upgrades we commissioned for the magnetosphere and heliosphere. They're incredible at rendering beautiful analytics. Take a look."

Chandra followed Rector's lead and took a seat at his terminal, sinking into the ergonomic seat. He rested his elbows on the desk and took the mouse in one hand, his eyes dancing from display to display.

A hand dropped onto his shoulder. "Better than what you had at the Prediction Center, isn't it?"

Chip Treadgold stepped into Chandra's peripheral vision and then sidled up to the workstation. He was wearing the same issued clothing as Chandra. He crossed his arms, revealing his new DiaWatch. He smiled.

"Higher tech, right?"

Chandra looked at Treadgold and over his shoulder at Rector. He scanned the room. The other workers were engrossed in whatever they were doing. He became acutely aware of the hum of the computers and the hiss of their internal cooling systems. His eyes drifted back to Treadgold and he nodded.

"Yes," he said. "Much more advanced. I didn't know we had some of these capabilities."

Treadgold chuckled, patted Chandra's shoulder, then squeezed it. There's a lot you didn't know."

CHAPTER 3

Jackie's fists tightened and she dug her fingernails into her palms. The same obstinate guard who'd denied her entrance to Johnson Space Center four days earlier was somehow less helpful.

She and her party stood exhausted at the front gate to JSC. In addition to the guard, a pair of armed soldiers stood watch. They didn't react to the guard's unwillingness to help. Instead, they stared off into the darkness as if programmed not to interfere, even when incompetence was evident.

The air was damp enough that Jackie was sweating despite the breezy chill that came with a late January cool front. She unballed her fist and wiped her brow with the back of her hand.

"I need to speak with Irma Molinares," she said. "Please get her on the phone."

The guard sighed. "As I've repeated several times now, protocol will not allow your entire party to enter the property. The only names I have on the list are yours and your children. That's it. We've been given strict instructions not to—"

Jackie stepped uncomfortably close to the guard. "Not to what?" she snapped. "Let the wife of a missing astronaut speak to the crew support for his mission? Are you seriously stupid? Did they give you a walkie-talkie and all of a sudden you think you have power? Do you—"

Marie touched Jackie's arm, gently coaxing her back a step. "Mom," she said softly, "he's only doing his job. It's not his fault."

Jackie bristled and then relaxed. She looked at Marie and then at the ground. "You're right." She nodded. "I'm sorry. I shouldn't have demeaned you. I need your help. I know you're capable of helping."

The guard stood unflinchingly silent. He tugged on his utility belt and shifted the buckle.

Jackie clasped her hands in prayer as she spoke. "Would you please call Irma Molinares? One call. If she doesn't answer or won't talk to me, we'll go away. I promise."

The guard shrugged. "One call?"

Jackie held up a finger. "One."

"Then you'll leave?"

Jackie pulled her clasped hands to her mouth. "Please," she whispered.

The guard sucked in a deep breath and exhaled loudly. He stepped into the booth and placed the phone call. Jackie could hear the muffled sound of the phone ringing on the other end. Once. Twice. Three times.

The guard looked over at Jackie and moved his finger to the telephone switch hook. It hovered over the button. Four rings. Five. Six.

"There's nobody—"

Jackie pleaded. "Two more rings?"

Seven.

"*MCC. Hello?*" came the muted voice answering the call. Jackie sighed with relief.

"Yes," said the guard and introduced himself. "I've got a visitor here looking for Irma Molinares." The guard paused, listening to the voice on the other end. "Jackie Shepard."

The voice said something Jackie couldn't understand and the guard moved the receiver from his mouth, cupping it with his hand. "They're getting her," he said and held out the phone toward Jackie.

His cheeks were flushed red.

"Thank you," Jackie said. She stepped to the booth and took the phone. "Again, I'm sorry."

The guard waved her off. "It's fine," he said flatly.

Jackie drew the phone to her ear. A familiar voice greeted her after a series of clicks.

"Jackie? It's Irma. Are you here at JSC?"

"Yes."

"Great," said Irma. *"I'll be out in a few minutes if you can hang on."*

"It's not just me," said Jackie. "I've got people with me."

The line was silent for a moment; then Irma said, *"Jackie, we explicitly told you that the invitation only included you and the chil—"*

Jackie was ready for the challenge. She'd thought about what to tell Irma during the long tense walk from her house to JSC. Over and again in her head, she ran through the conversation until she'd settled on pity and guilt. If NASA knew armed robbers had attacked them in her home, she hoped her appeal to their collective sense of mercy would lead them to forego their rules.

"I know what you told me, Irma," she replied. "I also know we had a violent home invasion last night. Three people died in my house. I wasn't about to leave anyone behind."

Another hesitation. *"How many people?"*

"Five plus me and the kids," said Jackie. "Eight total."

"Hang on," said Irma. She returned to the line an agonizing minute later. *"Okay. We'll accommodate all of you. For now."*

Jackie didn't hesitate or question what "for now" meant. She wasn't pressing her luck. She smiled wide, gave a thumbs-up to the group, and thanked Irma repeatedly. A half hour later they were inside the gate, crossing the sixteen-hundred-and-twenty-acre campus toward building 30-A.

Inside 30-A was the Mission Operations Directorate. It was adjacent to buildings 30-M and S, which housed the former and current Mission Control Center. NASA had set up cots in the hallways and in some offices, and the place looked to Jackie more like a Red Cross shelter than an administrative headquarters.

She walked along a hallway on the first floor, following an armed soldier and leading her children, Nikki, Betty and Brian Brown, and Pop and Nancy Vickers. They'd traveled what felt like a crowded maze, weaving in and out until they came to what looked to Jackie like a lobby. On the wall was a large circular emblem. Across the middle it read "Mission Operations". Above it, circling the logo along the top, were four Latin words: *"Res Gesta Per Excellentiam"*, "Achieve Through Excellence". Jackie's eyes lingered on the words and image of a rocket blasting into space. An image of Clayton flashed into her mind and she bit her lip, pressing hard with her teeth to fight back the wave of sadness threatening to force tears. Irma Molinares bounded around the corner, flanked by two men. They weren't the same men who'd visited her home.

Irma smiled sympathetically and extended her arms wide for a hug. "Jackie," she said. "I'm glad you decided to come."

Jackie reciprocated the embrace. "Thank you for letting my friends come along. I couldn't leave them. I—"

Irma pulled away and waved her off. "No further explanation needed. We've got space for all of you in one of the empty offices. It's sleeping bags and lumpy pillows, but it'll do."

"It'll be fine," said Jackie. She reintroduced the Browns and the Vickers, and the group followed Irma up a flight of stairs and into an office. A laminate desk and matching bookshelf were shoved into a corner next to the lone window. There were rolled cotton sleeping bags and small pillows stacked on the desk.

Pop Vickers pointed to the overhead light. "You have power here?"

"For now," said Irma. "We're not running on full power. We're trying to conserve as much as we can. Any other questions?"

"Bathrooms?" asked Betty Brown.

"Of course," said Irma. "Down the hall and to the right. No showers on this floor, but there is a lock on the bathroom door, so you'll have privacy enough to use the sink."

Betty twisted her lips with disapproval. "The sink?"

Irma shrugged. "While I know it's not ideal, it's the best we have right now. There is food in the cafeteria. It's open twenty-four seven. We're working odd shifts around here and there's always somebody on the job right now."

"What do we do when we're not eating, sleeping, or washing ourselves in the sink?" asked Betty.

"Good question," said Irma. "Nothing for now. But I'm certain we'll need each of you to sing for your supper, so to speak. Give us a couple of days to come up with something. Anything else? I'm sure you all would like to get some sleep."

"Thanks again," said Jackie. The group echoed her and began picking through the bedding.

"Jackie, I do need to talk with you privately," Irma said. "Can you come with me for a minute?"

Jackie glanced over at Nikki.

"I'll get them comfortable," Nikki said. "You do what you need to do."

"Thank you," Jackie said and turned to Irma. "What is it?"

"Follow me, please."

Jackie told Marie and Chris to get settled, make a bed for her, and that she'd be right back. She followed Irma and the two men out into the hallway and back down the stairs. They walked through a maze of corridors and out a side door, reentering a nearby building labeled 30-S.

Irma held the door for Jackie. "This is where the ISS program is housed," she said. "These men with me are with the ISS team and they've got some news for you."

An instantaneous lump formed in Jackie's throat. Her stomach dropped and she shuddered involuntarily. "What do you mean?"

Irma didn't answer at first, leading Jackie into what looked like a small control room. Jackie stood wide-eyed at the entrance, suddenly unable to move. There was a large flat-screen monitor on the far wall and a half-dozen manned computer terminals facing the monitor. The room was abuzz with activity, everyone seemingly hard at work. Jackie sensed an unnerving mix of urgency and anxiety.

The men checked with one of the terminal operators and then

turned back to Jackie. One of them glanced over at Irma. "You can tell her," he said.

Jackie swallowed past the ache in her throat. "Tell me what, Irma? What is going on?"

"Although we can't be one hundred percent certain about this," Irma said, "we are confident that it was Clayton in the Soyuz."

Jackie braced herself against the door frame. Her knees weakened and her vision blurred. "Oh my G—" She collapsed.

Irma caught her under the arms and helped her to the floor. "Get her some water," she called to the room.

Jackie blinked her eyes open, focusing on Irma's drawn face. Her brow was knitted tightly, her mouth ajar with concern. "Did...you...say..."

Irma, still holding onto Jackie, handed her a cup of room-temperature water. "Drink this," she said. "Don't talk."

Jackie sipped from the cup. "You said he landed?"

"Yes," said Irma. "We are confident he landed. And we believe he is alive."

Jackie's head felt heavy. Her legs tingled. "What?"

"Jackie," said Irma, "we think Clayton is alive. Your husband is alive and trying to get home."

CHAPTER 4

**WEDNESDAY, JANUARY 29, 2020, 12:06 AM CST
COUPLAND, TEXAS**

Bouncing in the cab of the truck, Rick Walsh adjusted the seatbelt at his waist. The dim headlights provided barely enough light to see the lines marking the highway. He looked out the window into the darkness, thinking about Nikki.

He'd never met a woman like her, and that was saying something. He'd met a lot of women. Too many. Those women, and his inability to honor his wedding vows, had ended his marriage and probably scarred his son, Kenny, more than any Armageddon. Rick was admittedly a serial womanizer. It bordered on pathological. His therapist had told him he suffered from a histrionic personality disorder, a need for constant attention and approval. He'd stopped seeing that therapist so he could date her. It didn't last.

Rick was restless. It was always as if he knew the end of the world was coming, and he couldn't live with the thought of not having sampled every candy in the box.

With the apocalypse upon him and a woman unlike any he'd ever met falling into his life, there was a sense of longing that went deeper than basic carnal desires. Rick ached to be with her again. He pinched the bridge of his nose and took a long breath.

Gus Gruber took one hand off the wheel and punched Rick in the arm. "What are you thinking about? It's like you're not even here."

Rick smirked at the retired firefighter who'd taken him in and given him a place to stay. He shrugged.

Gus tugged on the brim of his Mahindra ball cap and smacked his lips. He turned off the highway onto a side street. "We only got a couple more minutes until we're there. At least, that's what I heard on the radio."

"I still can't believe your radio works," said Rick, leaning an elbow on the door frame. "This truck too."

"Yeah, well," Gus said, "like your Jeep, this here Dodge was built before electronics filled every nook and cranny of an automobile. This is a 1974 D200. It's solid. No EMP is gonna kill this baby. And I keep my radio in a steel box. That way the magnetism don't kill it."

"Smart," said Rick. "What exactly are we looking for? And why at midnight?"

"FEMA camp," said Gus. "I keep hearing rumors. There's supposed to be one about ten minutes north of Coupland in Taylor. Best to go at night when they can't see us."

Rick narrowed his eyes. "FEMA camp?"

He'd been leery of leaving the relative comfort of Gus's property to begin with. Learning it was to search for a conspiratorial rumor made it worse.

Gus thumped Rick on the arm again. "Don't look at me like that," he said. "I know what you're thinking."

Rick raised an eyebrow. "What am I thinking?"

"You're thinking I'm some paranoid Jade Helm conspiracy theorist. That ain't so. I didn't buy into that FEMA camp martial law crap back in 2015."

Rick suppressed a yawn and tugged at the seatbelt.

Gus avoided a stalled car on the shoulder and turned north toward town. "I wasn't one of those people. I believe 9/11 was a legit terror act. I believe Sandy Hook actually happened, and we did put men on the moon."

"Then why are you a prepper?" Rick asked.

Gus slapped the steering wheel. "I knew it! Everyone thinks us preppers are right-wing nut jobs. It just ain't so. We're preppers because we're self-reliant. We take care of our own and we don't trust anyone else to do it for us when the sh—"

Gus slammed on the brakes and reflexively extended his right arm to brace Rick against his seat. The Dodge screeched to a stop. Rick jerked forward at his waist and slapped his shoulder sideways into the dash as the smell of burning tires filtered into the cab.

Rick grabbed his shoulder while trying to reposition himself in his seat. It was bruised at the least. When he rolled it forward, there was a sharp pain radiating out from the socket. He wasn't sure he hadn't torn something. He was so consumed with his injury he didn't notice what had forced Gus to stop suddenly until he turned off the ignition, cut the lights, and cursed aloud at the sight in front of them.

Rick followed Gus's stare to the brightly lit installation a hundred yards ahead. With the engine off, he could hear the constant, rumbling purr of diesel generators. They were powering what was best described as a fortified encampment. It looked as much a military installation as it did a prison.

"That's it," Gus said above a whisper. "It does exist. A freaking FEMA camp."

"How do you know that's what it is?" Rick said, playing devil's advocate. "It could be a prison."

Gus shook his head such that his cheeks flapped. "No. Prisons don't have uniformed soldiers and Humvees at their gates. That's a prison camp."

"For what?"

"People like us," said Gus. "No doubt. They don't want preppers running amok. They want to control things, suppress us. It's exactly what they were saying on the radio."

"They?"

"Sheesh, Rick. Are you thick? The government. The military industrial complex. The United Nations. You name it."

Rick wasn't sure what to think. On one hand he'd driven through the checkpoints. He'd seen the military presence and the caravans of heavily armed soldiers traveling the highway on his way to Coupland. He'd also been allowed to keep his weapons and supplies. It didn't make sense.

"Why would they have let me pass their checkpoints with weapons in the back of the Jeep if they were concerned about armed preppers?"

"You had what, a couple of guns?" said Gus. "And I doubt you're on any watch list. That's why they let you go. They figured you were too soft to be a threat."

Rick rubbed his shoulder with his thumb until a spark of pain stopped him. He flexed his hand, extending his fingers before curling them into a fist. He could do it, but it hurt.

Gus restarted the truck and, with the headlights off, eased the truck to the side of the road, parking it between a pair of seemingly dead SUVs. He shut off the engine again and quietly opened the driver's side door, reaching for the hunting rifle he had hanging in a rack covering the truck's back window. "C'mon, we need to check this out."

Rick reached across his body to open the door with his left hand and jumped onto the street with both feet. Gus was already ten yards ahead, moving like a hunter stalking prey.

"Hey," Rick called, "you think you oughta show up at the gates armed? You're liable to get shot, Gus."

"We aren't going to the gate," he replied and scurried off the road to the left. "C'mon, man."

The two of them ran alongside the southern shoulder of the road, darting between a Toyota Camry and a Ford F-150 to mask their approach. Gus stopped when they'd gotten within thirty yards of the perimeter, ducking behind a blue post office mailbox. A few feet from them, a large sign announced the entrance to the T. Don Hutto Residential Center. Beyond the sign was a ten-foot-high fence topped with looped razor wire.

"This place was an ICE detention center," said Gus. "I mean, that's what they said it was. It doesn't look like it now."

A group of soldiers armed with M4 rifles exited the fenced area and climbed into a Humvee. They were too far away for them to hear what they were saying before they cranked the engine. A shout from inside the fencing caught Rick's attention. He shifted his weight to see beyond the fence, but couldn't make out much of the scene. All he could see was the flash of camouflage running from the commotion. Someone was yelling, screaming about his rights. He cursed at what he called "fascist pigs".

Another voice, presumably a soldier, tried to quiet the man and ordered him to calm down. It didn't work. He grew louder and shrieked before falling silent. Although Rick and Gus tried working their way closer to the fence, they couldn't get a clear view.

"Can you believe this?" Gus whispered, wide-eyed. "This is like WWII Germany. What are they doing here?"

Rick swallowed hard. "What are *we* doing here?"

Gus shrugged. "I wanted to see it for myself. I didn't want to believe it, but—"

Another group of soldiers exited the perimeter fencing and marched toward a transport truck. They were discussing their operation loudly enough Rick could hear them.

"What's the sitrep?" asked one of them. "What kind of resistance are we looking at? I need more than the briefing they gave us."

Another soldier, cradling his rifle, spun around to walk backward. He addressed the group and they slowed to listen as he stopped.

Gus and Rick inched closer to listen. They stayed low and hidden behind a curbside UPS box.

"These operations are tougher than the last two," he cautioned. "We know the first target is armed. He's got at least a half-dozen people on his property. From social media posts before the first CME, he talked openly about his planned resistance. He's antigovernment. Typical stuff."

"And the second?" asked one of the soldiers.

"This target has a larger cache of weapons. He's self-sufficient, almost off the grid. We believe he's alone, but there's some intelligence from a checkpoint east of Coupland that he may have visitors."

One of the soldiers raised his hand. "How'd we find out about him if he's off grid?"

"A tip. Not sure who. Somebody who's already inside the camp gave us actionable intel during an interrogation."

Rick and Gus exchanged glances. Rick saw recognition mixed with fear in Gus's eyes.

"What are the rules of engagement?" asked another soldier.

"Same as before. Fire only if fired upon. Remember, these are American citizens. They're not the enemy. Yet. Our job is to detain them peacefully and then transport them back here without incident. Understood?"

The half-dozen soldiers barked their understanding of the operation. Then they marched across the street to the awaiting transport truck.

Rick whispered, "They were talking about you. They had to be, right?"

Still crouched on the balls of his feet, Gus steadied himself against the UPS box. He was slack-jawed and seemed to be searching for words.

"Gus," Rick pressed, "that was your place, wasn't it?"

"I-I-I don't know. It could be."

"It had to be. Coupland? Off the grid? Who else could it—"

"I don't know," said Gus with a raspy whisper. "It's too coincidental. We're sitting here when the guys about to raid my house are talking about it? That's like something out of a bad action flick."

"I'd call it lucky," said Rick. "Whether it's your place or not, we better get back. If they're coming for us, we need to be ready."

Loaded with soldiers, the transport truck pulled away from its parking spot near the fence and thundered around the corner toward the highway. Gus wobbled on his toes, blankly staring into space. He was mouthing something unintelligible. Rick reached out and touched his shoulder and Gus flinched back to reality.

"We should go," Rick said. "Now."

Gus, still dazed, led Rick back to the truck. He cranked the ignition and gripped the wheel with both hands, leaning forward as he drove.

"The headlights," said Rick.

Gus fluttered his eyes. He turned on the dim lights. "Thanks."

"You okay?" Rick asked, pulling on his seatbelt.

Gus nodded. "Yeah. I mean no. I don't know. You prepare for the worst. You always think you're ready for it. You do everything to be ready for it. Then it happens and it doesn't seem real. None of this seems real."

Rick watched the road ahead through the faint yellow fan of light beaming from the truck. Gus was right. No matter how prepared someone might think he was, he always failed to account for something. It was inevitable. Gus had done everything he thought was right: armed himself, became self-sustaining and virtually non-reliant on outside power and water. He hadn't accounted for his own government seeing preparation as a threat.

Who would?

"What are we going to do if they come for us?" asked Rick.

Gus shrugged and shot Rick a glance, his eyebrows arched with concern. "I'm gonna be ready," he said. "We're gonna be ready."

Rick scratched the thickening stubble on his chin. "What does that mean?"

Gus flexed his fingers on the steering wheel and adjusted himself in the driver's seat. "I don't know yet. I really don't know."

CHAPTER 5

MISSION ELAPSED TIME
75 DAYS, 7 HOURS, 01 MINUTE, 04 SECONDS
DENVER, COLORADO

Clayton sat on the side of his bed, his palms pressed flat against the thin cotton blanket that covered the thin foam mattress. His bare feet were flat on the cold floor. He stared at the wardrobe and matching desk on the opposite wall. The room had the feel of a motel room without the starving-artist paintings on the walls.

He shuddered at the sterility of it and edged from the bed to his feet. He fought against a flash of light-headedness and stumbled toward the desk, leaning against it for support.

"How did I get here?" he asked himself and searched his memory. He reached around to touch his lower back. "I hope I still have my kidneys," he muttered.

The last he remembered he was being interrogated by a group of overly-amped jerks who questioned his integrity, his veracity, and his loyalty to his country. They'd made it clear he wasn't welcome, but they weren't letting him leave. Gradually, the fuzziness was clarifying itself.

Clayton recalled he'd argued with the man named Perkins and the woman named Van Cleaf. He'd insisted he needed to get home to his family. They'd tried to calm him down. It didn't work.

He'd punched somebody. Perkins? Sergeant Vega? He wasn't sure, but he knew they'd restrained him and stuck a needle in his neck.

Now he was here in what was best described as a well-appointed cell. Stuck. No closer to home than he'd been on the ISS. Clayton scanned the room and settled on the door. He crossed the room and grabbed the handle. It spun but didn't open. He ran his thumb over a red light above the locking mechanism and tried the handle again. Nothing. As suspected, he was a prisoner.

A sudden well of anger exploded inside him and he kicked the door, pounding on it with his fists.

"Let me out of here!" he yelled, his voice scratching against the back of his throat. "You can't keep me here!"

As quickly as the outburst materialized, it ended. He was out of breath, and kicking the door had sent a vibrating pain through his injured leg. His heart pulsed angrily in his temples and across the back of his head.

He thought back to what Van Cleaf had said to him before he lost his cool. Without any empathy or hint of humanity, she'd smirked at him, her words dripping with condescension. "You don't understand, do you?" she'd said. "You can't leave."

That was the only moment since the first CME blasted the ISS that he lost faith. She wasn't giving him her opinion, she wasn't doubting his ability to traverse the rough terrain between Denver and Clear Lake, Texas, she was telling him with total certainty that he couldn't leave. She wouldn't allow it. It was fact. Pure and simple fact.

Recalling her words and how they'd sliced through his gut, they emboldened him and gave him new resolve. Who was she to tell an astronaut, a man who'd risked his life for the betterment of mankind, he couldn't do what he damn well pleased?

Clayton cursed and refocused. He exhaled, trying to ease the pounding in his head. He couldn't escape if he allowed his anger to consume him.

How could he engineer his way out of this? He stepped back to the desk, dropping into the rolling chair in front of it. He pushed back with his heels, wheeling across the floor to the bed. He pushed off the bed and rolled back to the desk.

His eyes searched the room. "How do I get out of here?"

He opened the drawers to the desk—empty. He checked the bedside table—nothing. He pushed himself from the chair and walked into the bathroom. He found a sink, toilet, and shower stall. He was checking the plumbing under the sink when he heard a magnetic click from his room followed by a man's voice calling his name.

"Clayton Shepard?"

He poked his head out from the bathroom and saw Perkins standing in the open doorway with a nine-millimeter pistol in his hands.

Clayton frowned and kept his distance. "What do you want?"

Perkins aimed the weapon at the ground in front of Clayton. Behind him, beyond the door, was the sergeant named Vega, also armed.

"You calmed down yet?" asked Perkins.

Clayton took a step from the bathroom. "You letting me go?"

Perkins shook his head.

"Then I'm not calm."

"That's problematic," said Perkins. "I'd like to be able to give you some privileges. I can't do that if you can't remain…amenable."

Clayton crossed the room to his bed and dropped onto his mattress. Perkins kept his weapon trained on the astronaut while Vega kept watch.

"We believe your story," Perkins said.

"Some of us don't," Vega chimed in.

Perkins shot Vega an angry look. "Keep the door open."

Vega scowled unapologetically.

"So let me go," said Clayton. "I'm not a threat to anyone."

Perkins lowered his weapon and holstered it at his hip. He stepped over to the empty desk chair and sat down, rolling himself close to the bed.

"Not now you're not," he said. "That would change if we let you leave the facility. You'd become desperate as the world falls apart and you'd come looking for us again. You'd bring people with you. That would be problematic for everyone."

"You like that word," said Clayton. "Problematic."

"It's appropriate."

"So what now?" Clayton asked. "Assuming I'm calm, assuming I've accepted your nonnegotiable proposal?"

"We get you acquainted with the technology available here. We find you a job. You contribute to the new society."

Clayton glanced at Vega. The soldier stood with his feet shoulder-width apart. He held the door open with a jackbooted foot. He looked as if he were holding in a fart. His attitude was as foul as it had been in the hospital room. Perkins, however, had softened.

"Your boss," he said, "Van Cleaf, said this is a secure facility designed to preserve civilization."

"That's correct."

"She said the world is dark," Clayton said. "Two CMEs were responsible for that. She said it would 'thin the herd'."

"Correct."

Clayton's eyes drifted across his cell. "It doesn't add up."

Perkins tilted his head. The corners of his mouth curled upward, as if he knew the answer to his question. He asked it anyway. "What doesn't add up?"

"This," Clayton said. "How is it you have this facility up and running a few days after a CME nobody wanted to admit was coming? How are you so sure the power is out everywhere? How can you know the herd will thin? It's too convenient."

Perkins looked Clayton in the eyes as he leaned back in the chair. He scratched the back of his head and folded his arms across his chest. It was clear he wasn't dignifying the astronaut's doubts with a rebuttal.

"How many people are here?" Clayton asked. "How big is this place?"

Perkins shrugged. "A few hundred," he said. "Maybe a thousand people."

"And the facility?"

"Five buildings," he said. "All of it underground."

"And nobody's allowed to leave?"

"Perimeter security like Sergeant Vega," said Perkins. "That's it."

Clayton nodded at Perkins and eyed Vega.

Perimeter security. That's how I get out of here.

"So we understand each other?" Perkins prompted.

Clayton sighed. "What choice do I have?"

"Good," said Perkins. "It's so much easier this way." He stood from the chair and tugged open the large velcroed pockets on his thighs. From one pocket he pulled what looked like an all-glass iPhone, from the other, he withdrew a smartwatch. He offered both of them to Clayton.

"You'll need these," he said. "The watch is called a DiaWatch. The device is a DiaTab."

Clayton took both and studied them "Dye-uh?" he asked. "What is that?"

"It's short for Denver International Airport. D-I-A," said Perkins. "Somebody in IT thought it was clever to name the proprietary technology after our location."

Clayton put the watch on his left wrist and held up the palm-sized glass tablet. "These are trackers, I'm assuming? As helpful as they are for me, they're more helpful for you or whoever else is trying to spy on me."

Sergeant Vega snorted. "Don't flatter yourself."

Perkins frowned at his colleague and rolled his eyes. "They do have a localized positioning system that runs through the internal Li-Fi system."

"Li-Fi?"

Perkins motioned to the overhead lights in the cell's ceiling. "It's like Wi-Fi, but uses visible light to transmit data. I don't know how it works."

Clayton flipped his wrist and the watch displayed its first message.

Hello, Clayton. Good morning.

He tapped the watch, and the time and date appeared. His stomach dropped.

"It's January twenty-ninth?" Five days had passed since the CME. Five days that at once felt like a minute and a month. Five days his wife was alone with the children. Five days closer to the herd being thinned. His heart racing, he considered what he'd already missed, how he'd already failed his family.

His fingers trembling, he tapped the DiaTab. In the upper right of the display he saw the battery indicator. It read one hundred percent. He ran his finger across it again and the screen glowed red. It showed the time and date and also a location.

ROOM 29-4 OFFAL LEVEL

Clayton looked up at Perkins. "29-4 offal level?"

"You're in room twenty-nine, building four."

"Offal though," said Clayton. "That's a slaughterhouse term. I've got family in Amarillo. Offal is what they call discarded parts."

"That's appropriate," snarked Sergeant Vega.

"I can't speak to that," said Perkins. "I don't know anything about it."

Clayton studied Perkins's face. As far as he could tell, the man was telling the truth. He looked down at the DiaTab and pressed the home button. It vibrated against his thumb and the screen changed to a control display.

OVERHEAD LIGHTS, LAMP, SHOWER, TELENET MONITOR

"Telenet?"

"Push the screen," said Perkins.

Clayton touched the icon and the screen changed to give the DiaTab the look of a remote control. There was a power tab, which he tapped, and on the wall at the foot of his bed, a large rectangular image appeared.

"Is that a television?" he asked.

"Telenet," said Perkins. "It's interactive. I'm sure you'll have more questions. The preprogrammed message will answer most of them. We'll leave you alone."

"Can I leave the room?"

"Not yet," said Perkins. "Once we've established your willingness to stay and work toward the common good, my bosses will consider giving you travel privileges. Until then, you'll be escorted everywhere. We'll be back to take you to breakfast."

The men left without saying anything else and the door shut behind them. A click and a red light told him the door was locked. Clayton stood up and faced the Telenet. He pressed his DiaTab and a welcome page appeared on the sixty-inch screen in front of him. There was a translucent infinity icon spinning and flipping in the lower right corner.

Hello, Clayton. Good morning. You have 1 new message.

Clayton pressed the message icon that populated on his DiaTab and looked back at the Telenet, where the woman who called herself Van Cleaf appeared. At least he thought it was Van Cleaf. The woman he'd seen hours earlier looked older. Her eyes had been sunken and framed with deep crow's feet, her cheeks sallow and thin with age.

The Van Cleaf on the screen was happier and tanned. Her eyes shone with hope. She sat in a control room, her head held back with confidence. She was easily five years younger, if not more.

"Welcome to your new home," she said gleefully. *"You are here because you are important. Please keep that fact in mind as I familiarize you with this facility."*

"Clearly she didn't record a version for the disposable innards like me," Clayton said to the screen.

"If you have questions, you may ask them by pressing the question button on your tablet. Speak normally and the Telenet system will record your query. I'll answer your question from a series of prerecorded answers. We believe we've anticipated most anything you might ask."

"I doubt that," Clayton mumbled and pressed the question button on the DiaTab. There was a haptic response and he felt the vibration in his fingertip. An audio wavelength appeared on the screen atop Van Cleaf's frozen face.

"Where am I?" he asked.

The icon at the bottom of the screen flipped and spun as the computer worked to populate the prerecorded answer. It stopped and Van Cleaf's image jittered before she spoke.

"You are in room twenty-nine, building four, on the offal level," she said. *"On this level you don't have keycard privileges or travel privileges."*

"Why am I on the offal level?"

The system cycled through the same series of steps. Van Cleaf unfroze. *"You are a threat to the safety and security of the facility."*

Clayton clenched his jaw. He wasn't the threat. "What are the other levels in this building?"

"You don't have access to that information at this time."

"Of course not," Clayton grumbled. "You're no better than Perkins."

"If you don't have any further questions at this time," Van Cleaf's avatar said pleasantly, *"I'll return to the original presentation."*

Clayton dropped onto the bed, half listening to the litany of instructions and directions. None of it mattered. He was a prisoner until he freed himself.

CHAPTER 6

WEDNESDAY, JANUARY 29, 2020, 1:00 AM MST
DENVER, COLORADO

Chip Treadgold pushed the button on the coffee maker and the machine gurgled into service. He plucked an extra cup from the stack to the right and offered it to Vihaan Chandra.

Chandra waved him off. "No, thank you. When we're finished here, I've got to get some sleep."

Treadgold smiled. "Suit yourself. I thought your circulatory system was fifty percent Arabica."

"I cut back," Chandra said. "I have trouble sleeping."

Treadgold took a yellow packet of artificial sweetener from a dispenser and ripped off the top. He poured it into the cup as the coffee maker finished its drip.

"Why did you bring me here?" asked Chandra. He motioned to the empty cafeteria, looking around the room for effect. "We could have talked in my new lab."

Treadgold shook his head. "Too many ears. We have a little more privacy here."

He led Chandra to a table at the center of the room and pulled out a seat. He blew on the coffee and drew a slurp from the steaming cup. He winced and sucked on his tongue.

"Too hot," he said.

Chandra sat opposite his boss and rested his elbows on the table.

He watched his boss take another sip of coffee, only to burn his tongue again.

"You ever notice people's predisposition toward stupidity, Chandra?" he asked. "Here I am taking a sip of coffee I know will burn my tongue, but I do it anyway. It's like when a waiter brings you a plate of food and warns you not to touch it because it's too hot. What do you do? You touch it anyway. It's stupid."

"I don't think it's stupidity," said Chandra. "I believe it's healthy skepticism. We choose to discover the truth for ourselves, despite what others might tell us it is."

A thin smile snaked across Treadgold's face. He blew on the coffee and took another cautious sip. His eyes stayed glued to Chandra's as he drank. Steam filtered from the cup into the air. There was something maniacal about it.

"Or," said Treadgold, "it's not stupidity or skepticism. Maybe it's something as simple as obstinance. People don't know what's good for them, even when told."

Chandra shifted in his seat, beads of sweat populating on his forehead. His loose collar suddenly felt tight at his neck. He tucked a finger inside the front of it and tugged. The room felt smaller than it had a moment ago.

"I'm not feeling well," he said. "Can we dispense with the philosophical debate and get to whatever it was that brought us here?"

Treadgold nursed the coffee and smacked his lips. "Okay. I didn't realize you were in a hurry. You know we technically have all the time in the world."

Chandra sat back in his chair, bouncing his knee up and down impatiently.

Treadgold rolled his eyes. "Fine," he huffed. "Clearly you have no sense of humor tonight. I'll get to the point."

"Which is?"

"I'm told you have a lot of questions about this facility. You aren't sure it's what's best for those sheltered here."

Chandra's eyes narrowed. "Who told you I had questions?"

Treadgold spun the cup on the table. He raised his eyebrows in question.

Chandra sank back in his chair. "The Telenet. It was the Telenet, wasn't it? You're tracking all of the questions."

"It's no different than Google recording your searches," said Treadgold. "Or Facebook inserting ads into your timeline based on your Internet searches."

"It's different," said Chandra.

Treadgold shrugged. "Agree to disagree. Regardless, I'd like to allay some of your fears."

"Go ahead."

"This facility, as I told you before, was first conceived decades ago. It was a product of two events. One was the Cold War. We were in the midst of a space race and an arms race with the Russians."

Chandra rolled his eyes. "I know what the Cold War was."

"I'm sure you do," said Treadgold. "I'm just giving you the background here."

"Go on."

"In May 1967, things came to a head. We were closer to war than we'd been since the Cuban Missile Crisis; however, nobody writes about it or teaches it in the history books."

"What happened?"

"Our surveillance radars in the polar regions stopped working," said Treadgold. "They were jammed. Convinced the Soviets were responsible, the Air Force prepped aircraft for war. They were ready to go. World War Three was on the horizon."

"I read about this in a journal a few years back," said Chandra. "Our earliest space weather researchers, military scientists, alerted command about the possibility of communications disruptions from a solar storm."

Treadgold raised his cup in a toast to his colleague. "I'm impressed. Yes, that single event convinced our government of the importance of monitoring space weather, how critical it is to national security. It also proved the need for a place to escape the ravages of both war and space weather."

"How so?"

"Even in the 1950s, we knew our reliance on electronics was accelerating exponentially. In the event of a nuclear attack, the resulting electromagnetic pulse, or a catastrophic solar event and its capacity to kill communications and power, society would collapse."

"Collapse?" Chandra echoed. "That's extreme."

"Is it though?" asked Treadgold. "We've seen estimates that every day without power costs the United States economy forty billion dollars. Every day. What civilization can survive a shock to the system like that?"

Chandra adjusted his chair. He sat forward and rested his elbows on the table.

"Remember, Vihaan, we were also in the midst of the Civil Rights Movement and the early years of the Vietnam conflict and—"

"War."

"Excuse me?"

"Vietnam was a war, it wasn't a conflict."

Treadgold smirked. "Whatever. The point is that we were engaged in fighting communism, among other things. Those in power during that tumultuous time decided we needed safe spaces for both continuity of government and for rebuilding society. They identified viable spots all over the country, and this was one of them. Although the work began, it was a cost-prohibitive effort. So during the Reagan administration, a public and private partnership was formed. That's where my employers came into the fold. We seamlessly integrated our efforts into all of the critical institutions—the military, the Departments of State and Energy, Homeland Security, and of course NOAA."

"Homeland Security didn't exist under Reagan."

"You're right, it didn't," said Treadgold. "Bush created the agency when it was apparent the Descent Protocol was too unwieldy. We needed a singular agency that—"

"Homeland Security was created because of 9/11."

Treadgold smiled. "*Sure* it was."

"So this is some vast conspiracy?"

"I wouldn't call it that," said Treadgold. "I would call it a coordinated effort to preserve our way of life in the face of a catastrophic event."

"What way of life is that?"

Treadgold's brow furrowed. "The American way."

Chandra leaned forward, resting his head in his hands. His fingers gripped his hair, tugging at the roots. His head was swimming. He squeezed his eyes closed.

"So instead of trying to maintain some sort of structure and help everyone survive," he said, "you callously calculated society would collapse? You left everything to chance and assumed the worst?"

"We didn't assume anything. We know it will collapse. We know that for a fact. It's already happening. We've merely separated the wheat from the chaff."

"How do you know?"

"We just do. Seriously, Vihaan, I'm beginning to question my decision to bring you here."

"Why *did* you bring me here?"

Treadgold's face relaxed and he finished his coffee, tapping the coffee cup as he tilted it back to drain the final drops. "My bosses gave the option of picking some last minute additions. People I thought would be of some benefit. Things were already in motion. I'd seen you hard at work since the first CME hit. I trust you. You've always been discreet. You don't have family. So I thought..." He shrugged.

Chandra slid his elbows from the table and folded his arms across his chest. He studied Treadgold's face, tracing the creases and folds with his eyes.

"Last minute?" asked Chandra. "I thought the decision to activate the protocol was made after I told you about the second CME? That's what you told me. You were surprised when I told you there was a new threat. You said—"

"I know what I said," Treadgold cut in forcefully. "I couldn't tell you that we were already headed underground, that we already knew a second CME was on its way. Did you think you were the only one who'd figured that out? You're good, Vihaan, but really."

Chandra sat back in his chair and dropped his arms to his sides. The ache in his stomach deepened and the nausea floated back to the surface. He swallowed the urge to vomit.

Treadgold reached out and grabbed his hand. "Don't you understand how lucky you are? How lucky all of us are to be here, to have a chance at making society better than it was?"

"All of us?"

"Yes, all of us."

"What about the prisoner? The man found wandering around outside?"

Treadgold let go of Chandra's hand and withdrew into his chair. The color drained from his face. He picked up the empty cup of coffee and then set it back on the table before squeezing it with his fist.

"I heard people talking about it," said Chandra. "Who is he?"

Treadgold took a deep breath and held it. He exhaled through his nostrils. He shifted his weight in the chair, scooting it while he cleared his throat. "He's an astronaut."

Chandra chuckled at the absurdity of the answer until he noticed Treadgold wasn't laughing. "Astronaut?"

"Yes," said Treadgold. "He was on the International Space Station. Somehow, and we don't understand how he did it, he managed to escape the ISS. He landed in Canada, found a working plane, and flew it until it crashed not far from here."

"Was he looking for us? Is NASA part of the…the…new world order?"

Treadgold shook his head. "Don't call it that."

"Is NASA involved in preserving the American way?"

"No. They ask too many questions and they're too transparent. They know the bunkers exist, that's about it. They weren't advised of any Descent Protocol procedures."

"So the astronaut just landed here by chance?"

"Seems so."

"Which one? I think we had three men aboard the ISS. Two

astronauts and one cosmonaut. They—"

"I'm aware of who was aboard the ISS. It's unimportant."

"What are you doing with him?"

Treadgold shrugged. "Nothing. He's staying here. He's in building four for now. Once he acclimates, he'll have a job like everyone else."

Chandra scratched his head. He rubbed his heavy, burning eyes and looked at his DiaWatch. It was late.

"I'm telling you all of these things in confidence," said Treadgold, pushing away from the table. "These are not things the general population knows about, okay?"

General population. Like a prison. "I understand," said Chandra.

Treadgold plucked the crinkled cup from the table and stood. "If you have questions, you come to me. Don't use the Telenet. It'll only cause problems."

The American way of life. "Okay," Chandra said. "I'll be sure to ask you first."

Treadgold motioned for Chandra to follow him from the cafeteria. The two rode the elevator silently and went their separate ways. Chandra accessed his room with his keycard. The overhead lights flickered on as he walked to the desk. He set down the DiaTab and took off his DiaWatch. He sat down on his bed, the mattress sinking under his weight, and took off his shoes. He spun his feet from the floor and lay atop the covers, resting his head on the cool pillow. He stared at the LED lights recessed into the ceiling of his cell. As he drifted off, he had no doubt he was in a cell. Chandra knew without a doubt that he, the astronaut, the strawberry blonde named Sally, the little scientist Henry Rector, and even Treadgold, whoever he truly was, were all prisoners here.

CHAPTER 7

WEDNESDAY, JANUARY 29, 2020, 5:08 AM CST
JOHNSON SPACE CENTER, HOUSTON, TEXAS

Jackie's eyes popped open and she sat up in her sleeping bag, bracing herself on the floor with her elbows. She was drenched in sweat, her heart pounding. Her chest heaved as she breathed in and out.

It was dark in the room, but her eyes had adjusted enough that she could see the outlines of the people sleeping nearby. Jackie felt for Marie. She was there. So was Chris. Both were snuggled next to one another in their nylon cocoons. Jackie exhaled.

They're okay.

Her dream had been too real, its tentacles still tickling the back of her neck as she sat there, reminding herself it had been a nightmare. As her heart rate slowed, she lay back on her pillow and closed her eyes.

Jackie didn't frequently remember her dreams. And when she did, they were farcical. They were reality laced with the fantasy she'd subconsciously stolen from the books she'd read. This one, though, stung with the reality of the nasty world in which she now found herself. Her children had disappeared while scouring makeshift tenements for scraps of food. She'd searched endlessly for them and couldn't find them. No matter what she'd tried or where she'd looked, they eluded her. It was a future she feared was all too real.

Awake, lying in the nondescript NASA office, Jackie's mind slid from the fear of what could be to the terror of what was. Her husband and best friend, Clayton, was the one missing. She'd told herself and her children, despite logic telling her differently, that he was coming home to them. Against the astronomical odds, he would find a way. It wasn't until Irma had told her he was on Earth she realized how unlikely it was she'd ever see him again.

"We are confident he landed. And we believe he is alive. Your husband is alive and trying to get home."

Irma's words repeated themselves in her mind as if they were the only verse of a song she could remember.

Alive. Trying to get home.

Jackie had learned that the Soyuz hatch was opened after crash landing. They'd been able to pinpoint the signal and knew that the Russian capsule had landed in Jasper, Canada, on or near the Columbia Icefield.

Using a surviving satellite, they'd found the capsule. They could even see footprints and a wide path leading away from it. There appeared to be a rudimentary camp. There was, however, no sign of life at the crash site. They'd made the educated guess the survivor had dragged supplies from the crash site toward a nearby visitors' center. There was no way to confirm any of it. And even if they had proof of life, getting help to the site would have been a gargantuan task that would have taken days or weeks. But Irma had told Jackie, regardless, they'd had a lucky break.

"Thanks to an atmospheric condition called 'tropospheric ducting', we are receiving radio signals from much farther than we would normally be able to hear," Irma had said.

"What does that have to do with Clayton?" Jackie had asked.

"One of our radio operators was monitoring a common frequency," Irma had explained. "We heard parts of a call that was reaching out to anyone listening. While we weren't able to connect, that operator made a note of the frequency and began recording all transmissions. By chance, he picked up on a brief, garbled conversation between two men."

Irma had shown Jackie the hand-scribbled transcription of the snippets of conversation they'd been able to hear clearly enough to understand the communication:

This is VA6CXX. I hear you, KD5XMX. Were you in an accident? I don't know my location yet. Name is Steve. Maybe I can help.

"The man's name is Steve," Jackie had said. "Why would you think he's talking to Clayton?"

"KD5XMX is Clayton's ham radio call sign," Irma had said. "We were listening to Clayton talk to someone named Steve Kremer. We found his identity by searching a manual log of North American amateur radio licenses. According to the license, he lives a few hours from where Clayton crash-landed."

Jackie looked at the words on the paper. *I don't know my location. Maybe I can help.* She wanted more than that. She wanted to know if the man named Steve had been able to help. She wanted to get on the radio herself.

Irma had insisted they had people working on it. They'd been trying unsuccessfully to hail Clayton or Steve. Nothing had worked. Then the temperature changed, the tropospheric ducting diminished, and their ability to hear anything beyond line of sight was gone. That snippet was all they had or would have. They were still monitoring the frequency, but the chance of hearing anything north of Dallas was miniscule.

Irma had told Jackie she thought the information would be comforting; they knew he was alive when he'd landed, he was mobile, and he'd made contact with others. It *should* have been comforting. It wasn't. It tore at Jackie's gut. It made her legs tingle with weakness. To Jackie, the idea that her husband was in Canada made him seem farther away than he was when he was orbiting the planet. At least when he was in space she could look up and feel close to him.

The thought that he could safely find his way however many thousand miles from the Canadian Rockies to southeast Texas was suddenly ridiculous. There were few cars, little available gasoline, and no airplanes.

Jackie shivered in her sleeping bag and pulled it up her neck. Her sweat had dried and cooled her skin, but she couldn't be sure it was the chill that sent the shudder through her body.

For the first time in a long time, she prayed for her husband. She had trouble forming the words at first, as if the guilt of seeking help was preventing her from speaking. She licked her lips and tried again, her words a whisper soft enough for only God to hear.

"I'm not devout," she said. "I don't go to church or help the poor. I'm not religious at all. In fact, you know I roll my eyes at those people who close their eyes and wave their hands while they're singing hymns."

Jackie's mouth curled into a self-conscious smile at the vision of the faithful parishioners she'd see on Sunday morning television as she flipped through the channels, looking for the ubiquitous reruns of *House Hunters*.

"I'm not asking for you to help me," she whispered, her eyes affixed to the ceiling. "I'm asking you to help Clayton, wherever he is."

A lump caught in her throat and she blinked back tears. She didn't believe her prayer would make any difference, but she felt helpless to do anything else. She jumped when she felt a cold hand on her cheek.

"Mom?"

Jackie pulled her hand from underneath the warmth of the sleeping bag and touched the soft hand on her face. "Marie? How long have you been awake?"

"Long enough to hear you pray," she whispered. "That's a first."

Jackie gently squeezed her daughter's hand. "It never hurts, right?"

Marie inched closer to her mother. "What did they tell you about Dad? We fell asleep before you got back. I tried to stay awake."

Jackie hesitated. She could be a realist and tell her daughter the unsanitized truth, or she could spin it, shine it up, and present an optimistic version. She smiled and stroked Marie's hair, pulling the strands behind her ear.

"Your dad is alive," she said. "He's back on Earth. He's—"

"But," interrupted Marie, her voice still a whisper. "I know there's a but coming."

Jackie's smile disappeared. "But he's in western Canada somewhere."

"Canada?"

"That's where he landed. He's made radio contact with someone who might be able to help him."

"How is he going to get home, Mom? Is NASA sending someone to get him?"

"I don't…"

"You don't what?"

Jackie ran her fingers along her daughter's cheek. It was damp. She thumbed away tears from beneath Marie's eye. Her own eyes welled. She squeezed them closed and opened them again to see her daughter had drawn closer, her face inches away.

"Mom!" she whispered forcefully. "You don't what?"

"I don't have an answer for that, honey. NASA isn't going to get him. By the time they go to where they located him, he'd likely be long gone. There's nothing we can do but wait."

A third muted voice joined the conversation. "We could go to Canada," said Chris. He poked his head over his sister's sleeping bag and draped his arm across her. "We could leave here and head north."

"When did you wake up?" asked Jackie.

He pulled on his sister's sleeping bag and pulled himself perpendicular to her, leaning his weight on her hip. "A couple of minutes ago. I heard you talking about Dad."

Marie shrugged off her brother, but he held onto her side. "Get off me, Chris."

"Chris," said Jackie, "please get off your sister. You can come over here."

The boy unzipped his bag and crawled across his sister. She groaned and gave him a healthy shove. He tumbled over his mom and landed on the floor.

"Mom!" he cried. "She pushed—"

"Shhhh!" Jackie said. "C'mon, kids, I'm not in the mood. Please don't aggravate one another."

"Sorry," said Chris, leaning on his mother.

"Sorry," Marie mumbled.

"Look," Jackie said, "the truth is we can't leave here. Not yet. We don't have transportation and we're certainly not walking to Canada."

"How is Dad getting here if he doesn't have transportation?" asked Chris.

Jackie buried her fear. She ignored the voice telling her Clayton wouldn't make it back to Texas, humoring her children. It was what they needed, and their needs outstripped hers. She faked what she knew was a convincing smile.

"Your dad always finds a way, right? He figured out how to get back to Earth. That was probably a lot tougher than getting from Canada to Houston. He'll find a way, kids. He always does."

CHAPTER 8

Rick Walsh woke up to the sound of men's voices. They were sharply barking military commands issued above a whisper that aimed to maneuver teams into right positions. They were coming from the other side of Brushy Creek on the southern side of Gus Gruber's property.

After spending several hours prepping the compound for a coming raid, Rick had reluctantly volunteered to be the lookout. Gus had stationed him near the creek, telling Rick that would be where he'd stage the assault if he were in charge.

The sun was another forty-five minutes from lifting over the rolling edge of the horizon. Gus had also told Rick the troops would hit them before sunup when everyone was deep asleep. He'd been right about that too.

Rick was leaning against a tree near the edge of the creek where it ran under State Highway 95. The trucks, two of them, were stopped on the highway at the start of the elevated portion, which ran across the creek from south to north. The noise had initially startled him and he'd dropped the radio resting in his lap. He groped the ground at his sides, finding it amongst the leaves and rot of the creek's steep but narrow embankment. He held it tightly with one hand and narrowed his eyes toward the voices and boot steps. Both were getting louder as they approached.

Despite the darkness, Rick could make out the fast-moving forms of at least a dozen men. They were splitting into three or four different groups, jumping from the highway to the ground below at different points.

Rick waited until the men passed him and keyed the radio he gripped tightly with one hand. Convinced the soldiers couldn't hear him, he turned on the transceiver and keyed the microphone.

"They're here," he said with his mouth pressed against the speaker. "Repeat, they're here. Do you hear me? Over."

The radio crackled. Rick looked at it and then pulled it to his mouth again.

"The soldiers are here," he said breathlessly. "Do you copy? Over."

Nothing.

Rick pushed himself to his feet and climbed up the creek's embankment toward the clearing at the edge of the trees. From there it was a straight shot back to a narrow wooden bridge to Gus's ranch. His thighs burning, he stayed low, crouch-running north. He knew he wouldn't beat the soldiers, but he didn't have to do that. It wasn't part of the plan. Up ahead, under the cover of trees, he saw a flash of light and slowed to a stop, quietly lowering himself to the ground, keeping his head up so he could see the light. It was coming from a team of soldiers. They were picking their way through the cover of the creek-side vegetation.

Perhaps he *could* beat them.

He held the radio close to his ear. It was silent. "C'mon," he said between his teeth, "answer the freaking radio."

He drew the radio back to his mouth. When he was about to try again, he realized he was on the wrong channel. He cursed himself, fumbling with the knob atop the radio.

"They're coming," he said hurriedly. "They're coming. Copy? Over."

The response was immediate. *"Copy. How many? Over."*

"Twelve. Three or four teams. All coming from the south and east. Over."

"Copy. Over and out."

Rick turned off the radio and scrambled to his feet. The light up ahead was no longer visible. Staying low, he resumed his awkward hunched-over run toward the creek crossing. The cold morning air tightened his lungs. He suppressed a coughing fit as he worked his way north.

He hadn't wanted to leave Kenny and his ex, Karen. He'd wanted to be there with them when everything got heated. Gus had convinced him he was the best to be the lookout. Despite Mumphrey's offer to take the spot, the ranch owner said he wanted Rick there. Rick had been with him when they'd seen the FEMA camp. Rick knew what they were up against.

Mumphrey had promised to keep a close eye on Kenny and Karen. He'd told them he'd go kicking and screaming. Rick was afraid of that, but he wanted to be a team player. Now, as his heart raced and his legs burned, he regretted not having been more selfish. Sure, Karen was a pain. But she'd earned that right. She'd earned more than that.

He knew she and Kenny were hunkered down in a crawl space underneath the main house. Lana Buck and Candace Bucknell were also hiding there. Gus thought it was the safest place to be if "things got violent".

Reggie Buck was positioned atop the garage on the northeastern corner of the property. Gus had armed him with his Remington .308 bolt action sniper rifle with a bipod and night vision scope. Reggie would be an overwatch covering the whole property.

Gus had activated all of the trigger alarms he'd installed on the perimeter fences. He'd armed trip wires between the greenhouse and garage, and between the greenhouse and main house. There was no way to cross from one to the other without setting off the wires.

Rick had protested the trip wires. "These are American soldiers we're talking about, Gus," he'd said. "You can't maim a soldier. That's treasonous."

Gus had laughed incredulously at the suggestion. "Treasonous?" he said, stepping uncomfortably close to Rick. "The US government is sending armed, professionally trained killers onto my land to forcibly remove me and imprison me? And *I'm* treasonous? You best rethink that position before I forcibly remove *you*."

Rick had held his ground. "I'm not telling you to go quietly and obey. I'm suggesting you not injure or kill anyone. You heard them. They said they'd only open fire if we did it first."

Gus had stuck his swollen finger in Rick's chest. "I know my rights. I'm an American too. They'll take me from here in a bag. You wanna leave? Do it. But all of you will end up in that camp, locked up and groveling for gruel. You want that? Leave."

Rick had apologized, not because he was sorry but because he wouldn't leave Kenny and Karen, and she wasn't leaving. She'd made that clear. Making one tortuously long trip in the Jeep was enough. Besides, Gus did have a point. The government had no right to do what it was doing. Martial law or no martial law, Off-the-Grid-Gus and his guns weren't hurting anyone.

Chugging as fast as he could, the winter-hardened ground crunching under his feet, he regretted not having stood up to Gus. He regretted not having taken Kenny and Karen, regardless of what she'd wanted, loading them into the Jeep, and going somewhere else.

More than that, he wished Nikki were with him. She'd have stood up to Gus. Heck, she'd have kicked his ass. Undoubtedly. On principle alone, she'd have sprung flat-footed into the air, snapped into a tornadic spin, and slapped his jaw with a roundhouse. Then she'd have drop-kicked Karen if she'd resisted leaving ahead of what amounted to a military invasion.

Rick caught a stitch in his side and he slowed, stretching as he walked cautiously toward the tree line. He was pretty sure he'd reached the general area where the wood-planked footbridge crossed the creek onto Gus's property, giving him access to the northeastern parcel.

He clipped the radio to his belt and, with his head on a swivel, approached the canopy of pines, scrub oak, and scraggly yaupon that tangled its way between the taller trees. His feet crunched on the leaf-covered ground and he stopped. He listened for chatter or the sound of boots. All he heard was the start and stop of tree frogs croaking.

Rick was unarmed other than the radio. It was his choice. He didn't want to shoot an American soldier. Though, as he wound his way through the brush, squinting to find his path toward the footbridge, he regretted not being armed. If he happened upon a soldier, or they found him wandering in the thin band of woods, it wouldn't end well. His breathing slowed, but his heart rate maintained its thick and heavy pulse against his neck and chest. A cold sweat chilled his forehead and the back of his neck. And then he saw him. Rick stopped cold.

On the eastern edge of the footbridge was a lone soldier. He was crouched low, bent on one knee. He held his rifle to his shoulder, his eye pressed against what Rick figured was a night-vision or thermal scope.

Rick cursed under his breath, frozen where he stood, afraid to move his feet and rustle the dead leaves that carpeted the ground. Clearly, he hadn't beat the team to his position. They'd moved faster than he'd anticipated. Still, he had to get across that bridge. He looked over his shoulder and back toward the highway. It would take him too long to run back and approach the property from the main entrance. He couldn't even move fifty yards south and try to cross the creek on foot. He'd make too much noise or get caught in what Gus had warned was a surprisingly swift current. His only option was going through the soldier.

Rick looked around at the ground. In the darkness, he found a palm-sized rock. Next to it was a rotted tree branch less than a foot long. Keeping his feet where they stood, he managed to reach far enough to grab both and hold one in each hand. He took a deep breath, sucking the cold air into his lungs before exhaling. There was no more time to wait.

Rick took a soft step forward, testing the leaves. Then another. He'd taken a half-dozen steps before the crunch gave him away. When the soldier swung around, Rick flipped the branch to the left.

It swirled through the air until it cracked against the side of a tree.

The soldier rose to his feet, the weapon still ready, and took a step forward. He swept the area with his weapon as Rick took another set of quick steps closer to the bridge. When he stopped, he tossed the rock in the same direction as the stick. It landed on the ground with a thud and the soldier advanced toward the sound, his movements silent and fluid. His rifle trained straight ahead, the soldier was jerking in a short, tight pattern as he scanned for the source of the noise.

Rick figured he was ten yards from the soldier and directly behind him. The footbridge was straight ahead. He had two options. He could make a run for the bridge and hope to cross it without taking a bullet in his back, or he could disarm a professionally trained soldier. The former option was far more appealing.

As he took his first step toward the bridge, the soldier swung back around. Rick felt the scope catching him in its sight. Instead of trying to hide, his instincts took him in a surprising direction. He played possum.

He raised his hands above his head. "Help," he whispered. "Sir, please help me. I'm trying to escape. These peop—"

"Stop!" barked the soldier. He kept the weapon trained on Rick and moved deliberately toward him. "Don't move. Move and you're toast. Got it?"

Rick stood motionless. He was no more than five feet from the footbridge, standing on the edge of the sharp creek-side embankment. "I got it," said Rick. "Please help me."

The soldier stopped two feet from Rick. He tilted his head away from the scope but kept the rifle leveled at Rick's chest. His finger was extended along the guard and not pressed against the trigger.

The soldier jabbed the weapon in Rick's direction. "Who are you?"

"My name is Rick," he said breathlessly. "I'm trying to get out of here. I—"

"Where did you come from?" The soldier's eyes were wide and bright against the dark smudge of mud-brown camouflage face paint streaked across his cheeks and chin.

Rick hesitated and stuttered an unintelligible answer. His shoulders were starting to burn from holding his hands above his head. His arms were heavy.

The soldier snapped, "Where?"

Rick motioned with his chin toward the other side of the bridge. "Over there," he said. "The other side of the creek."

The soldier glanced to his left and the footbridge behind him at the exact moment the distant sound of semiautomatic gunfire cracked in the distance. A cascade of echoing shots followed two short bursts. The soldier turned toward the sound, momentarily distracted.

It was enough time for Rick to step to one side and grab the rifle barrel with both hands. He yanked it as hard as he could, pulling the soldier off balance enough that when he applied leverage and shoved the butt at the soldier's face, it caught the man squarely on the jaw.

The soldier grunted and his head snapped forward to his chest. Still holding the barrel, Rick jabbed at him again and struck the soldier's collarbone with a sickening crack.

The soldier cried out in pain and dropped to his knees, losing his grip on the weapon. Rick, surprised by his success, stumbled back with the rifle in hand. He nearly tumbled onto his back but caught himself against a thin tree trunk.

The soldier was on his side in the dirt, his body splayed on the embankment above the creek. He was whimpering and cursing Rick.

Rick stood against the tree for a moment, stunned, before he shook free of his mental paralysis and bounded across the footbridge. He thought about disarming the soldier of his sidearm and radio, but didn't want to risk getting too close. An injured soldier was still a soldier.

Rick crossed the bridge and spun around, running backward for a few steps. He called back to the soldier in a hushed strain before turning back to run away from the creek.

"I'm sorry!" he called. "I hope you're all right!"

His face flushed at the idea of what he'd just said. Nikki never would have apologized. He wouldn't tell her about it.

"You're an idiot," he muttered to himself. His self-deprecation was interrupted by another snap of gunfire. Rick couldn't tell who was firing. He didn't know enough about guns to tell the difference by listening. The resonant echo also made it hard to decipher from where exactly the shots were originating. As he got closer, the high-pitched whine of the tripped perimeter alarms chirped and buzzed.

He reached the northern stretch of fence and climbed over it one leg at a time, dropping on the ground behind the garage. He puffed air from his cheeks, trying to catch his breath, and carefully worked his way toward the garage. Reggie Buck was supposed to be atop the garage's roof, perched there with a bipod and scope-equipped rifle. He looked up toward the pitch, straining to see Reggie, but couldn't spot him.

His job was to enter the garage and hop onto one of the two all-terrain vehicles Gus had stored inside his EMP-proof garage. But with the sounds of yelling came another short burst of gunfire from the south, closer to the garden and chicken coop. Ignoring the plan, Rick crouched low, his calves and thighs straining with exhaustion, and squeezed between the garage and the eastern fence line, moving south toward the garden and where he heard the most noise. He clung to the side of the garage for cover and so that Reggie didn't mistake him for a raider, until he came to the edge of the driveway that ran in front of the garage's entrance.

He stopped and pulled the rifle to his shoulder. Aiming south and squeezing shut one eye, he drew the other to the scope. His field of view filled with a hazy greenish glow. He swept the scope from left to right until he was aiming diagonally across the property toward the greenhouse. In the distance he could see two or three figures low to the ground. They were moving slowly, as if crawling on the ground. He swept back to the right and saw another signature. Someone was pressed up against the edge of the garden between its wooden edging and the fence. Rick stayed low and curled around the corner of the garage to look toward the front porch.

As he moved, he heard shouting from the greenhouse. For the first time, he could make out what was being said.

The first voice was definitely a soldier. "We don't want to hurt anyone!" he shouted above the squeal of the alarms. "We're here to help you. Please cease fire."

The second voice was Gus, much closer to Rick. Perhaps from the main house.

"Not gonna happen. Get off my land. Fourth Amendment. Read it."

Another rattle of gunfire pierced the air. Rick could see bursts of yellow-orange light from near the porch, muzzle flashes from Gus's weapon.

"Man down!" called one of the soldiers. "Man down!"

Instantly, a crash of weapons erupted around Rick. He resisted the urge to cover his ears and retreated. He ran north around the back side of the garage toward the rear of the house.

From above his head, he could hear Reggie engaged in the gunfight. Rick emerged on the western edge of the garage and dropped to the ground. He crawled toward the main house on his elbows and knees.

Strobes of light flickered in the milky smoke that hung low to the ground. It was like a war zone, or what Rick imagined how one would feel. The repeated *rat-tat-tat-tat* of military rifles vibrated in his bones. His ears were thick with a high-pitched ring. As he crawled west, scraping against the dirt to the house, he looked south. Gus was pressed against the greenhouse, using it as cover. He'd poke his head out and open fire on a moving target before retreating behind the Plexiglas building.

Rick looked forward to the lattice woodwork that covered the crawl space underneath the main house. He was halfway there when he saw Karen kick through one of the lattice panels. She scrambled from underneath the house and pushed herself to her feet as Rick heard a pair of rounds zip past his head.

"Karen!" he yelled, still on his elbows. "Karen! Get down! You're going to—"

A single shot struck her in her chest, spinning her around like a puppet on strings until her limp body collapsed to the ground. She was facing Rick with wide eyes. Her mouth was open and she gasped for air.

"Karen!" Rick screamed and scrambled to her side. He raised himself onto his knees and grabbed her body.

Staying as low as he could, he dragged her against the house. He sat against the lattice and pulled her into his lap. He stroked her clammy forehead with one hand while searching for the wound with the other.

In the surreal lightning storm of the gunfire, he could see the tears streaking from the corners of her eyes and down her temples. She was trying to talk but couldn't.

"Shhh," Rick said, fighting back tears himself. "Don't try to talk," he whispered. "It'll be okay. It'll be okay."

Finally, with both hands he ripped open her shirt and gasped. The wound was coursing blood. Rick fumbled around on her chest before he found the hole. He pressed his palm against it and Karen arched her back in pain. She gripped his leg with one hand, squeezing his calf. As quickly as she'd applied pressure, it weakened. Her body shuddered against his. Her eyes started to close.

"Karen," he said, his throat aching, "stay with me. Stay with me."

Her eyes widened for a moment; then her lids lowered. Her jaw slackened; her chest heaved once and then relaxed.

Rick pulled her head next to his and squeezed her limp body. "I'm so sorry," he whispered into her ear. "I'm so sorry for the pain I've caused you."

Rick knew she didn't hear him. She was already gone. The mother of his child was dead. Still, he gripped her familiar body against his, holding her for his comfort. A wave of guilt was washed away by a torrent of anger that exploded inside him.

This was Gus's fault. Karen would be alive if he hadn't opened fire. If he hadn't insisted on fighting back. Rick looked to the greenhouse at the instant Gus's body flailed wildly, responding to a barrage of bullets hitting him.

As he collapsed to the ground, a trio of soldiers approached in formation. One of them checked Gus's body then all three of them moved cautiously toward the house. The gunfire had stopped.

Rick inhaled the stinging smoke and moved Karen's body from his lap. Rolling over, he pulled himself under the house by using the opening Karen had created with her feet.

Almost immediately Kenny greeted him. The boy wrapped his arms around his father's neck, squeezing him tight.

"Dad," Kenny whispered, "what do we do? Where's Mom?"

Rick looked for the others, but couldn't see them. Mumphrey, Lana, and Candace were somewhere in the darkness.

"Where are the others?"

Kenny motioned over his shoulder. "Back there. Mr. Mumphrey said he had an idea. Where's Mom?"

Rick didn't have time for new ideas. He grabbed Kenny's face with his hands and looked his son in the eyes. Their noses touched as he spoke.

"Let's get out of here," he said. "Now. I'll worry about Mom."

"But—"

"Now!" Rick said. He looked to his right toward the back of the house. It faced the northern edge of the property. "Go that way."

Kenny didn't argue. He nodded, his eyes wide with fear, and he began crawling toward the back of the crawl space. Rick followed right behind him, focused solely on getting Kenny away from the danger. As he moved along the ground, dodging plumbing and gas lines, he could hear a muted conversation from outside the crawl space. It had to be Reggie Buck. Despite its volume, his voice was pitched with fear.

"I'm coming down," he called out. "I'll drop the weapon. I'll drop it."

Rick scurried to the edge of the crawl space where Kenny was waiting for him. Mimicking Karen, Rick kicked out the wood lattice and the two of them moved into the open. Rick realized then he'd left the rifle next to Karen's body. He was unarmed.

Rick looked to the woods directly beyond the fence before staring Kenny in the eyes. "All right," he said to his son between heavy breaths. "We're heading straight for those trees. When I tell you to go, you run. You don't stop; you don't look back. I'll be right behind you. Once you get into the trees, count as you run. Once you get to fifty, stop and hide. I'll find you."

Kenny's glassy eyes searched Rick's. "What about Mom? Where is she?"

Rick clenched his teeth. He took a deep breath. "Three."

"Dad!"

"Two."

"But—"

"GO!"

Kenny scowled but pushed himself to his feet and started running. Rick waited until Kenny cleared the fence; then, crouched low, he worked his way around the western side of the main house. He was met by the hum of the large natural gas generator that sat next to the porch. Rick stood up and eased his body between the generator and the porch, moving closer to the front of the house.

When he neared the corner, he could hear voices over the generator's hum. He didn't recognize one of them. The other was undoubtedly Mumphrey.

"Like I said," came the familiar phrase, "we're coming out. We're not armed. There's five of us."

Rick clung to the wall, staying out of sight. From his obstructed view he could see six soldiers. All of them were ready to fire, their weapons trained low at the house.

"One at a time," a soldier responded, his words clipped and sharp. "Move slowly. No quick moves. We *will* shoot."

A pair of thumps and a crack later, Mumphrey emerged, his hands up. The soldiers put him on his knees and frisked him.

A pair of soldiers helped Mumphrey back to his feet.

"How many more?" one of them asked.

"Like I said—" Mumphrey adjusted his shirt and brushed off his pants "—there's five of us. Me, three women, and a boy."

Rick curled back behind the house and stepped between the generator and porch. He'd heard enough. He ran until he hit the fence, climbed over it, and dropped to the other side, falling to the ground. He scrambled to his feet and bolted for the woods. He hit the trees and started counting. When he hit twenty-five, he slowed to a walk and picked his way through the yaupons and holly bushes that littered the brush.

Breathless again, he called to his son with a strained whisper. "Kenny?" He squinted, trying to find his son amongst the tangle. He stepped carefully, his breathing heavier than his feet.

"Kenny," he called, "it's Dad."

A short figure appeared from behind a thick pine.

Rick shifted his weight and spun toward the soft whimper. The boy lunged at his dad and wrapped his arms around Rick's waist. Rick held his son against him and tried to catch his breath.

Kenny looked up at Rick, his eyes seemingly knowing the answer to a question he didn't have to ask.

Rick loosened his son's hold and knelt in front of him, his knees sinking in the soft dirt. He gently placed his hands on Kenny's shoulders, prepared to embrace him.

"Your mother," Rick said, "she…she…"

Kenny's eyes danced from Rick's eyes to his chest and back. His chin quivered. "There's blood on your shirt, Dad."

Unable to look at it, Rick held Kenny's gaze with his own. Tears burned his eyes, cascading down his face. His chest felt tight. Telling Kenny the truth would make it real. Saying it out loud made it permanent.

"She…your mom…"

Kenny's expression flattened. "She's dead."

Rick pulled his son into his body. He needed consolation as much as what he offered Kenny. Karen didn't deserve the life she'd lived or the death she'd endured. Rick felt responsible for both. He didn't know what to tell his son. The words wouldn't come.

Kenny's body stiffened against Rick, resisting his father's efforts to hold him. But when Rick was about to let him go, Kenny melted. He buried his head into Rick's neck and sobbed. His little body shuddered and he gasped for air on the edge of hyperventilating. Rick resisted the urge to emotionally collapse. His son's cries emboldened him, reminding him of the need to be strong. He held his son for what felt like hours. It was likely minutes. The sun was beginning to peek through the veil of branches and leaves that surrounded them.

"What do we do now?" Kenny asked. His swollen eyes were red with sadness and exhaustion. "Where do we go?"

Rick sighed. In the distance, he recognized the rumble of the military transports. He knew where they were headed. Mumphrey, Candace, and the Bucks were on their way to the camp. He was sure of that and it left him with no options.

"I think we need to go get Mr. Mumphrey," he said. "He'd try to get us."

Kenny wiped his eyes with the backs of his hands. He didn't ask where they were going or how they'd free Mumphrey. Rick wondered if shock had taken hold.

He thought of different things to say to his son to try to make him smile, to lessen the immediacy of the pain he felt. Nothing felt right. Nothing seemed appropriate. So Rick Walsh pushed himself to his feet and took his son's hand.

"We gotta go back to the ranch," he said. "We need a ride."

CHAPTER 9

The food was better than anything he'd tasted in months. Clayton savored the maple flavor of the bacon, the strong, freshly brewed coffee, and the hearty crunch of granola. He couldn't get enough.

"It's not going anywhere," said one of his uniformed guards.

Clayton held the spoon inches from his mouth. "What's not going anywhere?"

The guard snorted a laugh through his nose. "The food. You're eating it like it's got wings, feet, and a place to be."

Clayton shoveled the spoon into his mouth and squirreled the granola into his cheek. He followed it with a swig of coffee. When he'd emptied his mouth, he aimed his spoon at the guard. "Funny that you say the food's not going anywhere. The same applies to everyone and everything in this place."

The guard smirked. "Ungrateful, aren't you? You could be up there."

Clayton shrugged and plucked the last piece of the bacon from his plate. It was slightly overcooked and crispy. He relished the last bite and ignored the glare from the guard.

They were sitting in the corner of what they called the "feed" level in building two. Apparently building three's cafeteria was suffering from power issues, so they'd made the longer train trek to this bunker. Clayton had to admit that, despite its Orwellian feel, the underground complex was impressive. It reminded him of a subterranean International Space Station, a series of tunnels and levels connected together to form a human-sized gerbil habitat. The only thing missing was microgravity.

The cafeteria was crowded, in large part due to the inaccessibility of the feed level in building three, and was a study in people. Clayton watched men, women, and children as they moved through the space. He studied their faces and their body language. Incredibly, nobody seemed concerned. They drank their coffee and ate their granola. They talked amongst themselves. Some laughed, others were engrossed in their DiaTabs, tapping and scrolling through whatever it was on their screens.

He scanned the tables, expecting, for some reason, to see a familiar face. And then he did. A young girl with gentle blond curls. She was lanky but athletic as she crossed the room with her tray of food. There was a confidence there. Her eyes were large and round and her cheeks carried a hint of cherub, as if there was a trace of baby still there.

Clayton froze. His heart thumped. Sweat bloomed at his temples and the back of his neck. He dropped the spoon into the bowl.

The guard reached out and touched Clayton's trembling arm. "Hey," he asked. "You okay?"

Clayton's gaze narrowed and everything blurred but the girl. She walked toward him. He smiled at her. She didn't see it.

Clayton waved at her. "Carrie?" he said. His voice trembled when he called again. "Carrie? It's me. Clay."

The girl didn't respond. She turned left into the crowd and disappeared. Clayton stood at his seat and craned his neck to see the girl. He cupped his hands around his mouth.

"Carrie!" he yelled.

Many of the nearby diners turned to Clayton and stared. The guard stood and forcefully gripped the astronaut's shoulder. "You need to calm down," the guard said.

Oblivious to the guard and the growing numbers of staring eyes, he stood on his toes. A glimpse of the girl flashed between a pair of adults. He called for her again and waved his arms. "Carrie!"

"Who are you calling?" the guard asked. "Do you know someone here?"

Clayton shrugged his shoulder from the guard's grip and looked at the man as if he had three eyes. He pointed into the crowd. He was wide-eyed. "It's my sister," he said.

"The little girl?"

Clayton glanced at the crowd, noticing the confused stares from those around him. He looked back at the guard's knitted brow and the concern evident in the frown lines that framed his face. Clayton's face reddened. He could feel the heat in his cheeks. He sank to his seat and buried his head in his hands.

"Oh my—" he said weakly. "I-I'm sorry."

Clayton's twin, Carrie, died when they were fourteen. They were fraternal twins on their way home from soccer practice. She'd been the star, a starting forward whose kicks sent the ball exploding like a rocket from her strong right leg. Clayton played sparingly on their select team as a defender. He'd always believed he'd made the invitation-only team only because of Carrie. He'd only recently grown taller than her and was still awkward with his gangly arms and legs.

Their coach had ended practice early when storm clouds gathered above the park and distant thunder threatened with increasingly frequent rumbles.

He'd called shotgun and got the front seat next to their mother. Carrie had reluctantly taken the backseat behind their mother as the clouds emptied and the rain began falling in sheets.

"Do either of you need to go to math tutoring?" their mom had asked, pulling out of the soccer park's parking lot. "I can take you on the way home. I don't want to have to go out twice in this weather."

"I'm good," Carrie had said, yanking the seatbelt across her body and clicking it into place.

Carrie had never needed to go to tutoring. She'd been taking geometry and was acing it. Clayton was still a year ahead of most classmates, taking algebra, but needed the extra help a private tutoring center provided.

"I do," he'd said. "I've got a test on axioms of equality tomorrow."

"I can help you if you need it," Carrie had offered. "I don't mind. I like property equations."

"Thanks," Clayton had said. "I'd rather go to tutoring. We already pay for it."

Their mother had chuckled. "We pay for it," she said. "That's a good one."

"You know what I mean," Clayton had said.

His mother had turned the windshield wipers to the fastest interval. Instead of turning left to go home, she'd turned right onto the four-lane road that ran parallel to the park, and accelerated into traffic. A flash of lightning flickered an instant before a crash of thunder reverberated through the car.

Sitting in the feed level of building two, Clayton could still feel the thunder in his chest all these years later. He could hear the shrill squeal of the tires on the wet pavement and the sudden, violent jolt of the pickup truck slamming into the rear door of the driver's side of the car.

He remembered his unconscious mother bleeding onto the deflated air bag, her body uncomfortably pushed into his. There were the strangers who pulled him from the tangled metal of the car, the firefighters who rescued his mother, the medics who tried unsuccessfully to save Carrie's life.

Since that day, Clayton's fraternal twin had remained frozen in his memory as a gifted fourteen-year-old. He'd sometimes see her in crowds.

She was at his high school graduation and at the rehearsal dinner the night before he and Jackie got married. She'd been amongst the tourists in Red Square on his first trip to Moscow. She'd stood outside the State History Museum, her white coat a stark contrast to the gold-spired red building. It always took him a moment to realize she wasn't really there, that he'd seen her in someone similar. It felt real in the moment. It was as if she was always there at the most critical, life-altering moments of Clayton's life.

He'd never talked about it. He'd kept it from Jackie and hidden it from the litany of doctors with whom he'd visited during his time at NASA. If they'd ever suspected he occasionally "saw" his long-dead twin sister, he'd have washed out of the astronaut corps many times over.

This vision was different, though. He was thoroughly convinced, in that moment, that he'd seen his sister. Clayton bit his lower lip, lifted his head, and looked over at the guard.

"Sorry about that," he said, trying to play it off. "I was confused for a second. Maybe it's the concussion."

The guard's eyes twitched. Clayton pushed his chair back from the table.

"Can I get one more serving of granola?" he asked. "Is there enough?"

The guard nodded with what appeared to be a newfound sympathy. "You're not supposed to make a second trip, but I don't care. I'm sure you're hungry. How long did you say you were up in space?"

Clayton picked up his bowl and set the spoon on a napkin. "About ten weeks. A little longer than that."

"Did you get stir-crazy?"

Clayton shook his head. "Not really. We had the whole world on our porch."

The guard smiled. "Don't worry about the bowl," he said. "Get a clean one up at the buffet."

"Can I get you anything?"

The guard thanked him and declined. Clayton wove his way from his corner table to the buffet on the opposite end of the cafeteria. He joined the line next to a tall woman, who smiled at him before running her long fingers through her strawberry blond bob.

"It's busy," she said to him. "I had to come over here from building three."

Clayton picked up a bowl and held up four fingers. "Building four," he said.

A man ahead of the strawberry blonde leaned back and looked at Clayton. He held a plate of eggs. "Did I hear you say building four?"

Clayton hesitated but answered, "Yes. The offal level."

The man stepped from the line and let the woman move ahead of him. He sidled next to Clayton and lowered his voice. "Offal level? What's that?"

Clayton shrugged. "Some sort of holding area. I guess they'll move me at some point."

A nervous smile crept across the man's face and he leaned into Clayton. "Are you the astronaut?"

Clayton took a step back from the inquisitor. "Who are you?"

The man nestled the plate of eggs against his chest and extended his right hand. His eyes brightened. "I'm Vihaan Chandra. I work for the Space Weather Prediction Center. Well, I did. Now I'm here."

Clayton gripped the bowl almost tightly enough to break it. He took another step back from Chandra. He didn't take the scientist's hand. Instead, he shook his finger at him and chastised him through clenched teeth. "You were in Boulder. You knew what was coming and you dismissed it as an anomaly. You blamed the equipment. Two of my friends died up there because—"

"Whoa!" Chandra held up his hand in surrender. "I didn't—"

Clayton turned away from Chandra and started back to his table, but the man grabbed his arm and stopped him. Clayton jerked free of his hold.

"I can help you," Chandra said softly.

Clayton tugged on his shirt sleeve at the cuff and straightened it. The woman, the strawberry blonde, was standing with Chandra now.

"What's going on?" she asked. "Is everything okay?"

Chandra kept his gaze on Clayton. There was a deep sadness in the man's eyes. The deep creases at his temples and across his forehead revealed recurring pain and unrelenting stress.

Clayton squared his shoulders. "How can you help me? How do you know who I am?"

Chandra, one hand still raised in peace, stepped closer to the astronaut. "I know you're an astronaut because I heard about you," he said under his breath. "I know you're here against your will. I would guess you want to leave. I want to leave too."

"You didn't answer my questions."

Chandra glanced over Clayton's shoulder. He spoke through pressed lips. "Not here. We have company."

"Everything okay?" Clayton's guard asked, approaching the trio. "I saw a little scuffle. You cut in line, Shepard?"

Clayton nodded. "Sorry about that," he said to Chandra. "Won't happen again."

Chandra's eyes skipped from Clayton to the guard and back. "I'll come find you if it does."

Clayton took the hint. "Go ahead," he dared the scientist. "Room twenty-nine. Building four."

The guard tugged on Clayton's shoulder. "C'mon," he said. "You don't need added attention."

Clayton gave Chandra a knowing glance and then followed the guard back to his table. "I didn't get my granola," he complained. "I'm still hungry."

"You'll have to wait until lunch," said the guard. "It's time to head back to your room. You've already had too much excitement for one meal."

***

Chandra watched the astronaut leave the cafeteria without returning to his table. "Shepard," he mumbled. "Clayton Shepard!"

"What was that about?" asked Sally. "I'm lost."

Chandra slid back into the buffet line and grabbed a yeast roll. He set it on his plate next to the eggs and looked at his breakfast. Suddenly, he wasn't hungry.

"Vihaan?" Sally asked. "Who was that?"

Chandra took a glass of orange juice and led Sally to an empty table. He noticed the crowd was beginning to filter from the room.

He offered Sally a seat, slid into his, and then pulled the chair close to hers.

"That was Clayton Shepard," he said. "He was an astronaut on the International Space Station."

"So?"

"He was on the station when the first CME hit," said Chandra, working hard to contain his excitement. "He managed to leave the station and get back to Earth. Now he's here."

Sally waved her hands with frustration and pursed her lips. "I'm missing something here, Vihaan. You're not making sense."

Chandra exhaled and slowed down. "Somehow, he landed near here. I don't know the details. But he's being held here against his will. He's in some sort of cell. You saw he had a uniformed guard with him."

"Maybe he's dangerous," Sally suggested.

"No," Chandra said, "he's an astronaut. He's not dangerous."

"Why was he mad at you? Had you met him before?"

"No," said Chandra. "It's a long story. It has to do with the CME and data that my people gave to—it doesn't matter. He doesn't know me."

"You said you could help him. Help him do what?"

"Escape." As soon as he said the word, he regretted it.

Sally's expression morphed. Her features squeezed tight. Her eyes disappeared beneath her brow. "Wait, what?" she said, raising her voice. "What are you talking about?"

Chandra placed his hand atop hers. "Shhh, don't call attention to our conversation."

Sally looked around the room and then glared at Chandra. "Look, you seemed like a nice guy. You have a sadness in your eyes that makes you...approachable. But you're freaking me out here. I don't think—"

Chandra pulled his hand away. "Okay, that's fine. I'm not going to try to convince you. I shouldn't have said anything. I don't know you. Never mind."

Chandra pushed himself from the table, leaving the eggs, the roll, the juice, and Sally behind. He hustled out of the cafeteria to the elevator. He stepped inside, cursing himself for having said anything. He didn't know her. Now she could go to their superiors and get him in trouble.

The uniformed guard attending the elevator interrupted his mental self-flagellation. "Where are you going?"

"Sorry," said Chandra. "Transfer level, please."

The guard hit the button, but before the elevator doors closed, a hand slid between them and they reopened. It was Sally. She stepped inside and stood next to Chandra without acknowledging him.

"Transfer level, please."

The guard pressed the button and closed the doors. The elevator whisked them up a level and glided to a stop. The doors whooshed open and Chandra waited for Sally to exit first. She stepped into the corral and walked a half-dozen steps toward the train tracks. Once the elevator doors shut behind Chandra, she turned around and stopped.

"I'm sorry," she said. "I shouldn't have talked to you that way."

Chandra kept walking. "It's fine," he said. "Not a problem."

Sally spun on her heels as he passed her and walked at his pace. "You're mad at me."

Chandra glanced at her as he approached the tracks. "I'm not mad. I don't know you, Sally. We met yesterday."

Sally frowned. "Look, we're going to be here a while. We both need friends. I want to be your friend."

Chandra sighed. The tracks rumbled as the next train approached. He could hear its engine growing louder as it neared the building two platform. He stepped toward the edge of the floor closest to the tracks.

Sally touched his shoulder. "Can we be friends?"

He looked over at her. Her eyes were wide with remorse. Her long eyelashes flicked as she looked up at him and brushed the hair from her forehead. Chandra was good at a lot of things—math, science, technology. He wasn't good at reading women. He never had been. His wife, Anila, had called him oblivious to her advances. She joked that if she hadn't made the first move, they'd never have exchanged more than pleasantries.

Something, though, told him he could trust Sally. Who could blame her for being freaked out at the mention of escaping their hi-tech refuge? He was certain that ninety-nine percent of the people living in the bunkers thought the setup entirely benevolent. Ninety-nine percent of them didn't know Treadgold.

"Okay," he said. "We can be friends."

The train roared to the platform and a gust of wind blew Sally's hair into her eyes. Chandra reached out and brushed it from her face. She smiled. The train screamed to a stop and they boarded, the only ones in their cabin. The doors shut and the train accelerated. An automated voice filled the space.

"You are departing building two," it said pleasantly enough. It was different than the sterile voice he'd heard the day before. *"Our next stop is building one, followed by building five. If building one is your destination, please prepare your belongings and be sure you have possession of your DiaTab, DiaWatch, and keycard."*

Chandra had his arm wrapped around a stainless floor-to-ceiling pole in the middle of the car. "Why do you think we have keycards?" he asked, shaking his wrist. "We have the watches and the tablets. I mean, they could just use the technology in those devices. We could swipe them across the entry panels. We wouldn't need the cards."

"I hadn't thought about it."

Chandra shrugged. "It seems redundant."

"Yeah," Sally agreed. "I guess so."

They rode in silence through the first three stops. Uniformed soldiers climbed aboard at buildings five and four. Sally smiled at them when they boarded. They ignored her.

The automated voice chimed through the cabin. *"Our next stop is building three, followed by building two. If building three is your destination, please prepare your belongings and be sure you have possession of your DiaTab, DiaWatch, and keycard."*

"This is us," Sally said.

The train slid to a smooth stop and the doors whooshed open.

Two of the guards exited the car. Sally and Chandra stepped off the train and walked together to the elevator, taking it down four floors to the "open/intact" level.

Sally walked close to Chandra as they made their way along the hall toward the T-intersection at its end. When they reached it, Sally paused.

"What are your plans today?" she asked.

"I'll go get ready for work," he said. "I'll spend most of the day in the lab, I guess. I'll see you at dinner?"

She smiled broadly. "Sounds great," she said. "I really am sorry, Chandra."

"It's fine. See you later."

He waved goodbye and walked toward his section of the floor. When he reached the end of the hallway, he looked back over his shoulder. Sally was gone. He retraced his steps and hustled to the elevator, pressing the button like an arcade game.

"C'mon," he said, urging the elevator to arrive.

The doors finally opened and he reentered the car. The guard raised an eyebrow and smirked.

"Forget something?"

"No," said Chandra. "I'm late for work. Transfer corral, please."

The doors slid shut and within minutes Chandra was back on the train headed to building four. Three stops later he was almost there. He was sprinting from the train by the time the doors had finished opening.

The elevator was already open when he arrived. "Level five, please."

The guard pressed the button for the lowest level. The doors slid shut and the elevator lumbered downward. Chandra was sweating. His heart rate was elevated, his mouth dry.

He was certain the guard would ask for some sort of clearance, but he didn't. He was sure he'd need to swipe his card or flash his DiaTab. He didn't. The elevator slowed to a stop and its doors opened to reveal a large dimly lit space. Stencils painted on the wall provided vague directions and Chandra followed them along a narrow hallway until he reached another large space. On either side of the space were six doors. At the far end, another hallway led to what Chandra assumed was another set of cells. The rooms were consecutively numbered in descending order beginning with the number thirty. Across from it was room twenty-nine. Chandra looked over his shoulder into the corridor through which he'd just speed-walked and approached the astronaut's room.

He knocked on the door and pressed his cheek against it. "Hey," he called, trying not to speak too loudly, "it's me. I'm the guy from the cafeteria. I'm here to help you."

From behind the door he could hear shuffling and footsteps. The astronaut was coming to the door.

"I can't let you in," said Clayton.

"It's okay," said Chandra. "I'm here to help. My name is—"

"No, I can't let you in because I can't unlock the door," said Clayton. "I'm a prisoner, remember?"

Chandra sighed. "Oh, I didn't think about that."

"You can't open the door?"

Chandra tried the handle. He took out his keycard and swiped it across the magnetic pad on the wall. He held up his DiaWatch and touched it to the pad. Nothing worked.

"Sorry," said Chandra. "I don't have access."

"Then how are you supposed to help me?"

Chandra looked around the space. There weren't any cameras, at least none he could see, and there wasn't any other noise, aside from the hiss of the cool air circulating through the ventilation system overhead. If there were other prisoners, they'd be banging on their doors by now.

"I think we're alone," said Chandra. "Have you seen any other prisoners?"

"Hostages, you mean?" Clayton corrected. "No. I think I'm the only one for now."

Chandra considered Clayton's terminology. It was more appropriate, and it applied to almost everyone in the bunker system whether they knew it or not.

"We're all hostages," said Chandra. "That's my take. That's why I want to help you out of here. I want to leave too."

"I don't understand," said Clayton. "I've got a family. I need to get home. That's why I want to leave. Why would you want out of here? You've got shelter, food, protec—"

"This place isn't what it appears to be," said Chandra. "This is some sort of government attempt at depopulation. They want to start over with a new society. They want the people on the surface to cannibalize each other and—"

"Cannibalize?"

"Figuratively," said Chandra. "They want to control and eliminate as much of the outside world as they can. That's just what I know. I'm sure there's more that—"

Clayton banged on the door and Chandra jumped back, his heart racing.

"You have got to get me out of here!" said Clayton. "I have got to get home."

Chandra took a step closer to the door and touched it with his fingertips. Clayton's anxiety and frustration were palpable, as if he could feel it oozing through the door.

"I'll get you out of here," Chandra promised.

"If you can't get me out of the room, how do you expect to get us both out of this underground labyrinth?"

"I'll figure it out," Chandra answered.

He ran his hands through his hair and scratched the crown of his head. He stepped away from the door and looked over his shoulder again. A feeling of dread was growing stronger, a sense that he was running out of time. He thought about the people he'd met. Who could help him? Not his boss. Treadgold would do everything he could to keep everyone underground and in the dark. He couldn't trust Sally, not yet. Besides, her expertise was telemetry and guidance. She wouldn't have access to anything that could help him inside the bunkers. Maybe once they were back on the surface she could help.

Van Cleaf? No. She was every bit a part of the scheme as was Treadgold. He didn't know her anyhow. He only knew her name.

There was Henry Rector, the lab supervisor. He seemed too squirrelly to be any help, even if he was sympathetic to the cause.

Chandra muttered to himself, "Who else? Who else?"

"What?" asked Clayton. "I can't hear what you're saying."

"Sorry," said Chandra. "I'm just trying to figure out who might be willing to help me with the security system. I need—" Then it hit him.

Bert Martin!

Bert Martin was the Australian security system analyst. He'd seemed nice enough when they'd met outside the Jeppesen Terminal. He'd been as anxious as Chandra. It was true he didn't know Bert much better than anyone else, but at least he had the necessary expertise.

"What?" asked Clayton. "You stopped talking."

Chandra pressed his hands and cheek against the door. "I've got an idea," he said excitedly. "I think I know someone who might be able to help us."

"Who?"

"I don't want to say it aloud," said Chandra. "I'll be back. I promise. I'm going to get us both out of here." Chandra started to back away from the door.

"Hey!" said the astronaut. "What's your name?"

"Vihaan Chandra. You can call me Vihaan."

"I'm Clayton," said the astronaut. "Clayton Shepard."

"I know," said Chandra. "You're the spaceman."

***

Clayton banged his fists on the door. "You're the spaceman," he whispered to himself. " I'm the idiot who wasted time and risked my life trying to rescue two dead crewmates."

He backed away from the door and crossed his room toward the desk. He clenched his fingers into tightly wound fists and then flexed them outward. He wanted to punch somebody.

The spaceman.

Clayton paced in the room. He was stuck here, and as much as he could blame others for his predicament, he knew deep down it was his own doing.

He should have evacuated the ISS the minute the power blinked. He'd repeatedly compromised his own life for the sake of two dead men, taking an ill-advised spacewalk that defied his training, carrying their bodies into the Soyuz, and then dragging them across a glacier. He'd unwittingly attracted wolves with their decaying corpses. Worse than all of that, however, was the time he'd wasted.

He'd spent hours aboard the ISS, awaiting the right pressurization before taking the walk and then hours more acclimating to the station once he'd returned. He'd taken hours more to traverse the icy descent from the frozen glacier field than necessary, dragging a makeshift travois with an injured leg susceptible to infection.

Every step along the way he'd taken actions that were contrary to what his mission should have been, should still be: getting home to Jackie, Marie, and Chris. Had he done what he was trained to do, what his instinct should have been, he might be home now. He certainly wouldn't be a hostage stuck five or six stories underground. He'd have avoided the second coronal mass ejection, or at the least he would have crash-landed in Texas somewhere much closer to home.

For a brilliant man who loved his family, he hadn't acted like either. He'd been selfish, off-task, and stupid.

He stopped pacing and sat on the edge of his bed. There was a growing ache over his right eye and along the right side of his head. Clayton squeezed his eyes closed and took a deep breath.

He pictured Jackie with the kids, all of them cursing his name for not having come home yet. He could see them in the house, eating by candlelight and sleeping together in the large California king bed in the master bedroom.

He could see Jackie giving the children chores to keep them occupied. Assuming there was no power, she'd have them cleaning the kitchen after meals and taking out the trash so it didn't pile up in the house.

Marie and Chris would resist reading books, but Jackie would insist. With no Snapchat, Instagram, Kikk, or YouTube, they'd have no excuses. She'd probably start Marie on the dog-eared copy of *Grapes of Wrath* she kept by the bed. *Animal Farm* would be a good starter for Chris. He might not note the fascism subtext laced into the narrative, but he'd like the story. It was short enough to hold his attention. Both books would be remarkably appropriate given the real-world circumstances in which they found themselves.

Maybe they'd play board games, Monopoly and Life. Jackie was ruthless at both. She'd amass properties to the brink of bankruptcy before draining everyone else of their funds. Chris loved being the banker. Marie was always the Scottie dog.

"Who am I kidding?" he said aloud, the pain in his head throbbing. He swung his feet from the floor and lay down on the bed on his left side. He hoped the pain, pulsing with the stress of an elevated heartbeat, would lessen.

Who am I kidding? They don't have time for games or classic literature. They're busy surviving.

Given Jackie's instincts, she'd probably taken in neighbors. She'd loaded her Glocks, barricaded the doors, and filled the bathtubs with water. She'd be fending off those who'd do them harm, not bargaining or explaining radial authoritarian nationalism.

Bile slid into his throat. He wasn't sure if the nausea was from the sudden headache or the thought of his family fighting without him. He opened his eyes and stared at the wall opposite the bed. His DiaTab was perched on the edge of the desk. Clayton remembered what he'd said the first time he'd sat at the desk the day before. He'd asked himself an important question he hadn't yet answered.

How do I engineer my way out of this?

He focused on the DiaTab. There were answers in that machine. He knew it.

There wasn't anything he could do about what was already done. There was no point in dwelling on it. He needed to look forward, do what needed to be done to get out, and yet again find a way home.

Fighting the jolt of pain in his eye and head, he got up and crossed the room to fetch the tablet. He palmed the device and carried it back to his bed. The DiaTab was meant to be an all-in-one communicator, data-finder, and tracker. It had restrictions built into its software that would prevent the average user from manipulating its functions in a way those in command didn't want it to function. There had to be a back door into the device that might give him a better idea of where he was and how he could get out.

Clayton was no hacker, but he was an engineer with a love for all things technology. He'd bought the first-generation iPhone on June 29, 2007. When it died, he took it apart and studied its guts. He'd been among the first with a Google Pixel. He'd purchased two of them, one to use and one with which to experiment. He'd experimented with TOR and had built a PC from scratch that ran both Microsoft and Apple operating systems. Some guys played softball or ran marathons, others hunted and collected guns. He was a tech nerd and knew enough to be dangerous. Although he'd tried to get Chris interested, it hadn't taken.

He thumbed awake the DiaTab's screen and tapped his way through a series of applications until he found an icon labeled MANAGE. He tapped the MANAGE icon and nothing happened. He held the icon for several seconds. Nothing.

He held the icon and the DiaTab's home button at the same time and the haptic response vibrated against his finger. The screen was replaced with a display that resembled a telephone keypad. Underneath the keypad were the words ENTER AUTHORIZATION.

Clayton's initial excitement at having accessed the MANAGE application was ebbed by the need for a passcode. He had no way of knowing how many numbers or letters were required. It could be four, six, or more. Still, he gave it a shot.

I-L-L-U-M-I-N-A-T-I. Enter.

The keypad flashed red.

"Worth a try," Clayton mused.

Instead of wasting his time deciphering the impossible combination, he tried something else. He remembered the iPhone had a glitch in an early version of its ninth-generation operating system. There was a combination of tasks that would bypass the locked passcode.

By asking Siri, the phone's digital assistant, the time, it would generate a clock on the screen. A user could then tap the clock, a plus sign, and then enter gibberish into a search bar to ultimately bypass the lock and gain access to the home screen of the phone.

Given this device was relatively new and probably functioned with a variety of bugs, there had to be a backdoor into the MANAGE application. For close to an hour he manipulated the device in countless ways until finally a combination of taps and holds and verbal commands overloaded the software.

At first he thought he'd ruined the device. The screen went black for nearly a minute. When it awakened, it displayed a screen Clayton hadn't seen before. There was a grid of new applications, all of them under the heading MANAGE.

His headache having subsided, Clayton scrolled through the options. Each of them had toggle switches that would allow the user to turn the various functions on or off. All of his were in the on position except for one. Those activated included Li-Fi connectivity, GPS/GLONASS, Voice-Activated Auto-Record, Data Transmission Interval, and DiaWatch connect. The only option turned off was one labeled KeyCard.

He hovered his thumb over the screen, deciding which one to tap first, considering the benefits and pitfalls of each application. If he turned off the tracker or the Li-Fi connectivity, they'd suspect he'd tampered with the device. The DiaWatch connect was a convenience. He wouldn't change any of those applications.

He did tap the VAAR and DTI toggles, turning them off. They wouldn't miss recorded and transmitted conversations from a man who was supposed to be in a solitary environment. He could only hope his device hadn't already transmitted his conversation with Chandra. If it had, there was consolation in the thought that whoever monitored the transmissions couldn't filter through every conversation happening within the bunker compound.

That left the KeyCard toggle. Clayton's eyes drifted from the screen to the magnetic pad adjacent to the room's entry door. He tapped the toggle, turning it on, and walked over to the door. He swiped the device across the pad and a metallic click accompanied a green light.

The door was unlocked.

Clayton reached for the handle but stopped short. If he opened the door, alarms might sound. They'd know what he'd done, that he'd figured out the device and could roam undetected through the maze of hallways and rooms until he figured a way out.

The likelihood of escaping alone, though, was zilch. He'd need help. He'd need Chandra. It was better to wait and be smart than rush and be foolish. Now wasn't the time to open the door, but simply knowing he could was satisfaction enough. He waited until the door clicked again and the light at the pad turned red, turned back to the desk, and set down the DiaTab. He'd give Chandra a chance to help him.

CHAPTER 10

"Remind me why we're doing this?" Jackie panted. She and Nikki were on their third lap around a loop composed of three intersecting roads on the JSC property. Nikki was a few beats ahead of Jackie as they turned left onto Avenue B from Fifth Street. She slowed to answer her new friend.

"Just because the world went to pot doesn't mean we have to do the same," she said. "I'm thinking zombies are coming any minute now. We'd best be able to run."

Jackie laughed. "Right," she huffed. "Zombies."

The former mixed martial artist's strides appeared effortless. It was almost as if Nikki floated from step to step.

"Seriously," Jackie called, "can you slow it down a bit? I'm not as young as you are."

Nikki slowed, but not because of Jackie's breathless request. Up ahead of them, stepping into the women's path, were two men. They stood in the road with their arms folded across their chests.

Jackie caught up with Nikki. "Can I help you?" she asked, bending over to catch her breath.

Both of them looked at Jackie. "We need you to follow us," said one of them.

Jackie gulped a breath of air and motioned toward Nikki. "Can she come with me?"

The men looked at each other and shrugged. "That's fine."

"What is this about?" Jackie asked. "Is it something urgent? Something about my husband?"

She realized as she followed them that they were the same two men who'd visited her home with Irma Molinares.

"We're going to the Communications and Tracking Division," said one of them. "You'll want to see it for yourself."

The men walked briskly, not waiting for either woman, even though Nikki kept pace. When they neared the entrance to building forty-four, Jackie sped up. One of the men was holding the door for them; the other was inside awaiting them. Jackie stepped across the threshold into the dark space. It took a moment for her eyes to adjust.

"Follow us," said the man who'd held the door. He was the taller of the two. It struck Jackie as they wove their way through the first floor that neither man had ever introduced himself.

"What are your names?" Jackie asked. "You know mine. You know Nikki here."

"I'm Bowman," said the man leading them to wherever it was they were headed.

The other man called from behind the group, "I'm Perry."

"So Bowman and Perry," Nikki asked, "what's with the cloak-and-dagger stuff? Why not just tell us what the deal is?"

"No cloak-and-dagger," Perry said, opening the door to a large room that looked like a mini version of master control. "We'd just rather not have to explain things more than once."

"Or out in the open," said Bowman, shutting the door behind them. "You never know who's listening."

Jackie and Nikki exchanged glances. Irma Molinares was standing at the far end of the space. She smiled at the women and moved toward them. The men offered Jackie and Nikki seats in front of a desk equipped with four large computer monitors. Each of the screens displayed different information. It was gibberish to Jackie.

Bowman sat on the edge of the desk nearest Nikki. He spoke softly, as if he were a third-grade teacher explaining quantum mechanics to a toddler.

"These screens display for us critical systems information about any given mission," he said. "Typically, of course, the information isn't something we share with anyone outside of the group of people who need to know."

"Understood," said Jackie.

"I am aware that Molinares told you we know the Soyuz hatch was opened and that we have some satellite imagery that tells us he left the Soyuz. We know it was him because of an intercepted radio communication in which he used his amateur radio license callsign."

"Yes?" said Jackie.

"Typically, we'd be able to communicate with our Russian partners," Bowman continued. "They're the only ones who can see the descent module after separation. Most of the telemetry ceases because much of the instrumentation is jettisoned. But they have these Luch relay satellites that—"

"She doesn't care about that," Irma interrupted. "Stick to the basics."

"Okay," said Bowman. "The basics…"

Perry stepped toward the desk. "Once the parachute deploys, the module starts checking in with GPS and GLONASS satellites. That's the only telemetry data it sends and it goes to the Russians."

Nikki raised her hand. "What's GLONASS?"

"It's the Russian version of GPS," said Bowman. "It stands for Globalnaya Navigatsionnaya Sputnikoyava Sistema."

"You don't have access to it?"

The men looked at each other. "Not technically," said Bowman. "That data gets transferred to an international satellite system for search and rescue. It's called COSPAS-SARSAT. That way the Russians can find their capsule even if they lose it on the way down."

"The crew has a GPS receiver and a satellite phone in their survival kit," Perry said. "It's been in there since 2003. There was a ballistic entry and—"

"The basics," Irma reminded them.

"The bottom line is," said Bowman, "the Russians would be more likely to know where he is than us. All of that, however, depends on the satellites' functionality. And since the CMEs hit, the satellites aren't what they were."

"We can neither confirm nor deny," Perry said with the hint of a smirk, "that we have ways to circumvent the Russians' exclusivity."

"While most of the satellites have failed because of the repeated blasts of electromagnetic energy," said Bowman, "a satellite called SBIRS miraculously survived."

"What's SBIRS?" asked Jackie.

"SBIRS is a space-based infrared satellite system. It is intended as an early missile warning system that—"

"Like Star Wars?" Jackie cut in. "President Reagan's big idea forty years ago?"

Bowman smiled. "Yes, exactly. The satellite has nuclear-hardened components. It's always on, and it's easily maneuverable."

"So what have you seen with this SBIRS?" asked Jackie. "I have to assume this setup is leading somewhere?"

"Yes," said Perry. "Typically our military runs the system. They have an asset here who works with us. We put that asset to good use when we first detected the Soyuz had separated from the ISS."

"The infrared system is incredibly helpful," said Bowman. "That's how we spotted the Soyuz landing site in the Columbia Icefield in Canada."

"In conjunction with some other specialized technology, it helped us learn that your husband moved from the landing site to a visitors' center at the edge of a large glacier," added Perry. "We also know he left that area in a vehicle. Heat signatures revealed that, somehow, the person he connected with on his ham radio found him and picked him up."

"Heat signatures?"

"Typically, we wouldn't be able to see it. But because there is no traffic on the roads, we were able to detect trace increases in ambient temperature. As we said, the infrared system is incredibly helpful."

"So you know where he is?"

"We think we do," said Bowman. "Your husband is remarkably resourceful. I mean, remarkably. It's amazing."

Jackie rubbed her sweaty hands together and clasped them in her lap. "Where is he?"

Both men answered together. "Denver, Colorado."

"Denver? How? Why?"

"He managed to secure a working aircraft," said Bowman.

"He found a plane and flew to Denver?"

"Yes," said Perry. "We believe the second CME damaged the plane mid-flight."

Jackie suddenly felt heavy. Her arms, her legs, her head—all were hit with the weight of what she worried Perry was about to say. She sank back in the chair, only half aware of the words flowing from the men detailing what they thought had happened to her husband. Nikki grabbed her hands, squeezing them for support.

…survived a crash…could be injured…disappeared…no evidence of a body…

"Mrs. Shepard?" asked Bowman. "Mrs. Shepard, are you all right?"

Irma Molinares put her hand on Jackie's shoulder. "Jackie?"

Unable to respond, it was as if reality was slapping Jackie with increasingly powerful waves. Despite having prayed for information, for a sign that Clayton was coming back to them, she now wished she knew nothing. It was better to imagine her husband finding his way home. Having proof that he was on his way and struggling was worse than ignorance.

Several months before he'd lifted off on his doomed mission, she'd been at a local HEB grocery store. She was waiting for a batch of freshly made guacamole and was scanning Marie's Snapchat story on her iPhone when an alert flashed on her phone. It was from a local news station promoting its early afternoon newscast.

Remembering Columbia and its crew sixteen years later. The exclusive story tonight at five.

"Sixteen years?" she'd said aloud. "How can it be that long?"

They weren't in the astronaut corps in 2003. Clayton hadn't even thought about it. They were pregnant with Marie and had only just purchased their first house. But she remembered that day as if she'd been in Mission Control.

It was a Saturday. The weather was beautiful. The seven crew members had all but completed their eighteen-day mission. They were sixteen minutes from landing at Kennedy Space Center. They'd crossed the California-Nevada state line at twenty-two times the speed of sound, but sensor readings were already indicating issues. Mission Control called the shuttle to report anomalous tire-pressure readings. The commander, Rick Husband, responded. His transmission was garbled. MCC asked him to repeat.

"Roger," said Husband. *"Uh, bu—"*

That was the last communication before the shuttle burned up in the blue skies over Texas and Louisiana. Camcorders caught the fiery disintegration and it was aired on television. It was a nightmare. Husband, William McCool, Michael Anderson, Kalpana Chawla, David Brown, Laurel Clark, and Israeli astronaut Ilan Ramon all died. They were among the twenty-two men and women who lost their lives either training for or executing a space mission.

While Jackie stood waiting for her guacamole, she recalled how she'd felt that day, how she'd imagined the shock, pain, and denial of the family members awaiting their loved ones' safe return from orbit. The cook handed her the plastic tub of deliciously mixed avocado, onions, tomatoes, cilantro, jalapeno peppers, limes, salt, and black pepper. She blankly thanked him and smacked the sour taste growing in her mouth. She'd never transposed that sense of loss onto herself. Until that moment, standing in the grocery store, she'd not considered the emotional burden of sending her husband into space. Even if he made it into orbit safely strapped inside a tube laced with explosives, and he survived months orbiting around the planet in an inhospitable vacuum, there was no guarantee he'd land on Earth intact.

The acidic ache in her gut she'd felt that day in the grocery store returned as she sat in the JSC's building forty-four. Her husband had survived a fall from space but might not have survived an airplane crash.

Nikki snapped her fingers in front of Jackie's face. "Jackie!"

The astronaut's wife snapped from her trance and sat forward in her chair. There was no use dwelling on what might have happened to her husband. She could wallow in self-pity, or she could control what was within her power.

She forced a smile. "I'm fine," she said. "Clayton is fine. Like you said, there was no body at the crash site. So he had to walk away, right?"

Perry, Irma, and Bowman exchanged glances before looking down at their feet. None of them wanted to say what they were thinking collectively.

"What?" said Nikki. "Tell us what you're not telling us. We've spent the last ten minutes listening to irrelevant crap like GLONASS and SIBRS. The least—"

"It's SBIRS," Perry corrected.

"What?" snapped Nikki. She'd adopted a fighting stance. Her arms were flexed, her hands tightened into fists. She stood with one foot behind the other as if to prep for a nasty axe kick with her rear leg.

Bowman, perhaps sensing her aggression, responded for Perry. "He was saying it's SBIRS. The satellite. It's not SIBRS. That's all."

"Whatever it is doesn't matter to me. You guys are more than happy to geek out on us with your *Battlestar Galactica* nonsense, but when it comes to telling Jackie something she really needs to know, you're hesitant."

"We don't think he walked away," Bowman volunteered. "We didn't say that."

"Then what did he do?" asked Jackie.

"There's some additional data we've been tracking," said Perry. "It fits with why there's no sign of your husband at the crash site."

Nikki threw up her hands. "Sheesh! No wonder people think you faked the moon landing. You hem and haw and—"

Jackie reached out and put her hand on Nikki's side. "It's okay," she said softly. "I appreciate your advocacy. But let them talk. They'll get around to telling me whatever it is they can't seem to articulate. Right?"

Nikki's shoulders dropped; the tension in her muscles relaxed. She nodded at Jackie and glared at the others.

"We believe there is a government bunker not far from where your husband landed—"

"Crashed," corrected Jackie.

"Crashed," Bowman acknowledged. "We know from satellite data we've collected over the years that there are emergency bunkers at various spots around the country."

"Other countries have them too," added Perry. "They started with the Cold War."

"One of them is in Denver," Bowman said, "under the airport."

Jackie looked to Irma for confirmation.

"Yes," said Irma. "Underground."

"If that's the case," said Jackie, "then why can't you communicate with them? They're a government facility; you're a government facility. You should be able to check with them and find out where my husband is."

"We wish it were that simple," said Irma. "The problem is that bunker isn't supposed to exist."

"They left us out of the loop," said Bowman. "That is to say, we don't have a way to get in touch with them. They've closed themselves off, as have other bunkers in West Virginia, Virginia, Pennsylvania, and California."

"Wait," Nikki interrupted. "This makes absolutely no sense."

Perry folded his arms across his chest. "What doesn't make sense?"

"This whole grand conspiracy thing," said Nikki. "That stuff is all make-believe. I was an MMA fighter. I know make-believe when I see it."

"But you just said you understand why people think we faked the moon landing," said Perry. "I mean—"

Nikki rolled her eyes. "Really? That was hyperbole."

96

Jackie stood. She walked from the group to the corner. She drew her hands to her face, covering her mouth and nose.

"So," she said, her voice muffled behind her hands, "you call me in here to tell me my husband is alive but missing and that he's probably stuck underground in a secret bunker shut off from the outside world?"

"We thought you should know," said Bowman. "We know it's not much."

"But it's something," Irma piped up.

Jackie paced in the corner, her hands on top of her head as she walked. "It's something," she said. "You're right about that."

Nikki planted her hands on her hips. "What's the bunker for? Who's in the bunker?"

"We don't know exactly," said Perry. "We're not cleared at that level."

Bowman nodded. "We're guessing if you know the answers to those questions, you're probably in the bunker."

"Still doesn't make sense," said Nikki. "Our government's been gridlocked for years and you're telling me they're smart enough to populate some vast network of secret bunkers with the rich and powerful?"

"That's what we're saying," said Irma. "We think most of the people at headquarters in DC are hiding in one. Nobody here or at KSC can get ahold of anyone there. What's left of our secure communication is getting no response."

Jackie walked back to the group. She ignored the pit in her stomach, the overwhelming sense of dread that threatened to suffocate her. "All right," she said, drawing the attention of the others in the room. "This confirms three things for me."

"What?" asked Nikki.

"First of all," she said, "it tells me that no help is coming and things are only going to get worse. If those in power are hiding underground, they know more than we do."

Nikki agreed. "What's the second thing?"

"Maybe I'm delusional," she said. "I just can't accept that I'll never see my husband again. But when you told me he's being held underground in a place his family can't go, it makes me believe he's more determined than ever to find his way back to us. That's how I'd react. If I had a breath left in my lungs, I'd be fighting against someone keeping me from my family and doing everything I could to outsmart them. I don't know how he'll do it, but I honestly believe in my heart he'll come back."

Perry raised his finger. "Statistically—"

Nikki stepped toward Perry. "Statistically you should be quiet. You guys have said enough."

"What's the third thing?" Bowman asked.

"The third thing is that I know we can't stay here. Not forever. This powerless, messed-up world is our new normal. We've got to adjust. Staying here doesn't allow us to adjust."

Irma shook her head. "Don't be so rash, Jackie. It's safe here. You said it yourself. It's going to get worse out there."

"I'm not being rash," said Jackie. "I'm being realistic."

CHAPTER 11

WEDNESDAY, JANUARY 29, 2020, 10:20 AM CST
COUPLAND, TEXAS

The bodies were gone when Rick and Kenny snuck back onto Gus's property. There was a dark, irregular stain on the dirt outside the main house. Another larger blotch colored the ground between the greenhouse and the front porch.

Rick tried to distract his son, but Kenny saw both drying pools of blood. He knelt down at the one by the house, reaching toward it with his trembling fingers.

He looked up at Rick, his eyes swollen with tears. His voice cracked. "This was Mom," he said. "This is where she…died?"

Rick squatted beside his son, placing his hand on the boy's back. In so many ways Kenny had matured. But as the fourteen-year-old mourned his mother, Rick saw the child in him. A boy always needed his mother.

"C'mon," Rick said. "We need to get to where they took everybody. We need to rescue them."

"Why don't we just leave, Dad?" he asked. "Why don't we go back to Houston? We could go to Mom's house and stay there. We'd be safe there."

Rick sighed and helped his son to his feet. "You're right. We could do that. We could run. But I've done a lot of running, son. You know that. You know I've made bad, selfish choices."

"You have," Kenny said, "but you're all I have now. It's just us. We can't go save people we barely know. It's stupid. I can't lose you too."

Rick winced at Kenny's words, his son's acknowledgment of his shortcomings. He couldn't blame him for owning his feelings and, surprisingly, the boy hadn't yet blamed Rick for his mother's violent death.

"You're not going to lose me," said Rick. "I'll tell you what. After we save Mr. Mumphrey, Candace, and the Bucks, we'll stick to ourselves. We'll pick a spot and stay put. We'll ride this thing out together. You and me."

Kenny wiped his nose with his shirt sleeve, dragging a web of snot. Rick pulled his own sleeve over his palm and wiped his son's face. Kenny looked down at the dark stain and sucked in a ragged breath.

"All right," he said. "We go save them and then we come back here, Dad. That way we're close to Mom too."

Rick wasn't sure coming back here was the right idea. Then again, there weren't too many good ideas to which Rick had ever attached himself. His life was a series of questionable choices. Why not make another one for the sake of his son's cooperation and sanity?

"All right," he said. "Deal. Now let's get out of here."

They crossed to the yard toward the greenhouse. Rick had parked his Jeep at the front of the property. As he approached it, his heart sank.

"Motherfu—" he said through clenched teeth.

"What?" Kenny asked. "What's wrong?"

Both the front and back tires on the passenger's side were flat. Rick jogged to the side of the Jeep, hoping his eyes were playing tricks on him. They weren't.

Both of them were ripped from gunfire. The Jeep was useless.

"Can't you change the tires?" asked Kenny.

"I've only got one spare," said Rick. "I could fix one but not both."

"What do we do?"

Rick motioned toward the back of the property. "We go find out what Gus was keeping in the garage. He said he had plenty of transportation in there. Let's hope it's true."

Rick led Kenny to the garage and they hoisted the large bay door, revealing a pair of older model cars, an aged pickup truck, and a pair of ATVs in the deep, climate-controlled space. They were hit with a strong chemical odor.

Kenny scrunched his nose. "It smells like gasoline in here."

Rick knelt on the floor. Underneath two of the cars were pools of evaporating gasoline. He stood up and walked over to the sides of the vehicles, which were parked in tandem. Both of them were decorated with several bullet holes. He looked over his shoulder at the exterior wall of the garage and saw a half-dozen tight circles of light where the rounds had penetrated the building.

"Yeah," he said. "These two are no good. Guess that leaves us with the pickup and the ATVs."

"I can drive an ATV," said Kenny. "Let's take those."

Rick shook his head. "Assuming we rescue all four people, we need space for them. The ATVs wouldn't hold more than two riders each."

Kenny frowned. He walked over to the smaller of the two ATVs and gripped one side of the handlebars.

Rick moved across the garage to the pickup truck. It was a sun-faded gray with hints of rust along its wheel wells and the edges of the tailgate. The bed was covered in a thick black plastic liner. Lying on the liner was a pair of long four-by-twelve pieces of wood. He looked back over his shoulder at Kenny playing with the ATV.

"Hey," he said, "I have an idea. Let's take both."

Kenny's eyes widened with excitement.

It couldn't hurt to have two travel options if one failed, Rick figured. He still had no real idea how they'd approach the FEMA camp.

After checking to make sure the old truck would start, he pulled open the tailgate, and he and Kenny dragged the ends of the boards to the ground, creating a ramp for the ATV. They crossed the garage to the four-wheeler.

Rick checked the printed starting instructions on the vehicle's fuel tank, which was positioned between the front seat and the handlebars. He hopped into the driver's seat, bouncing on the responsive shocks, and turned the key to start the machine.

"We need to make sure it works," he said to Kenny and pushed the start button.

The engine cranked and revved. The ATV purred, ready to go. Rick gave his son a thumbs-up, waved at him to back up, and accelerated toward the back of the pickup. He stopped at the edge of the wood planks and turned off the ATV, hopped off the vehicle, and adjusted the steering wheel.

Five strenuous minutes later, they'd managed to get the ATV into the bed of the truck. Rick picked up the boards and slid them next to the four-wheeler.

Kenny searched the garage and found a bag full of bungee cords, which they used to strap down the ATV. They climbed into the cab of the truck.

"This truck is old," Kenny remarked. "There's no seatbelt."

"Yeah," said Rick. "It's a manual. And it stinks too, doesn't it?"

The truck smelled like mothballs and dust, as if someone had stored his grandmother's clothes in the cab.

"It is what it is, son," he said. "Let's work with what we've got."

"Are you taking a gun?" asked Kenny.

Rick released the emergency brake, pressed the clutch, and shifted the truck into reverse. He extended his right arm on the back of the seat behind Kenny's head and looked out the rear window. He pressed the gas and accelerated from the garage and onto the driveway.

"No," he said. "The less reason we give anyone to use their weapons, the better."

Rick shifted into first gear and drove away from the property. He looked over at Kenny leaning on the door with his elbow. The boy was staring out the window at the passing landscape.

They drove the mileage between Gus's ranch and the FEMA

camp, the T. Don Hutto Residential Center. It took twice as long as it had when Rick had gone the night before. He was driving slowly, cautiously. When he guessed they were a quarter mile from the entrance, he slipped the truck into neutral and drifted to a stop off the edge of the road at a cluster of yaupon. They were across the street from a church and the Taylor Police Department. It was as good a spot as any.

He shut off the ignition and took the keys. "Let's go."

The two climbed from the truck, locked the doors, and Rick took the keys from the ATV. He pulled open the tailgate. He drew the wood planks to the ground, positioning the tops of them underneath the ATV's tires and then climbed into the bed. He hopped onto the four-wheeler and started it. He carefully backed the vehicle down the boards and to the ground. He shifted into a low gear and told his son to hop on the back.

"We may need this thing more than I thought," he commented.

With Kenny's arms around his waist, he drove a couple of blocks to West MLK Junior Boulevard and made a wide left turn. The fifty-horsepower engine roared and echoed across the empty street, reverberating against the single-story buildings that lined either side of the narrow two-lane street.

The noise was too much of a risk. Rick took his hand off the accelerator, braked to a stop, and turned off the ignition.

Kenny let go of his father's waist. "Why'd you stop?"

"Too noisy," Rick said. "C'mon, help me push this thing off the road."

Kenny climbed off the machine and helped his dad guide the ATV into the dirt lot of an old cotton processing place called the Williamson County Gin. The gin was a collection of tin-roofed buildings that looked like something straight out of the early twentieth century.

"What's a gin?" asked Kenny. "Is it like vodka? Do they make alcohol here?"

Rick grinned. "Not this kind of gin," he said, stuffing the keys into his pocket. "This is a place where they took cotton and separated the fiber from the seeds. Before the gin they had to do it by hand."

"Oh," said Kenny, sounding disappointed.

Rick motioned for his son to follow up along the edge of the street as they worked their way west toward the prison camp. If he had his bearings straight, they'd take the street until it ended; then they'd have a choice to cut north and west along the streets or venture into the grassy fields that surrounded the camp and its high fencing. Kenny jogged to keep up with his father's quick pace and longer legs.

Rick looked over at Kenny. The boy was the spitting image of his mother: deep, penetrating eyes, thick hair with a hint of a wave, and a dimple-framed smile. It was surreal to him that Karen was dead. He couldn't grasp the emptiness her sudden, shocking death would carve in their son. He slowed a beat and nudged Kenny's shoulder with his.

"Remind me to tell you about Eli Whitney when we have more time," he said. "He changed the world."

"Eli who?"

"Whitney," said Rick. "He invented the cotton gin."

Kenny looked up at his dad. "Okay," he said. "I'll ask you when we're not trying to break into a prison camp to rescue four strangers."

He also had his mother's sarcastic wit.

Rick patted his son on the back and they neared the end of the street. Low-hanging power and telephone lines drooped from house to house on either side. Both were useless. The houses were modest, but the yards were, for the most part, manicured. The driveways featured older cars and trucks. Some of the houses were surrounded by waist-high chain-link fences. It looked like a normal small-town Texas neighborhood. But when Rick paid closer attention, he noticed that wasn't exactly the case.

Trash cans at the curb were mostly on their sides, refuse spilling into the street. It appeared as though animals, or humans, had rifled through the cans. Most of the cars in the driveways had shattered windows. Some of them had their trunks open.

The homes' windows in most cases were open or broken. There

was clothing strewn across several yards. The sweet and sour scent of rotting food filled the air. As they approached the last house, Kenny stopped and looked over his shoulder.

"What is it?" Rick asked.

"It's the middle of the day," Kenny said. "We're in a neighborhood. I haven't seen anybody. No parents, no kids, no dogs or cats. It's like a ghost town."

Rick didn't know what to say. His son was right. It *was* like a ghost town. They stood at the edge of the street and looked back from where they'd come. Rick imagined he was looking at the past and the future all at once. He swung back toward the open field at the end of the street. Two hundred yards in the distance the complex rose.

"Which way?" Rick asked his son. "Should we try to approach it from the field or the street?"

Kenny shrugged and squeezed his brow. "Why are you asking me?"

Rick put his hands on his hips and looked north on the road marked Doak Street. His eyes scanned west across the field. There was nothing but fencing and buildings. It was a wide-open grassy field with no protection. If they took that route, they'd definitely get caught. He was squinting, his hand over his eyes to block the late morning sun, and searching the fence line for some sort of effective approach when Kenny tugged at his shirt.

"Dad," he said, his voice hushed. "Look! What are they doing?"

Kenny was pointing southwest to a spot fifty yards south of the fence. Right along the edge of a thicket of tall trees, there was a group of men digging with shovels. The men weren't in uniforms.

"I'm not sure," Rick said. "But those aren't soldiers."

Rick waved Kenny to follow him, and instead of running through the field or marching north on Doak, they jogged south. Rick clung to the edge of the street, his eyes constantly moving to watch for anyone who might spot them. They made their way a quarter of a mile south to the end of Doak Street before turning west. They were past the tree line and moving along Rio Grande Street. There were no houses and the grass grew taller, and there was more vegetation behind which to hide. They inched their way closer to the tree line and found a dry creek bed that snaked its way through the trees and toward the south edge of the complex.

They slowed along the creek bed and walked. Rick was winded and sensed Kenny was in worse shape. He was on the verge of wheezing from the dry, cold air they'd been forcing in and out of their lungs.

Rick whispered, "You okay? Can you keep going?"

Kenny rolled his eyes. "I'm fine, Dad. Don't worry about me."

Rick patted his son on the back and pressed forward. He led his son down a shallow embankment, crossed the dry bed, and then climbed a steeper incline to the other side. No sooner had they reached the north side of the bed than they could hear the men digging and talking. Rick held his finger up to his lips and motioned for Kenny to get down. Both of them squatted behind a thick oak.

"How many is this today?" asked a heavyset bald man that reminded Rick of a prototypical carnival strong man. The man was wearing a white tank top and dark sweatpants. He was leaning on his shovel.

"Four," said a taller man wearing a baseball cap, who was thinner and less muscular. "Or five."

A third man with a shock of jet-black hair and a matching lumberjack beard climbed out of a hole and tossed his shovel onto the ground. He grunted and then took a swig of water from a large plastic jug. Rick looked at the ground. He could see at least five large holes that sank shoulder deep into the earth.

"That's not as many as yesterday," he said. "I think yesterday was eight."

"How's it happen?" asked the tall man.

"Who knows?" said the strong man. "I don't ask questions. I just do what they tell me."

"Smart," said the lumberjack. "I've seen them take people into rooms and those folks don't come back."

"They just pull 'em from the yard?" asked the tall man.

"That's what I heard. I also heard some are from the raids, the people who don't want to surrender."

The tall man wiped his brow with his arm. "I heard a lot these are people fighting for rations. You know they're not giving people enough."

The strong man picked up his shovel. "I'm telling you," he said, "you mind your business. Keep quiet. Do your job. You'll survive."

Kenny pressed his cheek to the back of Rick's head behind his ear. "What are they digging?" he whispered. "What are they talking about?"

Rick put his finger to his lips. Now wasn't the time for a conversation, however hushed. If his son hadn't picked up on the fact the men were digging graves, there was no point in telling him. Not yet.

The men kept digging until an army green truck rambled from the fence, through a gate, and rolled to within a few feet of their work. Uniformed soldiers climbed from both sides of the cab. Neither of them acknowledged the men. They disappeared behind the truck. Minutes later they emerged with four more soldiers and a rectangular pine box.

Rick felt Kenny's hand grip his shoulder and squeeze. His son had figured it out. This was a graveyard. These men were undertakers.

"Hey," barked one of the soldiers, "all of these holes ready? They all dug to specs?"

The strong man nodded. "Yes sir," he said. "All of them."

"We've got two to drop," said the soldier. "I need all of you in a hole so we can ease them into place."

The men obliged without saying anything. One by one, the trio climbed into a hole. The soldiers eased to the side of the hole and then tipped the coffin at a forty-five-degree angle. They grunted and argued, and it took some effort, but they managed to get the box into the hole.

The soldiers marched to the back of the truck and appeared with a second, smaller box. They didn't struggle as much to lower it into the same grave as the one before it.

The soldier who'd done all of the talking bent over at his waist and put his hands on his knees. He extended his neck to look down into the hole. He crinkled his nose. "We could get two more in there, I guess," he said and stood up straight. "We'll be back in a couple hours. Keep digging until then."

The strong man climbed from the hole and wiped a dirt stain onto the belly of his white shirt. He helped the other men back to the surface before walking to the truck. "You want us to fill the holes, sir?" he asked the soldier. "You know, like a proper grave?"

The soldier opened the truck door and stood on the tread, hoisting his arm onto the roof of the cab. He surveyed the holes, counting them with his finger. "Nah. We won't fill them until later in the week. People seem to be dropping like flies in there. Somebody got sick. It's spreading fast. The elderly can't take it. They're dying of dehydration by the hour. We'll need to fill those holes to the brim before we cover them back up. Too much work otherwise."

The soldier ducked into the cab, slammed the door, and backed away. The truck spun in the dirt as he shifted into drive and sped back to the compound. The three men stood still, leaning on their pitched shovels until the tall one said what Rick figured the others were thinking.

"Disease?" the man asked. His head was cocked to one side and his eyes were nearly squeezed shut. His question had the tone of disbelief. "You buy that?"

The lumberjack shrugged. "Could be," he said. "We're all crammed in there like sardines. Somebody gets sick, everybody else is exposed."

"Yeah," said the tall man, "I guess. But I don't know about—"

"Best stop asking questions," said the strong man. "Just dig the holes like they tell us, and get your rations when we go in at night. Sleep, go back to work, and dig."

The other two grimaced, grabbed their shovels, and started digging.

Rick motioned to Kenny and backed away from the men. They walked back to the dry creek bed and lay down along the steep embankment.

"I got an idea," Rick said, keeping his voice barely above a whisper. "We head back around to the front of the complex and surrender. We let them put us in the camp."

The color leached from Kenny's face. He opened his mouth, his eyes filled with fear, his pupils shrank to pinpricks.

Rick put his hand on his son's, reassuring him he knew what he was doing. "It's okay," he said. "They're not going to hurt us. We'll surrender with our hands up. Worse comes to worst, they rough me up a little looking for a weapon. They won't find one."

Kenny stammered, "Th-th-then what?"

"Then we find our friends," said Rick, "and we get them out."

CHAPTER 12

MISSION ELAPSED TIME
75 DAYS, 16 HOURS, 13 MINUTES, 17 SECONDS
DENVER, COLORADO

Clayton stared at the man in his cell. He was trying not to blink. It was out of principle. He wanted to show the man he wasn't intimidated.

"So you had a visitor," said Sergeant Vega, repeating himself. It was a statement of fact, not a question. He and Perkins had been in the cell for five minutes. Clayton hadn't said a word.

Although Clayton's eyes stung, he held his focus. He sat on the edge of his bed and gripped the corner of the mattress.

Vega glanced over at Perkins and rolled forward in the desk chair, closer to the bed. He narrowed his gaze. "Look, Perkins can do his thing if you want. We can head back to a place less comfortable than your suite and do this the hard way."

Clayton blinked. "The hard way? Really? That's laughable. You sound like an actor in a low budget Netflix movie."

Perkins was leaning against the wall next to the desk. He sighed and stood up straight. "We know Dr. Vihaan Chandra came to your room," he said. "We know he spoke with you through the door. We have digital recordings of the conversation."

"And we know he wants to leave," said Vega. "We also suspect you'd like out of here as well. So we put two and two together. You two are planning something. What is it?"

Clayton scooted back on his bed and leaned against the wall, pulled his knees up to his chest, and considered his lack of options. It wasn't worth playing the game anymore. It also wasn't worth being entirely forthright.

"Yes," said Clayton, "he came here. You heard the conversation, so you know I don't want to be here. I've asked to leave; you've refused. You're treating me like I'm a criminal. Of course I want out of here. How is any of this a surprise?"

Vega leaned back in his chair and glanced over at Perkins. Both men crossed their arms, as if it were part of the drill. The sergeant looked back at Clayton. "It's not a surprise," said Vega. "But we need to impress upon you how critical it is for all of us that you not try anything, that you don't collude with Dr. Chandra to attempt an unauthorized egress from the facility."

Clayton smirked. "Unauthorized egress? You sound like my stockbroker when he tells me a big loss is just the market retracing gains."

"As we've tried to make clear, for our security and yours we cannot have anyone leave," Perkins said. "It puts everyone here at risk."

"I still don't follow that logic," said Clayton. "If I leave, if Dr. Chandra leaves, who cares? We're two fewer mouths to feed."

Perkins stepped toward the bed and stood next to Vega. "We cannot have people outside this facility know it's here. It's as simple as that. You leave and people find out."

"So what now?" Clayton asked, waving his hand around the room. "What am I supposed to do? Just sit here and wait for the world to end?"

"The world already ended," said Vega. "We're trying to rebuild it. We're—"

Perkins put his hand on Vega's shoulder. "Be patient. We'll find a job for you. In time, you'll understand why we're doing what we're doing and how, ultimately, it's what's best for all of us."

"Does Dr. Chandra know all of this? Have you talked with him?"

"He's our next stop," said Perkins.

The two men left Clayton's room. He checked the door behind them. It was locked. He pulled his DiaTab from his pocket and considered letting Chandra know what was coming, then decided against it.

"Better not," he mumbled. "They're tracking us."

Still sitting on the bed, he extended his leg and kicked at the desk chair. He connected with his heel and the chair rolled across the floor, stopping once it hit the desk. The sound echoed in the cell. He fumbled with the device, thumbing open a series of screens. Clayton imagined the walls of his room were closing in around him. The space was getting smaller, more confining. Being patient, as Perkins suggested he be, wasn't an option. He couldn't sit around waiting for something to happen.

Chandra had promised a plan. He'd told Clayton they'd figure out a way to escape. Clayton, though, wasn't going to wait for the good doctor any longer, not with Vega and Perkins on his trail. He had to figure out his own way out of the subterranean prison. There had to be a way.

"It's not that I'm so smart, it's just that I stay with problems longer," Clayton said aloud, quoting Albert Einstein. "I can't use the elevators, they're guarded. Everything electronic is guarded. Every—"

Wait!

"Could it really be that simple?" Clayton bit the inside of his cheek, considering the right question to ask. What query was the right one, the one that wouldn't arouse suspicion or set off alarms?

Clayton made certain the DiaTab's tracking and recording tabs were turned off. He activated the keycard function, pressed the microphone, and activated the Telenet.

"Please show me the emergency exits," he said, holding the device like a walkie-talkie.

The icon spun in the lower right portion of the Telenet's display for a few seconds. Then a schematic drawing filled the screen.

Clayton's eyes widened. "Bingo."

It was a map of the entire complex. A series of exits and stairwells were illuminated by flashing circles that highlighted their locations.

He stood from the bed and walked to the screen. "Where am I?" he asked the DiaTab.

The icon in the lower right spun and spun. A message appeared on the screen and Clayton spoke the words aloud.

"Unable to locate. I guess that's good."

The schematic on the screen was equivalent to an aerial view of the underground complex. Clayton traced his hand along it, marveling at its size. There had to be miles of interconnecting tunnels that joined five rectangular buildings. In the center of the buildings, which were positioned in a rough pentagonal pattern, was the track system. Its overhead design resembled the meteorological symbol for a hurricane. In the center was the loop that ran to each of the five buildings. At opposite ends of the circle were offshoots that ran away from the main loop. The one at the northern end of the loop curved away and to the east. The southern track curved to the west.

Clayton pressed the DiaTab. "Show me the location of room 29-4 offal level."

The icon spun for a moment; then the aerial schematic rotated away from Clayton, revealing a multilevel frontal view of the complex. It zoomed in on building four and highlighted his room with a flashing circular emblem.

"Where is the closest emergency exit to room 29-4 offal level?"

A second flashing circle highlighted an exit door on his level. It led to what looked like a tunnel and a stairwell. The tunnel appeared as though it led to building three, running parallel to the circular train track. It led to the stairwell between buildings three and two. He traced the path on the screen with his finger. He could find the doorway, the tunnel, and the stairwell. That would be easy. However, from the stairs, he couldn't tell where he'd need to go to reach the surface. Clayton stepped back from the screen. He tapped the DiaTab against his chin, surveying the map in front of him. He needed to be careful about the question he asked next.

Even though his locator and tracker were off, and Big Brother likely wouldn't know who specifically was asking the questions, he'd already mentioned his room number. How many people would be looking to escape a place they'd entered voluntarily a couple of days earlier?

Clayton shook his head. It didn't matter now. He'd already showed his hand. If they were watching him, they'd already be in his room. He threw caution to the wind.

"Where is the surface exit?"

His eyes focused on the spinning icon at the bottom of the screen. He stepped forward, willing a response from the system. After a few seconds, the icon dissolved and a pair of flashing circles at the tops of two buildings strobed the locations of the complex's surface exits.

There was one at what looked like the main airport terminal. Clayton traced his finger along a suspected path to that exit from the closest stairwell in building three. He'd have to get on a train to get there. That wasn't going to happen.

The other exit was atop building five. There was no obvious path to that exit that didn't involve an elevator and an escort. Clayton scanned the screen, his eyes dashing from one side of the schematic to the other. Although he didn't see anything that looked like an analog escape route, he knew there had to be one. If for no other reason, somebody would need a nonmechanical exit to repair damage to the elevator if—

"That's it!" Clayton exclaimed. "Where is the building five mechanical elevator access?"

The system hesitated. The schematic disappeared and was replaced with Van Cleaf.

"I'm sorry," she said. *"I don't understand your question. Could you rephrase it, please?"*

"Building five," said Clayton. "Please show me building five's elevator access."

Van Cleaf's image froze and she repeated herself. *"I'm sorry. I don't understand your question. Could you rephrase it, please?"*

Clayton's brow furrowed. He scratched the top of his head with the DiaTab.

"What can you tell me about building five?"

The system replayed the same message a third time. This time, however, it followed the nonanswer with a question of its own.

"I cannot determine your DiaTab location," it said. *"Please be certain your Li-Fi connection is active. If it is not, I can adjust it at your request. Would you like me to adjust your Li-Fi connection?"*

The image of Van Cleaf in a control room sat idle on the screen. Her recorded avatar was awaiting his response. Clearly, it wasn't going to answer anything about building five. The people in charge didn't want information about that structure available to the herd. Clayton ignored the question and tried again to locate the mechanical access to building five's elevator. This time he asked for the information without mentioning building five.

"Where are the emergency exits?" he asked. "Where do they connect with surface exits?"

The system whirred for a moment, then responded as requested. The screen revealed a three-dimensional schematic that gave him an implausible and complicated path to freedom and took him back to the screen where he'd been previously.

"Where is the elevator's mechanical access?"

A glowing circle immediately flashed at the bottom of building five.

"Please magnify."

The schematic grew in size and zoomed into the bottom floor of building five. Clayton leaned in, not sure that he was reading the schematic description correctly. He rubbed his finger across the screen and then ran it up the wide elevator shaft to the top floor of building five. A smile spread across his face.

The elevator in that building was wide enough for freight. In fact, the schematic labeled it as such. On the top floor was a level labeled GARAGE.

If Clayton could find his way there, he might not only escape, he might have a ride home. It was a long shot. But there it was: hope.

CHAPTER 13

WEDNESDAY, JANUARY 29, 2020, 11:40 AM MST
DENVER, COLORADO

Vihaan Chandra's thighs rubbed together, burning, and he adjusted himself as he walked. Much more friction and he worried he might catch fire. His belly jiggling, he moved as fast as he could toward Bert Martin's room. It was also in building three, but on the opposite end of the floor from his. He licked a bead of cold sweat from his upper lip and hurried past a uniformed guard. If anything, the apocalypse would force him to lose the weight he'd gained after his wife's death. It hadn't happened yet. He told himself he was merely retaining water.

Chandra's eyes swept back and forth, suspiciously checking over his shoulder with each man he passed. People were on their way to lunch and it was more crowded than he'd seen it previously.

He located Martin's room, according to the Telenet directory, and knocked on the door. He checked over his shoulder, bouncing in place like a little boy who had to go to the bathroom.

"C'mon, c'mon, c'mon," he whispered. "Answer the door."

On cue, Bert Martin opened his door. His hair was wet and tousled, and he was wearing a T-shirt and some sweatpants, his feet bare. He smiled at Chandra and pointed at him. "The weatherman, right?"

"Yes. Vihaan Chandra."

Martin snapped his fingers. "Right. Vihaan. I remember. Good to see you, mate. Everything good?"

Chandra looked over his shoulder. "So sorry to just show up, but could I come in?"

Martin shrugged. "Sure."

Chandra moved past Martin into the room. He walked to the back of the space, which was identical to his own, and then back toward the door when Martin closed it. The door hummed and clicked as it locked.

Martin shuffled toward the desk and dipped his hands into his pockets, leaning his shoulder against the wall. He was quiet for a moment and then reached out and stopped Chandra from pacing.

"You okay?" he asked. "You don't look okay."

Chandra took a step back from Martin in the small space between the desk and the wall. He planted his hands on his hips and then ran his fingers through his hair. Finally he crossed his arms in front of his chest and exhaled loudly, searching for the words. He couldn't trust Bert Martin. He didn't know him, really. He moved toward the door.

"I shouldn't have come," Chandra said. "I shouldn't have bothered you."

Martin chuckled. "Well, now you've piqued my interest. You can't leave without giving me a nibble of the bait, now can you?"

Chandra stopped at the door and turned around. "I'm just not sure who I can trust and who I can't," he said. "We aren't friends. I'd hate to put you in an awkward position. It's best if I go. Just forget I came here, okay?"

The smirk evaporated from Martin's face. A look of concern replaced the mild amusement. "Now you've worried me, mate."

Chandra sighed and his shoulders drooped forward in exasperation. He looked at Martin, studying the man's face. There was no telling what he was thinking. Chandra wasn't that intuitive. His wife used to tell him that unless the data was staring him in the face, he'd miss it.

"All right," said Chandra, "what does it matter? I'll end the suspense."

"Good on you," said Martin. "Go ahead."

Chandra started pacing again. He talked with his hands as he explained to Martin what he'd experienced, what he'd learned. He told the Australian about the exclusion of billions of people and how those in charge, whoever they really were, wanted most of the world's population to die off. They wanted to start fresh with bountiful resources and less human pollution. The whole thing smacked of an Orwellian coup predicated on an "advantageous" catastrophic event or events. When he was finished with his incredible story, he stopped pacing and stood in front of Martin, picking at the fabric of his pants above his knees.

"You think I'm crazy?" he asked. "You think I've lost it?"

"No," said Martin. "I don't."

Chandra sighed with relief. "Really? I know it sounds so fantas—"

"I already knew most of what you told me."

Chandra's jaw dropped. He found himself struggling for words, as if he were choking on air. He stepped back from Martin, bumped against the bed, and lost his balance. He fell back onto the bed and pushed himself up with his elbows, still unable to speak.

Martin stepped toward the bed. "All of us knew," he said. "I'm surprised you didn't. We all have special skills the new society will need once we resurface."

Chandra slid to the edge of the mattress. "I don't understand. You knew?"

Martin answered, but Chandra didn't hear him. He was thinking back to the welcome reception in the cafeteria. Nobody around him seemed surprised when the speakers talked about their predicament. Nobody was upset or asking anxiety-laced questions.

They all knew. Everyone but him.

Martin was still talking when Chandra refocused on his host. "—did you not know?"

"What?" asked Chandra.

"How did you not know? I thought everybody was briefed

twenty-four hours before the transport here. We all knew about the second CME. We knew what to pack and what to leave behind."

Chandra's mind drifted again. He recalled his breathless meeting with Chip Treadgold after he'd first discovered the existence of a second CME. Treadgold had acted as if it were news to him.

"Another geomagnetic storm, bigger than a G5, is on its way," he'd told his boss.

Treadgold had sunk back into his chair, pretending to worry. "You're certain?" he'd asked. "What's the Kp index?"

Chandra had stood there, data in hand, and reluctantly relayed the truth. "Well above a nine."

"Holy mother," Treadgold had said. "How long do we have?"

Chandra recalled the meeting and how his boss had lied to him. He'd known all along that the second CME was coming. Hundreds of people already knew, and he'd feigned ignorance and surprise when Chandra had confronted him with the information.

Bert Martin waved his hand in front of Chandra's face. "You there, mate?"

Chandra blinked back to the present, anger swelling in his chest. He rose to his feet and tightened his hands into fists. He looked Martin in the eyes.

"I didn't know," he said through his teeth. "I didn't know what this was. All I knew was that I'd have a chance at surviving the second CME. I didn't realize I'd be trapped down here while innocent people were systematically abandoned."

Martin took a step back, his brow furrowed with concern. His eyes narrowed and danced aimlessly around the room. "What do you mean trapped?"

Chandra shook his fists. "We can't leave! We are not allowed to leave. I already told you this."

Martin cocked his head sideways. "That's not true," he said, seemingly trying to convince himself. "I mean, who would want to leave? But you're wrong. This place was designed to keep people out, not the other way around."

"I'm not wrong," said Chandra. "It was designed to keep people inside. And that's why I'm here asking for your help. I need to get out of here."

"My help?" he said.

"You're a security expert, right?" said Chandra. "You told me you helped put together the security for this place and—"

Martin waved his hands and backed farther away from Chandra, shaking his head. "I'm not sure I can help you. I don't have access to shutting off what needs to be shut off for you to circumvent—"

"I don't need you to shut it off," Chandra said. "I just need to know how I can get out. Please help me."

Bert Martin was the one pacing now. He drew a hand to his mouth and marched toward the bathroom, retracing his steps to the door. "We didn't design the system to trap people. We were told it was to keep people out. I don't understand. Why would they lie to us?"

Chandra smirked. "A better question is 'Why would they tell us the truth?'"

Martin made another pass from one side of the room to the other, mumbled something unintelligible, and disappeared into his bathroom.

"Will you help me?" Chandra called to Martin.

Martin emerged from the bathroom with a towel over his face. He exhaled into the fabric and drew the towel over his head, draping it around his neck. His face was flushed.

"I don't like liars," said Martin, gripping both ends of the towel at his shoulders. "I don't like being lied to. I hope you're not the one who's lying here, Dr. Chandra."

Chandra stood up. "I'm not lying."

Martin squeezed his eyes closed and crinkled his nose. "Okay," he said. "I'll help you."

Chandra smiled and offered his hand to the security expert. "Thank you."

"You better go," said Martin. "If they're as sneaky as you say they are, they're probably listening to our conversation right now. But I have one question for you."

"Anything."

"Even if they are lying to us," said Martin, "even if they are trapping us inside, why would you want to leave? It's got to be worse out there."

"I don't know. But at least out there I have free will. I'd rather die on my feet than on my knees."

Martin crossed to the door, opening it. "I'll figure something out and find you. How soon do you need this?"

"Yesterday."

Martin shut the door behind Chandra after the scientist exited the room.

Chandra navigated the corridors back to his room, looking at the floor as he moved. He worried about exposing himself. Bert Martin was probably right; they could be watching and listening.

He was turning the final corner toward his room when a soft voice called his name. Chandra looked up. Standing outside his room was Sally. She was smiling and waving.

"What are you doing here?" asked Chandra.

Sally stepped back, her smile disappearing. "Well, hello to you too."

Chandra softened, if only to find out what she wanted with him. "Sorry," he said. "I'm just surprised to see you, that's all."

Sally folded her arms across her chest. "Oh," she said flatly. "I came to see if you wanted to walk with me to work."

Chandra studied her face. She appeared sincere. But he'd told her earlier when he left her that he was heading to work.

"Why?" he asked, not sure what else to say.

Sally huffed. "Never mind then, Vihaan." She spun on her heels and marched away, genuinely offended.

Chandra cursed himself for doubting her sincerity. "Sally," he called after her. "Sally, stop."

Sally stopped and turned around. "I'll see you at lunch, Vihaan. If you're in a better mood, you can sit with me. If not, don't bother."

She continued along the hall toward the path to the elevator. Chandra watched her quick, frustrated steps carry her until she disappeared around the corner. He held his key to the door and slid into his room. He grabbed his lab coat from a hook on the bathroom door. It was time for work.

CHAPTER 14

"What do you mean we're leaving?" Marie whined. "We just got here."

Jackie looked at the faces of everyone who'd slept in the small office. All of them, except for Nikki, shared her daughter's dumbfounded gaze.

"You brought us here to keep us safe," said Nancy Vickers. "You said it was safer here."

Betty Brown stepped forward, rubbing the back of her arms with her hands, as if she were trying to keep warm. "I agree with Nancy. You told us this place was better."

"People died in your house, for goodness' sakes," added Nancy.

Betty raised her voice. "That's right. People died. There's blood on the floor. There are holes in the walls."

"I think my ears are still ringing from the gunfire," said Nancy.

Pop Vickers put his arm around his wife's back and pulled her toward him. His eyes were sad. "Jackie," he said softly, "I'm confused too. We picked up and dragged ourselves here less than twenty-four hours ago. It makes no sense."

Jackie's eyes drifted to Brian Brown. He was sitting on a desk, his hands gripping the sides of the desktop as he rocked back and forth.

His lips were pressed flat, his eyes staring off into some imaginary distance. His mother, Betty, was rubbing her arms with nearly the same cadence as Brian's rocking.

Nancy, a reasonable woman, wore the confusion on her drawn face. Her eyeliner was smudged, her cheeks sunken and pale. The sagging skin at her neck was more evident.

Jackie's own children stared at her in disbelief. Marie and to a lesser extent Chris frequently rolled their eyes at her suggestions or guidance. They feigned aggrievedness when they didn't get their way. This was different. They were seriously bothered. Jackie, as only a mother could, felt the growing distance between herself and her children.

Jackie sighed. "I just think—"

"We know what you think, Jackie," said Betty. "You've made it very clear. We just—"

"I agree with Jackie," Nikki interrupted. "We should leave. We should go back to her house or even the Vickerses' house. We shouldn't stay here."

Betty's eyes scanned Nikki from head to toe and back again. "Of course you agree with her."

Nikki visibly tensed. "What is that supposed to mean, Betty?" she snapped.

Betty shrugged, apparently unfazed by Nikki's aggression. "I'm just saying you're a stranger. You have nowhere to go. You're going to hitch your wagon to the—"

Nikki clenched her fists and her jaw. She took a giant step toward Betty and jabbed her finger inches from the woman's nose. "Don't test me, woman. I'm grateful for your trigger pull in the house. That's where my love for you and your incessant complaining ends. I'm not going to—"

Jackie put her hand on Nikki's shoulder. "Stop. It's fine."

Nikki relaxed. "It's not fine," she muttered.

"Here's the thing," Jackie said. "My kids and I can stay here as long as we want to be here. The rest of you can't. You've got a few days at best, okay? Then somebody is going to kick you out or force you somewhere you don't necessarily want to be."

"So we stay here until that time," offered Pop. "Why not do that? Why not stay here until things start to get back to normal? A week or two, and we see where things stand. NASA will give us that, won't they?"

"It's going to get worse out there," said Jackie. "No help is coming. The power is not coming back. We will be on our own eventually. I think it's better to get back to our neighborhood and regroup."

"Shore up our defenses," added Nikki. "Make sure that when the shi—"

"So you wasted our time and energy by coming here to begin with," said Betty. "I just don't understand the logic."

Jackie bit her lower lip, considering how to respond. "I did what I thought was best, Betty," she said softly, "and it's exactly what I'm doing now."

Nikki looked at Jackie and stepped to Betty. "What would you do, Betty?" she said firmly.

"It's okay, Nikki," said Jackie. "I don't need you to defend me."

Nikki waved her off and glared at Betty. "No, it's not okay. You're not some Special Forces guru with a crystal ball and a flamethrower. You are doing the best you can. And so I am asking Betty Crocker here what she would do if she were in charge."

Betty lifted her chin. "First of all, I'm not Betty Crocker. Secondly, I have no idea what you mean by a guru with a flamethrower."

Nikki chuckled. "You have no ideas, period. You stand there in the corner and criticize. You're a naysayer and not a problem solver. You're just a…"

Jackie stopped listening to the bickering between Nikki and Betty. Her attention was focused on Brian. His rocking was more pronounced. He had a pained look on his reddened face. His mouth was squeezed tight and she could see from his white knuckles, he was holding the edge of the desk as tightly as he could. The louder the argument became, the faster he rocked.

"—a harlot," said Betty. "I see the way you looked at Rick. And right in front of Karen. So tasteless. I refuse to take any sort of criticism—"

Jackie raised her hands and shook them. "Stop," she said. "Just stop."

The room was silent except for the sound of Brian rocking while whimpering and murmuring to himself.

Jackie nodded toward Brian. "Betty," she said, "comfort your son."

Betty opened her mouth as if to tell Jackie to mind her own business. She pressed her mouth into a scowl and crossed the room to Brian. She leaned into him and rubbed his back while she spoke into his ear. His cadence slowed and the red drained from his face.

"Jackie, you don't have to justify yourself," Nikki said. "You don't owe anyone anything. You do what you want to do, without explanation, and if they want to follow, they can follow."

Jackie smirked. "Betty's probably right," she said. "We shouldn't have left the house."

Pop Vickers ambled over to the women. "I understand why we came here, and I guess I understand the logic for going back. You were kind enough to take us in, Jackie. We'll do whatever you think is best. Nikki is right."

Nikki blushed. "Thank you, old man."

"I don't understand it," Marie said. "We can stay here. They have food and water; there's even some electricity. Plus they have a lot of people with guns."

"Yeah, Mom," Chris said. "I'm good here. I don't want to go home. I don't want to go out there and have to deal with…"

Jackie coaxed her son to finish his thought. "Deal with what?"

"The bad people."

Jackie extended her arms and motioned for her son. Chris moped across the room to her and she wrapped her arms around him. She squeezed him and kissed his head.

"I understand," she said. "You and Nikki have traveled more than any of us here. You've seen more bad people than we have. But we don't have a choice, Chris. We have to go home."

"I'm scared," Chris said.

Jackie pulled back from her son and lifted his chin with her finger so he'd look her in the eyes. "I know. I am too. We all are."

Chris blinked back tears.

"I also know you're very brave," she said. "You're strong. Marie and I need you."

Jackie glanced at Marie, who was about to protest. She kept her mouth shut and smiled with one corner of her mouth. Jackie smiled back.

"Okay," said Chris. "We can go. I'm ready."

"I'm not ready," said Betty, her voice loud enough for everyone to hear. "Brian and I aren't leaving until they kick us out."

The room's attention focused on Betty before everyone, like the crowd watching a tennis match, turned back to await Jackie's volley.

Conscious of the eyes watching her, Jackie walked deliberately to Betty and Brian. She put her hand on Betty's shoulder and squeezed gently.

"I know none of this is easy for you," she said. "You know I respect you, Betty. I get that you do what you have to do. I can't fault you for trying to protect your family. It's all I'm trying to do too."

Betty inhaled and her body shuddered as she took a ragged, emotional breath. Her eyes moistened and her chin trembled. She ran her hand along her son's back and nodded at Jackie.

"I can accept that," said Betty, "and I do appreciate all you've done."

"We're staying too," said Nancy.

Pop met her words with the same look of surprise as everyone else in the room. "What? I just told Jackie—"

Nancy raised her hands, waving off her husband. "I know what you told Jackie. I understand why she's compelled to go home. I can't do it. I can't go back there."

Pop's open mouth curled into a frown. "It's our home," he said pleadingly. "We're talking about going back to our home."

"No," said Nancy. "That's not our home anymore," she proclaimed, her voice trembling. "That place is where our house is.

It's not our home."

Pop's frown slid into a supportive smile and he sighed. He put his hand on his wife's arm and rubbed it gently. "I understand. Bad things happened there. It's still fresh. You're afraid; I'm afraid. But we can't stay here. We're temporary guests."

Nancy stiffened. "I can't do it. It's more than fear. It's worse than that."

"We'll be okay," said Pop. "We'll—"

Nancy's jaw set. She folded her arms tightly across her chest. "I'm not going. And what is NASA going to do? Throw us to the wolves? They accounted for Jackie, her kids, and her husband. That's four people. If they leave and Nikki leaves, there's four of us left. It's you and me, Betty and Brian."

Pop looked to Jackie, seemingly coaxing her to help change his wife's mind. "I don't think that's how it works."

Jackie shrugged at Pop. She knew better than to meddle, and Nancy had a point. If Clayton were here with her, she might stay. It was definitely the safer of the options for the short term.

Pop's shoulders dropped. "Okay. We stay here as long as they let us. I'll try to make myself useful somehow and earn our keep."

Nancy's eyes brightened. "We're staying?"

Pop gave her a hug. She wrapped her arms around his back and squeezed her eyes shut. A smile crept across her face. "Thank you," she whispered.

"We'll miss you," said Jackie.

Pop placed his hands on both sides of Nancy's face and kissed her forehead. He shifted his weight and spun toward Jackie. He offered her a smile much less emphatic than the one still plastered on his wife's face.

"We'll miss you too," he said. "You be careful out there."

CHAPTER 15

Rick could taste the dirt on his lips. There were grains of sand between his cheeks and teeth. He tried freeing them with his tongue, but with his face pressed to the ground, he didn't have much range of motion. The jab of a rifle barrel between his shoulder blades didn't help.

The soldier at the other end of the weapon barked at him again. "Where did you come from?"

Rick winced at the pressure on his lower back from the soldier's boot. He spit out some of the sand and tried articulating as best he could.

"I'm from Clear Lake," he said. "I'm just looking for a safe place with my boy."

Rick couldn't see Kenny, but he could hear him talking with another soldier. They were twenty yards away, and Rick couldn't hear every word. But he made out enough to know his son was sticking to their agreed-upon story.

"—looking for water," Kenny said. "We're so thirsty."

Another jab in his back distracted Rick from eavesdropping. He grunted at the pressure. The soldier shifted his weight, increasing the discomfort and sending a sharp bolt of pain screaming down his right leg.

"Why are you walking?" asked the soldier. "You didn't come here from Clear Lake on foot. Where's your vehicle?"

"We ran out of gas," Rick said. "Ten or twenty miles back."

The soldier jabbed again. "We're not off a major highway. If you were headed to Austin or San Antonio, you wouldn't be in Taylor."

"We stayed off the highway," said Rick. "We tried to keep to ourselves and avoid trouble."

The pressure eased on his lower back and the soldier tapped Rick's ribs with his boot. "Get up. On your knees, hands behind your head. Keep your fingers clasped."

Rick did as instructed and looked over at Kenny. He was guzzling water from a canteen, two soldiers standing on either side of him. A third was on one knee in front of him. He was saying something Rick couldn't hear, but Kenny nodded, water dripping from his chin.

"What did the boy say?" called the soldier guarding Rick. He stepped in front of Rick, blocking his view of Kenny and the others.

"Said they ran out of gas ten miles back," one of the soldiers called back. "They came from Clear Lake. Looking for somewhere safe."

The soldier in front of Rick grunted and stepped to one side. Rick could see Kenny again. He'd returned the canteen and the soldier who'd been on his knee was standing.

Rick's guard used his rifle to motion toward Rick. "So, Lieutenant Turner," he said, "what do we do with them?"

"We do what we did with the others," the lieutenant answered. He'd been the one on his knee. He glanced back at Kenny and then marched toward Rick. "We take them inside, process them, and let the caretakers deal with them."

Lieutenant Turner waved for Rick to get to his feet. He stopped a couple of feet from Rick and eyeballed him. His bloodshot eyes narrowed as he studied Rick. He held out his canteen and Rick took it, thanking the soldier before swigging a mouthful of warm water. He swished the sand and dirt around in his mouth and swallowed it. He took one more swallow for good measure and returned the offering.

Lieutenant Turner took the canteen and recapped it. "C'mon," he said to his men. "Let's do this."

Kenny joined Rick at his side and the quartet of soldiers hustled them toward the front gate. A breeze-fueled funnel of dust and sand swirled around them as they approached the imposing entrance with its concertina wire and high metal chain-link fencing. It looked every bit the prison camp Rick knew it was intended to be.

Lieutenant Turner stopped at the guarded entrance. A baby-faced soldier with a black MP wrap on his bicep stood on the other side of the fence. He dispassionately asked the officer a few questions about their guests and then unlocked the gate. It swung wide and the escorts pulled Rick and Kenny back to make room, then ushered them into the camp.

"Holy mother," Rick breathed when they passed through the narrow entry. His eyes widened at the third-world conditions surrounding him. What wasn't evident from outside the fencing was the scope of the facility and the sheer numbers of people surviving within it.

The facility itself was a series of nondescript, unremarkable buildings. In between those buildings, filling every inch of the ground, were countless numbers of what could only be described as refugees. It had been five days since the CME had knocked out the power and sent the world spinning down the drain. Just five days. The deeper into the camp they walked, the worse it seemed to get.

"How is this possible?" asked Rick aloud. "Why is this place…"

The soldier next to him chuckled. "Such a piece of sh—"

"Hey," scolded Lieutenant Turner, "we've got a kid here. Watch the language."

"I've heard worse," Kenny quipped, apparently unaffected by the filth and suffering around him.

"Still," said the lieutenant, "he shouldn't talk that way."

"How did it get this way?" Rick asked. "It hasn't been a week."

"People are pigs," one of the soldiers remarked. "They don't pick up their trash after we give them food. The toilets stopped working on day two. The port-a-potties can only handle so much."

They turned a corner toward a building closest to the rear of the property. "Day two?" asked Rick. "Why were people coming here on day two?"

The soldiers looked at each other but said nothing. One of them pointed toward the building.

"We're taking you there," he said. "We'd normally have processed you up front, but there are issues preventing it."

"What issues?" asked Kenny.

"The building is also our MASH. A couple of our guys got hurt. They're getting fixed up."

"MASH?" Kenny echoed as they stopped at the building's entrance.

"Mobile Army Surgical Hospital."

The lieutenant guided them into the dimly lit building and it took a moment for Rick's eyes to adjust. When they did, he gripped Kenny's shoulder, signaling his son to stay quiet. He then shook his head to the people sitting in plastic chairs along the wall to his right.

Reggie Buck and his wife, Lana, were sitting next to each other. Her head was resting on his shoulder and her eyes were closed. Reggie's head was resting against the wall. His mouth was curled into a pronounced frown until he saw Rick. His eyes widened with recognition and he started to say something. He stopped and nodded in Rick's direction before leaning his head against the wall again.

Candace Bucknell was sitting backward in her chair, her arms folded across its back and her chin planted on her hands. She didn't notice Rick at first. When she did, she looked away from him, apparently understanding his desire she not acknowledge him.

The only one he didn't see was Mumphrey. The man he'd come to save wasn't there. Rick walked past the group to the end of the room. The soldiers stopped him at a desk and requested his personal information: full name, hometown, age, height, weight, and general health questions. There was a uniformed woman sitting behind a desk stacked with paperwork.

"Why do you need this stuff?" he protested. "I just want some water and some food. We're only passing through."

The soldiers exchanged glances. Lieutenant Turner dismissed the others and turned to the woman. "We've got a couple more visitors we need you to process," he said. "Can you take them now, or do they need to wait?"

She looked at Rick and Kenny; then her eyes shifted to the trio sitting along the wall. She offered a flat smile to the lieutenant. "I can take them now. Those people are on a hold. There's another one in the interro—"

"Go ahead, then," the lieutenant interrupted loudly. "Take them now."

Rick smiled at the woman. "We don't need to go through all of this. We're only here for some food and water. We'd be willing to work for it. Anything. We could even dig ditches."

"Everyone gets processed," said the lieutenant. "And I don't know if I made this clear before, but there is no passing through. Once you're here, you're here. It's for your own safety."

"We're here forever?" asked Rick. "That doesn't seem right."

"You're here until you leave in a pine box," said the lieutenant. He nodded at the woman behind the desk and marched out of the building into the sunlight.

Rick looked around. There were no soldiers in the main room of the building. It was just the trio along the wall, the woman behind the desk, Kenny, and him. The woman motioned to a chair opposite her. He pulled it out and sat down.

She was looking down at the paperwork in front of her, her pen poised above the top of the page. "I'll need a name. Spell it for me."

Rick leaned on the desk. It creaked against the floor, sliding away from him as he put his weight on the edge. "Is there someone being interrogated?" he asked softly. He motioned toward a door to his right.

The woman looked up from the paper. Her eyes darted to the door and back to Rick. "I shouldn't say. Could you give me your name?"

The woman's eye twitched. Rick glanced at the name embroidered on her uniform. "C'mon, Miss Cooper," he said. "I'm not going to tell anyone. It's just you and me here."

"It's Private First Class Cooper," she corrected him. "And I can't."

Rick winked and glanced at the sidearm on her right hip. "First class is right," he said. "But you already know that. I'm sure you stay just as busy fighting off men as you do filling out paperwork."

"Dad," whined Kenny, "don't bother the pretty woman."

That's my boy, thought Rick.

PFC Cooper blushed and tried unsuccessfully to suppress a smile. "Your name, please?"

"How many people are in there? Are they waterboarding?"

"No," she blurted. "He's just asking the man about…"

"About?"

Her smile disappeared and her eyes narrowed. "Nothing. Please, you're being difficult. Do I need to call the lieutenant?"

"I'm just trying to make small talk with a pretty woman," he said. "Arrest me if you must."

Kenny chuckled. "Gross, Dad. She's not interested. She's working."

Her sharp features softened again and she rolled her eyes. "Name?"

Rick sighed. "Okay, I give up. It's Jon."

Kenny nudged his father. Rick leaned back from the desk and dropped his hands. Out of sight of PFC Cooper, he tapped on Kenny's leg and pushed gently. Kenny took a couple of steps back.

"John?" she asked. "J-o-h-n?"

"No," Rick said. "It's J-o-n, short for Jonathan."

"So it's Jonathan?"

"Yes. Need me to spell it?"

She smiled at him. "No, I've got it."

PFC Cooper looked back down to write and Rick stood up, leaning on the desk. His weight pushed it another inch back toward the wall. The soldier stopped writing and pushed her palms against the desk. She easily shoved it away from her body and it screeched on the floor.

Rick apologized and leaned in. "Sorry, I think you spelled it wrong." He reached across the desk to point at the paper, knocking a stack of papers onto the floor to the soldier's left.

PFC Cooper stared in disbelief at the mess on the floor, her mouth agape. "Really?" she said, exasperated. "Just sit back down, please, and I'll—"

When she leaned to her left to pick up the mess, Rick shoved the desk toward the wall, using enough force to pin Cooper against the wall, eliciting a shriek and grunt from the soldier as she struggled against the desk. With her right hip exposed, Rick leapt across the desk and reached for her sidearm.

Cooper blindly flailed, unsuccessfully trying to keep Rick from her weapon. He unsnapped the holster, pulled the nine millimeter in a fluid motion, and rolled off the desk onto his feet. Behind him he could hear the confused shouts from the Bucks and Candace.

With his weight no longer on the desk, Cooper managed to free herself from the space, dropping to the floor on her knees. She gasped for air and grabbed at her ribs, cursing Rick and his mother.

Rick leveled the gun at the injured soldier. "Stay on the ground," he snapped. "Don't get up. Hands behind your head."

"I can't," Cooper whimpered. "My ri—"

Rick stepped toward the woman, aiming the gun at her head. "Now!"

Wincing, she raised her arms and moved her hands to the back of her head. Keeping the weapon trained on her, Rick moved around the desk to the back wall where he'd pinned her. With his back to the wall, he turned to his compatriots, ready to bark orders, when the door to the interrogation room swung open.

Rick took three quick steps toward the door, maintaining his field of vision, and swept the gun from the woman to the man emerging from the room. He was tall and muscular. His hands were balled into fists.

"What is going on out—" The color drained from his face when he saw Rick. His eyes moved to the injured PFC and back to Rick, his eyebrows twitching as he tried to make sense of the scene in front of him. He started to reach for his weapon.

"Don't," Rick said. "Put your hands above your head."

The man complied and Rick motioned toward Reggie Buck. "Reggie, please relieve the man of his weapon."

"What are you doing?" Lana protested. "Too many people have already died."

"Nobody needs to die," Rick assured her. "But we're not staying here as prisoners."

"Gus is dead," said Candace. "He tried to stop them."

"I'm aware," said Rick.

"Look, son," said the muscular soldier, "I don't know what's going on here, but you need to calm down. We can talk this through."

"Not gonna happen," said Rick. "Reggie, get the gun."

Reggie looked at his wife, at Rick, and back at Lana. The space between her eyes crinkled, she bit her lower lip, and she shook her head. Reggie put his hand on her thigh and squeezed. He smiled weakly and looked back to Rick. He stood, carefully approaching the soldier from behind. He deliberately withdrew the sidearm from the soldier's holster, deftly removed the magazine from its grip to check if it was loaded, and stepped away. He jammed the magazine back into place and returned to his seat. He rubbed Lana's back then thumbed a tear from her cheek with his free hand while keeping the pistol trained on its owner.

Rick motioned to the open door with his weapon. "What's in there?" he asked the muscular soldier.

The soldier's face reddened and he glowered at Rick. He rested his clasped hands on the top of his shaved head and remained silent.

Rick took a step toward PFC Cooper. He swung the weapon around and pressed it against the top of her head. She pressed her lips together to suppress a cry. Lana Buck gasped.

Rick focused on the muscular soldier and repeated the question more forcefully. His voice was lower and more measured as he jabbed the muzzle at Cooper's hairline. "What. Is. In. There?"

The voice that answered wasn't the soldier's. "Rick?" a frail voice called from inside the room. "Rick? That you?"

Kenny peeked into the room. "Mr. Mumphrey?" he said, his brows arching with confusion.

Rick felt an instant spike in his blood pressure. He gripped the handgun more tightly, his finger drifting toward the trigger, and he swung it around to the muscular mute in front of him. He took three strides toward the soldier, ready to combust.

"Back up," he spat, pushed past the retreating soldier, and turned into the room. It was empty except for two chairs, a single overhead light, and a bound and beaten Mumphrey. The old man was bleeding from his swollen lower lip. One eye was purpled and closed. His head bobbed as he worked to maintain enough strength to hold it upright.

Rick rushed to his side, knocking over the empty chair and sliding to his knees in front of his wounded friend. He set the gun on the floor beside the chair and worked to unravel the binds around Mumphrey's ankles.

"Like I said," Mumphrey slurred, "you're a good man, Rick Walsh."

His hands trembling, Rick moved to the back of the chair and struggled to loosen the knots at his wrists. "Shhh. Save your strength."

Rick struggled with the final knot, digging his finger between the strands to wiggle them free of each other. Mumphrey's breathing was labored. He rasped as he sucked air in and out from his open mouth.

"I didn't tell 'em anything." Mumphrey's voice was discordant. It didn't sound anything like the gravelly country drawl to which Rick had become accustomed. His friend sounded feeble. "Like I said, I didn't have anything to say. They were asking me about things I don't know."

Rick undid the final knot and looked over Mumphrey's shoulder toward the door. He'd forgotten about the two soldiers in the other room and cursed himself under his breath. Scanning the room, he saw a half-dozen more lengths of rope piled onto a wall-mounted shelf. He crossed the room, grabbed the rope, and tossed it onto the floor next to Mumphrey's chair.

"Reggie!" he yelled. "Guide our new friends in here, please."

Mumphrey's hands dropped to his sides, deep red rings decorating his wrists, and he mumbled something Rick couldn't understand.

Rick squatted on his heels and moved close to Mumphrey's mouth. The blood leaking from the old man's mouth wasn't from the nasty contusion on his lip. It was coming from inside his mouth. His tongue was bathed red. Rick tried to focus his attention on the task at hand. He checked the handgun and raised it toward the door.

The two soldiers were in the room now, walking ahead of Reggie. Both of them had their hands above their heads. PFC Cooper limped forward, her face contorted with pain. She was breathing through puckered lips and grunting with each exhale.

Rick swept the gun between the two soldiers. "You're going to be staying here for a little while," he said. "Stop right there."

"You're tying us to the chairs?" asked the muscular soldier.

Rick reached down and tossed a length of rope to the muscular soldier. "All right, Arnold," he said, "use that to tie her wrists the way you tied Mumphrey's."

The soldier hesitated but did as he was told. PFC Cooper was bent awkwardly at the waist, apparently unable to stand.

"Help her sit down on the floor," Rick snapped at the musclehead. "Help her get more comfortable."

Musclehead shook his head with incredulity. While he helped PFC Cooper to the floor, Rick called for Lana and Candace to join them in the room. He told them to shut the door behind them and lock it, which they did.

Lana gasped at the sight of Mumphrey and scurried to his side. She knelt beside him, whispering comfort to him as he tried to suppress a cough.

"Candace," Rick said, "please take the gun from Reggie. Reggie, tie up Arnold's wrists, please."

Candace took the gun and held it tightly with both hands, aiming it at the muscular soldier. Rick tossed Reggie some rope and within a couple of minutes the task was done. Both soldiers were back-to-back on the floor.

Reggie used another, much longer length of rope and wrapped it around both soldiers at their chests. When they protested, Reggie ignored them.

"We need something to keep them quiet," said Rick.

Mumphrey muttered something, raising his head.

Rick knelt down beside him. "What?"

Mumphrey smiled, revealing bloody gums that traced the outlines of his teeth. "Use my socks," he said with as much of a chuckle as he could muster. "I've been sweating a lot."

"I like that."

Mumphrey's color was somewhere between translucent and sallow. He suddenly looked ten, even twenty years older than he had the day before. Whatever the soldiers did to him was likely unfixable without a hospital or surgery.

"Hey," Rick said, stepping to the soldiers, "the lieutenant said there was a MASH unit near the entrance. That right?"

Neither soldier answered and Rick kicked the muscular one on the outside of his thigh.

The man grunted. "No," he sneered. "There's no MASH unit. It's a morgue. People don't get fixed here. That's the point."

Rick squatted on his heels. "What do you mean?"

"The sick go to the MASH unit to die," he said. "Then they take their bodies to building eight and stuff them into boxes. Nobody gets better. It's part of the plan. This is where you're all going to die." He nodded toward Mumphrey with his chin. "That one's gonna go first."

Rick clenched his jaw and braced himself on the floor with his left hand. He balled his right hand into a fist and jabbed it forward into the soldier's nose. It cracked under the force of his knuckles. Blood poured from the man's nose, across his lips and chin, and onto his uniform.

"You're all dying here," he growled, his chest heaving. "Sooner than later if I can help it."

Rick pushed himself to his feet and tucked the gun into his waist. "You can't help it," he said. "Reggie, give me Mumphrey's socks."

Rick took the socks, hot and damp with sweat and thick with ripe pungency, and forced one of them into PFC Cooper's mouth. She struggled against him, trying to kick him as he pinched her nose and stuffed the cotton past her teeth. Her eyes watered.

"I am sorry," he said to her. "You really are a beautiful woman. You're just on the wrong side of things."

The muscular soldier Rick called Arnold spat onto the floor and protested his fate. "You can't stuff that in my mouth," he whined. "I'll suffocate. I can't breathe through my nose. You broke it."

"I need help here," Rick said dispassionately, moving around to face the man. "Ladies, can you each grab a shoulder? Reggie, please hold his head still. You may need to grab him from the side."

While the others forcibly restrained the behemoth, Rick straddled the man's thighs and dangled the sock in front of him.

"We're all dying here," Rick said. "Isn't that what you said? Sooner than later?"

The man's eyes bulged with fear. He shook his head, blood spattering from his chin. "I won't be able to breathe," he said. "Seriously. You'll kill me."

Rick looked up at Reggie, who shrugged, and then eased himself to his feet. He backed away from the soldier who was still bound and restrained by the Bucks and Candace.

"All right then," Rick said. "I'm a compassionate man. I won't suffocate you. That would be an awful way to go. But I can't have you calling for help either."

Rick balled his right hand into a fist and then flexed his fingers, loosening his joints. He paced back and forth, measuring Arnold. He pulled the gun from his waist and aimed it at the soldier. He stepped forward; the soldier squirmed against those holding him. His eyes were wide. His blood-covered chin trembled. He was snorting through his damaged nose.

"Rick," said Reggie, "you don't have to do this."

Rick stepped to the side of the soldier and drew the weapon close to the side of his head. He held it there, between the man's temple and jaw.

"C'mon, Rick," said Candace. "This isn't who you are."

Reggie's tone was more urgent. "Rick, you—"

Rick ignored their pleas. In a single motion, he flipped the gun around to hold it by the barrel. He rotated his body to his right and, with all the force he could muster, swung the grip at the soldier's head. He connected just above the top of his jaw. The soldier's eyes rolled back and his head snapped from the impact. He was out.

Reggie and Lana helped him sit up, despite him being unconscious. A large knot swelled at the side of his head. Reggie checked his pulse.

"He's alive," he said, exhaling. "But you could have killed him."

"I could've," said Rick. "I probably should have. Look what he did to Mumphrey. And for what?"

Reggie stood and backed away from the bound pair on the floor. "Still—"

"We can debate my morality later," said Rick. "Right now we need to go. He won't be out of it for long. We've got ten minutes before he's lucid enough to call for help."

"Where are we going?" asked Candace.

"Building eight," said Rick. "That's our ticket out of here."

CHAPTER 16

MISSION ELAPSED TIME
75 DAYS, 18 HOURS, 22 MINUTES, 02 SECONDS
DENVER, COLORADO

Clayton closed the door to his room behind him and slid the DiaTab in his back pocket. He knew he could navigate the first part of his escape without having to rely on a digital map, and having the DiaTab turned off would further enable to him to move off the bunker's internal electronic grid.

His heart was pounding with excitement such that his headache had returned. The concussive impact from the plane crash was lingering, as was the ache in his leg. His stride was limp-free, though there was still a dull ache in the wound.

The astronaut knew he couldn't wait any longer. He needed to move. Having located his would-be accomplice Vihaan Chandra before leaving his room for good, Clayton knew he needed to climb one level to connect with the good doctor.

He walked hurriedly along a hallway, avoiding eye contact with anyone he passed. Clayton was certain someone would recognize him, call him out, turn him in, and put an end to his run. Yet nothing happened and nobody approached him.

Although he'd considered using the elevator to level four to find Chandra, and then working his way into the tunnel system, he knew there were fewer eyes on his level, fewer people who might see him entering a locked, rarely used door. At least, that was his thinking.

From memory he turned left and then right and found an unmarked door with an electronic key panel adjacent to it. Clayton pulled his DiaTab from his pocket and powered it on. He maneuvered through the screens until he found his way back to the administrative screen he'd hacked two hours earlier. Without turning on the locator, he activated the electronic key.

Clayton assumed, and prayed, that because this was an access door to an emergency exit, everyone's electronic key would work. In an emergency, he presumed, the control center could activate everyone's DiaTab's for access to areas they otherwise couldn't enter with their standard keycards. It was a leap, sure, but he needed to leap. Single footsteps wouldn't get him home.

He took a deep breath and exhaled, swiping the DiaTab across the panel. The panel lit and a metallic click preceded a hum at the door. He pulled the handle; he was through. He closed the door and turned off the DiaTab.

"That's one down," he said aloud, "and a zillion to go."

Clayton stuffed the DiaTab in his pocket and surveyed his surroundings. He was in a wide tunnel. It stretched fifteen feet across and was a good ten feet in height. It was concrete floor to ceiling, lit in a dim blue hue. It was enough light to see several feet ahead and Clayton began marching forward. Along the roof of the tunnel alongside the blue lighting were long stretches of metal piping. Some of it, Clayton imagined, was plumbing, though most of it was probably electrical. His steps echoing in the hollow rectangular tunnel, he kept moving. When he'd reached a T-intersection, he turned left, walked a few feet, and found another door. This one was labeled STAIRS and there was no key panel.

He gripped the handle and shouldered the door inward. It opened easily into a familiar-looking concrete and metal stairwell, much like he'd seen in parking lots and hotels. It was also lit in a pale, dim blue that washed the walls with a hue that made them look like walls at an aquarium.

He let go of the door and gently pushed it closed, then two at a time, bounded the steps toward level three. The adrenaline coursing through his body numbed the aches and pains he'd felt minutes earlier. So far, so good.

Clayton finished the flight of stairs and found the wall stenciled "Meteorology, Climatology, and Environmental Engineering" at the landing for level four. He tried the door that he assumed led into the secure area. It opened. But instead of being in the secure area closest to where Chandra was working, Clayton found himself in another tunnel. His eyes widened and for an instant his muscles froze with panic.

"It's all right," he told himself. "Not a big deal. Just another tunnel."

Clayton retraced the path he'd taken a floor below until he reached its end. There, he found a door with an adjacent keypad. He repeated his effort with his DiaTab, and the door clicked and buzzed. He pulled the handle and confidently walked through the opening.

The ambience was remarkably different. It was abuzz with activity, but nobody seemed to pay attention to him. They were engrossed with whatever populated their DiaTabs or seemed hurried and distracted from whatever was going on around them.

This is good, Clayton thought to himself. He pulled out his DiaTab, pretending to swipe its screen as he moved toward a bank of Telenet monitors, which appeared to display the outdoors. He presumed they were feeds from security cameras.

The floors clicked hollowly as he stepped across the large lacquered black tiles. Clayton stopped at the monitors, and from the corners of his eyes he watched the hive activity around him.

The people crossing the space all moved with a familiarity those in building three didn't seem to possess. True, he'd not seen much of the complex other than his cell and the cafeteria, but this space seemed different. It lacked the newness of the other areas, as if the orientation here had occurred some time ago. They walked with purpose and direction, their shoes squeaking as they crossed what Clayton assumed was a lobby.

He searched the walls for the stenciled guidance he'd seen

elsewhere but couldn't find it. There were no clues as to exactly where on the floor he should go. He turned on his DiaTab, hoping he could access the locator with the help of Telenet. His device was cycling when someone tapped Clayton on his shoulder.

"May I help you?"

Clayton turned to face a smallish bald man. He was tanned and a few wisps of hair crossed his smooth scalp. His left eye twitched. Clayton offered a smile.

"May I help you?" the man repeated. "You appear to be lost."

Clayton looked at the name stitched onto the man's white lab coat pocket. "Dr. Rector?" he asked. "Perfect. You're the man I was here to find."

Rector tilted his head suspiciously to one side. His left eye twitched again. "Is that so?"

"Yes," said Clayton. "I was sent here to have you guide me into the meteorological laboratory. Unfortunately, I'm having trouble with my DiaTab and I couldn't call up the right information to locate you."

Rector tilted his head in the other direction and narrowed his eyes. He pursed his lips and then motioned, craning his neck, toward the elevator on the other side of the lobby.

"You had clearance to come to this floor?" he asked. "To find me and the meteorological lab?"

Clayton nodded earnestly. "Yes. This place is like Fort Knox, am I right?"

Rector's expression flattened. He tucked his hands into his lab coat pockets and took a step back, away from Clayton. "What's your name?" he asked.

Clayton fumbled with his DiaTab, thinking of the best possible response. He wasn't about to give the twitchy scientist his real name. He'd be toast.

"I'm Alan Bean," he said. "I'm a liaison for Chip Treadgold."

Rector took another step back, his eyes widening, and tugged at his collar. His eye twitched again and he rubbed it with a knuckle. "Treadgold?" he said. "You work for Treadgold?"

145

"Yes," said Clayton, sensing an opening. "He's not going to like it if I'm delayed. I need to get a message to your lab and one of the technicians there."

"Which technician?"

"Vihaan Chandra."

"Huh," said Rector. "Alan Bean, you said? That name is familiar."

"It should be," said Clayton. "People know me."

Rector nodded. "Okay then, I'll take you there. Please stay with me, however. You cannot be unattended once we leave the lobby."

"Understood," said Clayton, exhaling with relief. "Lead the way."

Rector led Clayton past the monitors and into a darkened corridor. As they moved through the hallway, lights flickered to illuminate their path. Others in lab coats squeezed past them, scurrying in the opposite direction.

"Here we are," said Rector. "I'll bring him out. I can't have you in the lab no matter who you paint yourself to be, Mr. Bean."

Clayton stood in the hall and peered past Rector through the open door when the scientist stepped into the lab. He couldn't see much other than a couple of manned computer terminals.

In the way of the nonstop foot traffic, Clayton stepped out of the walkway and leaned against the wall. So far, so good. He nervously tapped a random rhythm against the wall with his fingers. Several minutes passed and Clayton looked back down the corridor toward where he and Rector had come from. The longer this took, the more vulnerable he was, the more likely it was Rector had figured him out and had led him to a trap. Then the door opened.

Rector poked out his head. "It seems he's not here," said the scientist. His left eye twitched. "He's on his way, though. So wait right there."

He slipped back into the closed lab and Clayton replayed his conversation with Rector in his mind and it hit him. Rector had his number.

Clayton cursed, pushed himself from the wall, and joined the flow of traffic leading back to the lobby. Within a minute, he was safely back in the tunnel and headed to the stairwell. Sweat formed at his temples and on the back of his neck. He cursed himself again.

"I thought I played the perfect Jedi mind trick on that lab-coated stormtrooper," he mumbled. "Thought I was clever using the name Alan Bean. Nope. Totally stupid."

He imitated Rector's voice. "Yes," he mimicked, "come with me. I'll lead you right to your destruction."

In is haste and arrogance, Clayton had given Rector the name of a legendary NASA astronaut. Alan Bean was on *Apollo 12*, the fourth man to walk on the moon, and in his later years, he became a painter.

Rector had said, "No matter who you paint yourself to be, Mr. Bean." He knew it was a lie.

Clayton's cover was blown. There was no telling where Chandra was. Getting out of the underground hell was going to be near impossible. He cursed again as he turned the corner, opened the stairwell door, and made his way toward the top level, where he'd find the emergency exit.

He was one flight from the top when he heard a door close on a lower level. It echoed up the concrete tube of the well. Clayton stopped, his hand on the cold metal railing, and listened. When the echo of the door dissipated, he could hear steps. More than one person was quickly ascending the stairs.

They were coming for him.

Clayton grabbed the railing and pulled himself upward. He looked over the railing and into the well. He could hear the steps, but he didn't see his pursuers. Faster he climbed until he reached the top level.

He reached the door and fumbled with his DiaTab, his sweaty hands making it tough to manipulate the screen. He swiped it across the keypad and the door clicked open. He knew the loud hum was a giveaway to the people chasing him, but he had no choice.

He pulled on the door and found himself in another tunnel. Unlike the other floors, this one offered Clayton two choices. He could go right or left. He exhaled and cursed, closing his eyes to imagine the schematic of the train system. He knew this tunnel would lead him parallel to the tracks and ultimately to building five.

He envisioned the layout. It was essentially a pentagonal shape with building one at the top. The building numbers increased clockwise. At the moment, he was in building three. He'd need to move to two, then down to one and five.

He started left. He tried running, but the ache in his injured leg had returned, throbbing when he put weight on it. Nonetheless, he pushed forward as quickly as he could, resisting the temptation to look over his shoulder every couple of steps. He kept reminding himself of the complexity of the tunnel system.

There was no straight line out of the bunkers. He'd successfully found his way from his cell to the emergency exit, which put him in building three. Now he was working his way to the building two stairwell. It would lead him deep underground to level five. At that point, there should be another tunnel leading to buildings one and five. From there, he could access the elevator's mechanical access and climb his way to the surface. At least, that was still his hope.

"It's like freaking M.C. Escher designed this place," he grumbled under his breath. "Up one, down two, over three, down four, up five. Ridiculous. Where are the stairs that have no ending and no beginning? Where are those?"

He kept chugging and had put at least a hundred yards between the entrance door and his position when he heard the echo of the door buzzing. His pursuers were in the tunnel with him.

Clayton checked over his shoulder and saw nothing, but accelerated his pace. Wincing against the now-stinging pain in his leg, he pushed harder against his good leg to propel himself along the corridor, which now curved to the right. He had to be getting close to building two.

A hitch in his side sucked the wind from his lungs and Clayton slowed for a moment. He licked his dry lips and stretched his right arm high above his head, working out the cramp.

He could hear the echoes of footsteps clacking off the concrete as the people giving chase kept moving. Clayton sucked in as deep a breath as he could and started moving again. He stopped when he heard a voice.

"Clayton! It's me, Vihaan Chandra. Please stop. Please wait for me. Clayton!"

Clayton did stop. He listened to the call twice more before deciding it was the scientist. He recognized the lilt of his voice even with the concrete echo distorting it.

"Who's with you?" he called back.

"Bert Martin," said Chandra. His voice was getting louder. "He's a security expert."

Clayton started walking toward Chandra. He didn't say anything at first.

"You there?" Chandra called.

"Yeah," said Clayton. "Who else?"

Chandra was huffing now. "Nobody."

Clayton saw their shadows first. They stretched along the concrete wall, cast there by the overhead tunnel lighting. There were only two shadows. Seconds later, the men emerged and approached him. All three of the men struggled for breath.

The man with Chandra smiled at Clayton and offered his hand. "Bert," he said. "Pleasure."

Clayton, bent over at his waist, took his hand from his knee and shook Bert's hand. "Nice to meet you. So you're a security expert?"

Martin shrugged. "I helped with the design here. I know some backdoors."

Clayton motioned toward the direction from which he'd come and started walking that way again. The men followed. They walked in silence for fifty yards or so, the only sounds their footsteps and heavy breaths.

"Backdoors," Clayton said out of nowhere. "That how you found me?"

"Not exactly," said Martin. "Your DiaTab was turned off. The tracker is disabled."

"I found a backdoor," said Clayton.

"Impressive, said Martin. "It's simple in design but not intuitive. Well done."

"I try," said Clayton. "So how did you find me?"

"I told Chandra about the tunnel and stairwell system that leads to building five," said Martin. "It's the only way out."

"For us," said Chandra. "It's the only way out for us."

"Essentially that's true," said Martin. "So when I saw you'd accessed the emergency exit key panel using your DiaTab in building four, I knew you had to have figured it out."

"We didn't know you'd be coming for me, though," said Chandra. "That was a surprise."

"It was probably not the best idea either," said Martin. "Because now they're looking for us. They know the two of you are scheming something. You trying to reach Chandra in his lab was a total tip-off."

Clayton pointed toward a door on the left side of the tunnel and the trio stopped. There was a keypad and Clayton pulled out his DiaTab to access it. Bert stopped him.

"Don't use that again," he said. "They're looking for you. Before, your access was hidden among a thousand alerts. Now they're zeroing in on it."

Clayton's eyes widened. "So they know we're in this tunnel?"

Bert smirked and held up a device that appeared similar to a DiaTab but was slightly larger. "Not exactly. I erased your last two key swipes and then ghosted them on two different panels. They think you're somewhere in building four."

"So nobody knows we're here?" asked Clayton.

Bert punched a key sequence into the access panel and the door clicked open. "Not at the moment," he said, ushering Chandra and Clayton through the open door. "But once they figure out I'm not where I'm supposed to be, they'll put two and two together."

"Can't you just shut everything down?" asked Clayton. "Then we have free access and they'll never track us until we're about to bolt."

"Not yet," Bert replied. "If I do it now, they have an override. It takes about fifteen minutes to reboot the system. I need to wait to shut down the system until we're almost free."

Clayton bounded down the stairwell, sliding his hand along the metal railing for balance. He looked at Chandra when he reached the second landing. "Where did you find this guy, and why is he helping us?"

"Chance and pity," said Chandra.

Bert chuckled nervously. "I'm helping you because this place is not exactly what I was told it would be. They never said it would be a prison. They never told me what their plans were."

"Thank you," said Clayton. "Whatever your reason."

The men descended three more flights. Moving swiftly down the well, they reached the fifth level, where the stairs ended. They couldn't go any lower.

"What now?" asked Clayton. "Don't we move to buildings one and then five?"

"That's the plan," said Bert. He entered a sequence into a door-side panel and it clicked. "These are default test codes. They activate every coded door. Nobody will have any clue which doors we've manually accessed or where we are."

Clayton swung open the door to move through. "Why are some doors coded and others not?"

Bert shrugged. "A handful of the stairwell and tunnel doors don't have codes. It's for ease of movement in emergencies, though all of them are within the secure perimeter of at least one other coded door."

"So when we reach building five, you'll shut off the Li-Fi?"

Bert slapped Clayton on the back. "Well done. Exactly. We'll power off the lights and embedded network. It'll reset fifteen minutes later."

Chandra was huffing as the men rounded the tunnel toward building one. He tugged on his pants to pull them up. Clayton slowed and kept even with the scientist, letting Bert take the lead.

"You okay?" he asked Chandra.

"Yeah," Chandra said breathlessly. "I'll be fine. I'm out of shape. My wife always told me to take better care of myself."

"You'll be okay," Clayton said. "We're almost there."

Chandra huffed and plugged along. He smiled weakly. His face was glistening with sweat in the relative warmth of the fifth level.

Focusing on Chandra distracted Clayton from the pulsing throb in his leg. It was getting worse and it only exacerbated his intensifying headache. He licked his dry lips and smacked his tongue. "We've got to get some fluids," he said. "I'm getting dehydrated. Chandra is sweating out his bodyweight in water. Any ideas, Bert?"

Bert was a good five or six strides ahead. Rather than stopping, he turned and walked backwards as he answered Clayton's question. "There's a storage closet near the elevator's mechanical access," he said. "If I remember correctly, there's a sink. We can get water there. We're ten minutes from it."

That ten minutes felt like thirty to Clayton. But the sink was there. All three of them quenched their collective thirst. Bert checked his DiaWatch and then tapped and swiped his version of the DiaTab. "All right. The elevator access is monitored. There are cameras and trip alarms. Once I enter a code on this tablet, all of that gets shut down. It also means we're climbing the elevator access in the dark."

"Wait, what?" said Clayton.

"We've got fifteen minutes to climb the ladder," said Bert. "Then the system reboots and they'll see us."

"Can't you shut it off again?"

Bert nodded. "Yes, but it has to come back on first and there will be a tracer icon on the security display, identifying where the system was shut down. So in that split second before I can shut it back down, they'll know where we are."

"Yeah," Clayton said. "Let's give that a go."

"Are we climbing to the top?" asked Chandra, his voice cracking.

"Yes," Bert replied.

"And that's where we'll find the garage," said Clayton.

"You know about the garage?" asked Bert. "Of course you do. Yes, the garage."

"That's how we get out of here," said Clayton. "And how I get home."

Bert's finger hovered over the tablet. "You ready?" he asked, eyeing both men.

"Ready," said Chandra.

"Ready," said Clayton.

Bert typed the sequence and the tunnel instantly snapped into darkness. "Let's do this."

CHAPTER 17

Jackie Shepard turned one last time, the third look back in a dozen steps, to wave goodbye to Betty Brown. They'd had their differences, but there was something final about her departure that filled Jackie with an unexpected melancholy.

She and Clayton had lived across from the Brown family for years. They were as familiar as the twisting, knotted crape myrtles in their front yard or the warped wooden driveway joint that Clayton repeatedly promised to fix but never managed to put atop his list of things to do. There was an odd comfort in the trees and the trip hazard and the neighbors across the street.

"Talk soon," Jackie said to Betty, more out of habit than a belief she truly would. Chances were they'd never see each other again. Jackie didn't know why. She couldn't put her finger on it, she just knew.

"Sounds good," replied Betty, a surprising lilt in her voice. Jackie surmised she too knew they wouldn't talk soon.

"C'mon, Mom," said Marie. "We gotta go. I want to get back to the house as fast as we can."

Jackie sidled up next to her daughter and nudged her. "For someone who didn't want to leave, you're in a hurry."

Marie rolled her eyes. "I *don't* want to leave. I think it's stupid. But

154

if we have to go, I don't want to linger in no-man's-land."

Chris, thumbs tucked under the straps of his backpack, was a couple of steps behind both of them. "No-man's-land? What's that mean?"

"It's like the part where people shouldn't be," Marie said over her shoulder. "Like the Wild West."

Jackie nudged her daughter again, less playfully than before. She shot Marie an arched-brow warning and spoke under her breath. "Don't frighten your brother. Not cool."

Chris jogged to catch up with them, his pack bouncing on his back. "Wild West?"

Marie looked at her mother and then at Chris. "I'm just kidding. They wouldn't let us leave if it was dangerous."

"Oh," Chris said, his squeezed expression relaxing. "I was gonna say you had me worried."

The three of them and Nikki approached the entrance gate. The same guard who'd given them access to JSC was standing outside the guard shack. He was still in uniform, though it looked worse for wear, as did he. His eyes carried the same blank stare as most people wore a week into the apocalypse.

Nikki stepped ahead of Jackie and approached the guard. "You have our guns?"

The guard slid inside the shack, motioning for Nikki to join him. He keyed open a black safe and swung open its door. Without saying anything, he handed Nikki the first of the two weapons they'd reluctantly surrendered when entering the complex.

Nikki took the Glock 17 and eyed the guard. "The mag better be full," she said. "Ammo is as precious as gold these days."

"It's all there," said the guard.

Nikki slid the magazine from the Glock's grip and checked it. She pressed the top of the spring-loaded bullets, felt it was at capacity, and slapped it back into the gun.

"Satisfied?" he asked.

She pulled the slide back to chamber a round then tucked the Glock 17 into her waistband at the small of her back, tucking it under her backpack. "I will be when I check the nineteen," she said, holding out her hand.

The guard clucked his tongue and reached into the safe. He withdrew the Glock 19, the second of their two weapons, and handed it over. Nikki took it and repeated the ammo check.

"We're all good here," she said. "I gotta sign anything?"

"No," the guard said. "A thank you would be nice though."

Nikki faked a wide smile. "Thanks," she said with a sweetness that dripped with sarcasm. "I appreciate you keeping our guns for us in a box and then kindly returning them to us."

He smirked and waved her out of the shack. "Much better. You know I'm just doing my job."

Nikki backed out into the street and hiked the backpack up onto her shoulders. She handed the Glock to Jackie and looked at the guard over her shoulder as they walked toward the main road. "We all are," she said.

Jackie pulled back the slide and tucked the gun into the front of her waistband. "What was that about?" she asked. "He give you any trouble?"

Nikki shook her head. "No. I didn't like the idea of handing over our guns, like we're criminals or something."

The group started trekking toward Jackie's house. They'd not been at JSC for twenty-four hours and already the world felt different. It was quiet. Even the birds were silent. There was no wind, and the humidity had returned. They'd walked about a half mile and the Space Center was no longer visible. The kids were ten yards ahead, their packs bouncing as they trudged forward.

"What time is it?" asked Jackie.

"I don't know," Nikki said. "Two thirty. Could be three o'clock. Why?"

Jackie spoke softly enough for only Nikki to hear her. "Something is off."

Nikki's eyes narrowed with concern. "What do you mean?"

Jackie shook her head, her eyes scanning their surroundings.

"What?" Nikki said, pressing the issue. "Is this intuition, or do you see something?"

"I don't see anything," Jackie said, "but it's like we're being watched."

"Huh," Nikki said. "I usually get the feels when something's up. I have a pretty good sixth sense. No alarms are going off though."

Jackie shrugged, focusing on their surroundings, trying to home in on whatever it was that made the hair on her neck stand on end. They were in the middle of the street, maneuvering amongst the abandoned cars and trucks. Most of them had shattered windows, their trunks popped open. Spare tires, random bits of clothing, and empty food containers littered the asphalt.

Occasionally she'd get a whiff of urine or something even more malodorous. Surveying the wasteland that was once one of the busiest thoroughfares in her Houston suburb, she unconsciously rested one hand on the protruding handgun grip.

How many days had it been? A week? No, less than a week.

Her surroundings looked so much worse than what she'd have expected only a week into the crisis. She stepped over the carcass of a dead, half-eaten cat and held her hand over her mouth. Passing another car, a bright blue Volkswagen sedan, there was a body wrapped in a blanket in its backseat. She couldn't tell if the person was sleeping or dead until it shuffled and tugged the blanket farther over its head.

Nikki snapped her fingers in front of Jackie's eyes. "You've slowed down. The kids are getting pretty far ahead of us. We should catch up."

Jackie took an elongated stride to kick-start her acceleration. The kids were side by side, helping each other through and around the obstacle course. Jackie smiled at Chris holding his hand out to direct Marie around some broken glass. She tiptoed around the trash and followed her brother closer to the shoulder of the road.

Her eyes drifted from the kids back to a shuttered strip center on the opposite side of the road. The doors were off their hinges at several of the stores. There were opened cardboard boxes of various sizes littering the parking lot. Nikki caught her attention again, though this time it wasn't to speed her up. She was screaming Marie's name.

Jackie snapped her attention to where she'd last seen her children. It took her a moment to process what she was seeing. There were two large figures, probably men, dressed in all black. One of them was holding Marie on the ground. The other had Chris by the back of the neck, keeping him from helping his sister. Instinctively she yelled for her children and took off running. Nikki was a good five yards ahead of her, but stopped short of the kids. Jackie couldn't understand why until she slid to a stop next to her friend.

The man on the ground was holding a knife to Marie's neck. He had her pinned with his weight. He was a large man, overweight but muscular. He was breathing heavily. Marie was lying awkwardly on the grass at the shoulder of the road, her backpack still attached to her shoulder by a single strap.

The man holding Chris didn't appear to have a weapon, but had an arm wrapped around his neck, holding the boy close to his body. Chris was struggling but wasn't strong enough to free himself or cause the man much concern.

"I don't want to hurt the girl," said the man, his voice shaky but earnest. Jackie believed him. He didn't want to hurt her, but he would if pushed to it.

"Let her go," Jackie urged. "Let them both go. We'll give you whatever you want."

The men exchanged glances. Their eyes were wild, unable to focus. The one holding Marie was shaking.

Jackie swallowed hard. "It'll be okay, kids," she said. "They're not going to hurt you. You're okay."

Both children whimpered. Chris stopped struggling. Tears streaked down Marie's face, dripping onto the backpack and the ground underneath her.

"Give us your stuff," said the shaking man. "Now! We don't want to hurt your kids, but you need to hand over your packs."

Nikki held her hands out in front of her. She took a step in front of Jackie, nearly moving directly between Jackie and the man holding

Marie at knifepoint. She spoke clearly, as if she was in control.

"You're right," Nikki said. "You don't want to hurt her. That would be very bad for you. What is it you want specifically?"

"Are you deaf?" the man holding Chris blurted. "We need whatever you've got."

"Everything," echoed the man on the ground.

Nikki's hands were still in front of her. Her arms were extended straight. "I can't do that," she said, glancing over her shoulder at Jackie. "We can't do that. Be reasonable, fellas."

The man on the ground chuckled, revealing a wide gap between what was left of his front teeth. As he spoke, it became evident he was injured. His lips were swollen, and the upper lip was split at the corner.

"Reasonable?" He cackled. "What's reasonable? Nothing's reasonable. Give us everything you have."

Jackie shrugged off her pack, ready to hand it over.

Nikki shook her head and took a step forward. "All right," she said. "We can bargain here, right? We can give you what you need and then you can give us the kids back."

The shaking man withdrew the knife from Marie's neck and pointed it at Jackie while he talked directly to Nikki. "You best follow her lead. Give us the packs."

Nikki took another step. "Yeah, you best follow my lead."

"Nikki," Jackie said, "these are my children. I—"

"Hang on, Jackie," she said, waving her hand. "These guys are reasonable. If I give them my pack, that's all they need. They're frightened because somebody took everything from them. They got taken and they're desperate. Am I right?"

The men looked at each other and then at Jackie. The trembling man holding Marie nodded. "It doesn't matter," he snapped. "What happened doesn't matter. I don't have time for this psychobabble bullsh—"

"Take my pack," Nikki said. "Let go of the girl and you get my pack. You're reasonable. I can tell you're a good man. You're desperate, that's all. You'll take what we give you. I'm giving you my pack in exchange for Marie there. Her name is Marie."

The man's eyes danced from person to person as he considered the offer. His features softened for an instant before they curled into an angry squeeze and he tightened his grip on Marie. "You're not telling us what's going to happen," he snarled. "I'm keeping the girl. You give the bag to Otto."

Nikki glanced at the other man. "Otto?"

The man nodded.

"Then let go of my son," said Jackie. "His name is Chris. Let go of Chris."

Otto loosened his grip on Chris and Nikki removed her pack and offered it at arm's length. Still holding Chris by his shoulder, Otto reached his hand out.

At the moment he opened his hand to take the bag, a percussive blast echoed in the still air and a red circle bloomed at his temple. Otto's mouth dropped open and he collapsed to the ground, blood leaking from the bullet hole in the side of his head.

Startled, the other man turned his body away from Marie, lifting up his torso and putting several inches between the knife blade and Marie's neck. Nikki, unfazed by the gunshot, pulled the Glock from her back and fired a trio of quick shots at the man as she advanced toward him.

He dropped onto his back next to Marie, gasping for air and grasping at the wounds in his neck and chest. Marie rolled away from him, scrambled to her feet, and ran to her mother.

Nikki took a final step forward and put one foot on the man's bleeding chest, putting a fourth bullet in his face.

"That'll end your misery," she muttered. Crouching down, she searched his jacket and pants for anything useful. The knife and a pack of matches was it. She looked back at Jackie and the kids. They were huddled together, crying and hugging, unaware of their surroundings.

Nikki looked past them back toward the path they'd traveled for the source of the gunshot that saved them. At first she couldn't see anything; then she saw a large figure approaching rapidly, carrying a rifle with him.

"Get down," Nikki said, brushing past the Shepards and toward the gunman. "Get behind that car. Now!"

Jackie guided the children behind a stalled Nissan and got low to the ground. Her arms were still wrapped around them, comforting them while they hid. She peered over Marie's head and around the rear of the car, finding Nikki marching toward an armed man. Nikki's arms were extended as she pressed forward with the gun leveled at the stranger.

"Wait here," she said to her children's protest. She tugged herself free of their persistent hands and drew the Glock from her waist. Still crouched low, she checked the weapon, making sure a round was in the chamber. Her children's faces were pale, their puffy eyes reddened from their tears. She bit her lip.

"I'll be right back," she said. "Stay here."

Before either child could argue, she was racing toward Nikki. Jackie held the weapon at the ground, gripping it with both hands. Seconds later she reached Nikki and the stranger. His hands were above his head. He'd put the rifle on the ground.

"—trying to help," he said with a deep Southern drawl. "I heard you scream."

"Back away from the rifle," Nikki said to the stranger. "Three big steps."

The man rolled his eyes and took three large steps, counting them. He was graying at the temples. His hair was disheveled and the shag growing on his face was wiry and unkempt. His eyes carried the same mix of shock, sadness, and exhaustion as most people. His face was long and thin, but beneath his long-sleeved Lyle Lovett concert T-shirt, he held onto the remnants of a spare tire. His faded jeans were ripped along one side and stained with dirt from the thighs to the shins. He wore canvas athletic shoes and dog tags around his neck.

"That good?" he asked. "Seriously, I'm on your side here."

"What side is that?" asked Nikki.

He shrugged. "Decency?"

"Where did you come from?" Jackie asked, joining the

conversation. "How did you see us?"

The man motioned over his shoulder to his right. "I was in that Volkswagen," he said, his words drawn longer by his accent. "The blue one. I was sleeping when I heard a noise. It was you two talking. Or maybe it was the girl down there. I don't know, but you woke me up."

"I saw you," Jackie said. "You were under a blanket."

The man looked at the ground. His cheeks flushed. "I've been sleeping where I can," he said, eyeing the women again. "Just moving along, that's all."

"What about the rifle?" asked Nikki.

"Protection," he said incredulously. "You both have guns, right?"

Jackie looked down at the rifle and then over her shoulder at the dead men on the shoulder of the road. It had to be fifty yards. "Military?"

He took the tags in his hands. "No, I'm a hunter. Deer, coyote, hogs. My wife was the soldier. These were hers. She'd have killed me if I hadn't helped you, so…"

Nikki looked back at Jackie. "Well, don't I feel like an ass?"

Jackie grinned. "Thank you," she said. "From both of us."

"Thank you," said Nikki.

"You're welcome," he said. "Can I grab my rifle? I mean, if I was gonna use it against you, I already would have."

Nikki eyed the weapon and then looked at Jackie. Jackie nodded her approval.

He stepped forward and bent down to pick up the rifle. "Thank you. Could I ask for a favor?"

"What?" asked Nikki.

"You have any food in those packs?" he asked. "I haven't eaten since my car died. I was on a road trip south to hunt in Edinburg and—"

"Of course," Jackie said and waved him to follow them back to the kids. "The kids will want to thank you too."

He sighed with relief. "Thank you. I'd be in better shape if the power went out after I'd bagged some game."

"Where are you from?" asked Nikki, trailing behind Jackie and the stranger.

"Oklahoma," he said. "Stillwater. I worked maintenance at OSU."

"Can't get home?" Nikki asked.

"Trying," he said. "Made it this far from Victoria, where the car died. About a hundred forty miles down, only five hundred fifty to go. You got far to go?"

"No," said Jackie. "A mile or two. We live near here. We're heading back home."

Marie and Chris emerged from behind the Nissan and stepped toward their mom, their eyes glued to the man with the rifle. They stood close to each other, holding hands. Chris was rubbing Marie's thumb with his.

"Kids," Jackie said, "this is Mr...?"

"Salt."

"This is Mr. Salt. He's the one who helped us."

"Thank you," they said in unison.

Chris pointed at the body of the man who'd been holding Marie. "Nikki killed that one."

Holding the rifle on his shoulder by its stock, Salt walked over to the body. He grunted and looked over at Nikki. "I saw you in the scope when I moved over to take him out. You did my work for me."

"You're welcome," said Nikki.

Salt walked back to Nikki, his eyes narrowed and his head tilted to one side. "Have we ever met before? You look really familiar."

"I don't think so," she said. "I get that a lot."

Salt wagged a finger. "I know you."

"She's Deep Six Nikki," Chris said.

Nikki, crouching in front of her open backpack, shot Chris a look. Chris smirked.

Salt's jaw dropped. "The MMA fighter?"

Nikki pulled a can from the pack. "You wanted food? How's refried beans?"

Salt took another step forward and then squatted next to Nikki.

"If you don't mind my saying, your fight against Laura Lingo was like watching a young Tyson against, well, anyone. I mean, you dominated her. You had that one move. What was it called? The shutdown something."

Nikki set the can on the ground and withdrew a box of uncooked pasta. "Shutoff valve," she said, shaking the pasta. "Noodles okay?"

Salt snapped his fingers and smiled. "The shutoff valve! That's right. Darn near suffocated poor Lingo with that move."

Nikki fished through the pack and found a six-ounce bottle of water. She set it on the ground next to the noodles and beans.

"I'll take whatever you got," he said. "I wasn't taught to discriminate. Given my current situation, I'm not about to start. You were a heck of a fighter, by the way. Heck of a fighter."

"I don't fight anymore," she said. "I gave it up."

Salt nodded toward the dead man on the shoulder. "I wouldn't agree with that. He probably wouldn't either."

Nikki found a package of tuna in her bag and added it to the haul. She looked at Salt and then at the dead man, his eyes fixed open with the same shock they'd revealed when she put the first bullet in his neck. She glanced at the kids. They were watching her dole out the food.

"Yeah." She shrugged. "It's not the same thing. You good with this? Some protein, some starches. They should give you energy."

"I've got a couple cans of kids' pasta too," said Jackie. "You have a can opener?"

Salt shook his head. "Just a canteen back in the car, the blanket, my rifle, some extra ammo and a couple of hand warmers. That's it."

Nikki pulled the dead man's knife from her bag and stuck it in the dirt at the shoulder of the road. "You can have this," she said. "It'll make do as a can opener."

"Y'all have been mighty nice," said Salt. He pushed himself to his feet and the women handed him the food. He cradled it against his chest, managing somehow despite still holding the rifle. "I appreciate you."

"We appreciate you," said Jackie. "Good luck."

"You too," said Salt.

He backed up a couple steps, turned around, and marched back to the Volkswagen.

Nikki zipped up her pack and heaved it onto her back.

"That man gives me hope," said Jackie, watching him walk away.

Nikki checked her Glock and adjusted it against the small of her back. "How so?"

"He helped us," said Jackie. "In a world where every stranger seems to be out for himself at the expense of others, he took a risk. He saved my kids."

"I guess," said Nikki. "Let's get going. These jerks put us behind."

Jackie adjusted the pack on her back. "We'll be fine."

If she only believed it…

CHAPTER 18

Kenny snuck a peek around the corner and slid back into hiding next to his father. "Is that building eight?" he asked. "It looks like there's an eight next to the door."

Rick peered past the edge of the concrete wall that gave them cover. "I think it is. Good eyes."

They'd successfully crossed the camp towards its southern edge. At times blending in with other prisoners, at times ducking for cover, they'd managed to move within a matter of minutes. They couldn't know how long they'd have before the unconscious, ungagged soldier would awaken and have the presence of mind to call for help.

Once that happened, they'd be screwed, so they moved as swiftly as possible. Reggie and Rick had helped Mumphrey together, each of them draping an arm across their shoulders and carrying him like a wounded soldier from a battlefield.

Mumphrey was in and out of consciousness. Blood dripped from his bright red lips, leaving an intermittent trail of their path across the camp. He occasionally mumbled or coughed. Otherwise, he was fading.

Rick eyed the others in the group. "We move fast, but we walk.

Running will call attention to us. Once we get there, we get inside and regroup."

"What if there are soldiers in there?" asked Candace.

"Reggie and I are armed. We do what we have to do."

"They're American soldiers," she said. "We can't just—"

"I know who they are," Rick cut in. "But thinking that way got Gus and Karen killed. It got Mumphrey beaten to a pulp. We have to do what we have to do. It's them or us. Damned if I let it be us."

Candace nodded. "Okay."

Rick took Mumphrey's arm, draped it across his shoulder, and held the old man's wrist. With the gun tucked in the front of his waistband, he took his other hand and held it around Mumphrey's back. When he adjusted his grip, Mumphrey lifted his head and turned toward Rick.

"Hey," he said, barely above a whisper, "I do appreciate you. You didn't have to let me tag along. Like I said—"

"Save your energy, Mumphrey," said Rick. "I know you're thankful. I'm thankful to have you."

Mumphrey smiled and lowered his head. He closed his eyes and pressed tears from the corners. They leaked down the sides of his face, mixing with the stain of blood on his stubbled chin.

"All right," Rick said to the group. "Ready?"

A chorus of subdued acknowledgements told Rick it was time. "Let's go."

Rick leaned forward and, together with Reggie, led Mumphrey at a brisk pace across an open courtyard. To their left was a small encampment of a dozen people huddled around a tent. They were sitting on the ground in clusters of two and three each, not paying attention to anything outside their own conversations. To their right was what Rick supposed was the mess hall. There was a long line of people waiting to go inside the building. Opposite them, others filtered out one at a time carrying small bags or pieces of fruit. Guards were positioned at both the entrance and exit, controlling the traffic. They either didn't notice or chose to ignore Rick and his companions.

They were halfway to their destination when a sharp pain exploded in Rick's lower back, sending jolts of electricity down his leg and into his side. His lower back was on the verge of seizing, but he ignored the tension and pushed forward toward building eight.

Kenny had hustled to his left side. He was moving his legs twice as fast as the adults to keep pace, but he was doing it. He looked up at Rick, his eyebrows knitted with concern.

"You okay, Dad?" he asked. "You need help?"

Rick adjusted his hold on Mumphrey. "Thanks, I'm good. Why don't you move ahead of us and check the door? Knock. See if they let you in."

Kenny's eyes brightened. "Okay," he said and sped up. He was on the verge of running but maintained a fast walk. He quickly reached the front of the building and paused at the entrance, looking back at Rick.

Rick nodded at him and Kenny knocked on the door. He stood there dancing in place, like a kid having to go to the bathroom, and knocked again.

"What are you going to do if they open it and let him in?" asked Reggie. "He's a kid."

"Exactly," huffed Rick. "He's a kid. They won't suspect anything. I just sent him there to see if the place is empty."

"Huh," said Reggie. "Good idea."

Kenny had knocked again by the time they'd reached building eight. He was still dancing in place. "Nobody's here, Dad."

"I know," Rick said. "You gotta go?"

"No," said Kenny. "I'm just anxious."

Rick loosened his hold on Mumphrey. Reggie held the ailing man upright while Rick tried the door. It was unlocked. He shouldered it open and hustled the group inside. He closed it but left it unlocked. Before he saw the contents of the space, he could smell it. Freshly cut wood spiced with the faintest hint of pine.

He turned around and saw palettes of rectangular coffins. The boxes were identical to the ones he and Kenny had seen the involuntary undertakers put into the ground.

Reggie helped Mumphrey to a chair and sat him down gently. "Coffins?" he asked. "I don't understand. Why are there so many coffins?"

"People keep dying," said Kenny. "My dad and I saw men putting them in the ground at the edge of the woods outside the camp. There were big holes. Deep holes."

Mumphrey raised his head and chuckled through what had become a gargling cough. "I'm not dead. I'm still here."

"What are we doing?" asked Candace. "What is this?"

Rick held up a finger. "Give me a minute." He walked from the group toward the rows of open pine boxes. Each of them had a lid leaning against its side. At the back of the room next to a rolling bay door were four that were closed. Rick wove his way through the collection to the closed boxes and lifted one of the lids.

The scent of pine was immediately replaced with the foul odor of rot. Inside the box was the stiffened body of an overweight middle-aged man. His eyes were closed, but his mouth was open. His blue-tinged skin looked almost cartoonish. Rick stared at the corpse for a moment before shutting the lid. He stepped sideways to another closed box and found a body inside that one too. He looked up from the coffin, recognized the disgust on the adults' faces, but ignored it as he revealed his escape plan.

"We get in the coffins and pretend like we're dead," said Rick, crossing the large room back to his friends. "They'll come and move us, drop us in the ground, and leave us there overnight. Once the sun goes down, we climb out and head back to Gus's ranch."

Reggie frowned. "You're kidding, right? Climb into coffins and let them bury us alive?"

"They won't bury us," Kenny said. "We heard the men say they're leaving the graves open until they fill them. They're not putting the dirt back in the holes until tomorrow."

Reggie looked at Kenny then Rick. "Seriously? This is your big rescue plan? You break in here to help us escape in coffins?"

Rick nodded. "That's my plan."

"God help us," said Lana.

169

"I don't think I can get into one of those boxes," said Candace. "I'd freak."

"We don't have time to debate this," Rick said firmly. "They're going to come looking for us any minute now. If we're standing around talking about it, they'll find us. They'll lock us up or execute us. I'm getting in a box. You want to do something else, be my guest."

Kenny shrugged. "I'm getting in a box."

Mumphrey raised his trembling hand. "I might as well get a head start on this dying thing. I'm in."

"You're not dying, Mumphrey," Rick insisted. "Once we get out of here, we'll get back to Gus's place. He's got medicine and all kinds of first aid there. We'll get you fixed up."

"Like I said," said Mumphrey, "I'll get a head start. Drop me in one of them boxes."

Rick rolled his eyes and helped Mumphrey to his feet. He led him across the room, careful not to trip on the rows of empty coffins as they moved to those closest to the ones already occupied. Mumphrey climbed into the box as if getting into a bathtub and lay down.

"This ain't so bad," he said. "Almost comforting."

"Try not to cough if you can help it," said Rick. "That'll give you away."

"I'll try," said Mumphrey. He laid his head back and closed his eyes. "Shut me in."

Rick lifted the lid and slid it atop the box. It settled in the carved grooves along the edges. "Can you breathe?" he asked.

"Does it matter?" came the muffled response.

"Just try to conserve air," Rick said.

"Kenny, you and I are last. Anyone else?"

Candace exhaled and ran her fingers through her hair, pulling at the roots. "Me," she said. "What choice do I have?"

One by one, Rick helped the group into their coffins. He was last and found one next to Kenny. He climbed into the box and lifted the lid on top of it, using the tips of his fingers to maneuver the lid into the grooves. It settled in place with a thump and Rick was in the dark.

He lay there for a few minutes figuring now would be a good a time as any to take a nap. The exhaustion overtook his aching body and he drifted off to sleep. When he awoke, the casket was shaking, rattling from the vibrations of a loud rumble.

At first, Rick forgot where he was. His pulse quickened and he tensed. He reached out blindly trying to grab onto something. His hands found the pine, scraping across its smooth-hewn edges. Before he pushed on the casket lid, he remembered where he was. Once he'd caught his breath, he realized he must be in the back of the military truck on his way to the gravesite.

He had no concept of how long he'd been asleep nor any knowledge of whether any or all of the others were with him. His initial fear was replaced with anxiety and nervousness with not knowing if he'd made the right decision.

He strained his ears to listen for any clues. The rumbling of the truck's engine and the knocking of his casket against something next to it was all he could hear. Then both stopped. A squeal told him the driver had applied the brakes. A moment later his body jerked as someone moved the coffin. He felt the friction of the box sliding against something underneath his back and pressed his boots against the box frame to brace himself as the coffin rolled to one side. Outside the box, men grunted.

"All right," one of the men said. "Let's lower this one in."

Another voice, coming from beneath Rick's casket, called up to the pallbearers. "How many you got this time?"

"Eight. This will be it for the day. We do another haul in the morning and you can fill in the graves then."

"Leave 'em open overnight?"

"Yeah. They're not going anywhere."

The blood rushed to Rick's head as the coffin tipped diagonally. His feet were a good two feet above his head. Gradually they evened out and Rick's body shook with the rattle of hitting bottom.

Sweat stung his eyes and he squeezed them shut to ease the

perspiration elsewhere. It didn't work, so he blew from the top corner of his mouth. All that did was move the sweat into his eye. A wave of panic washed over him as he considered how long he'd have to wait in the box, in a hole six feet deep in the earth.

To distract himself, he paid attention to the grunts and complaints of the men moving the caskets. Then he thought about the others. He counted again in his head. There were six of them: Candace, Reggie, Lana, Mumphrey, Kenny, and himself. That meant that two of the arriving caskets did contain dead bodies. Rick hoped none of his group was left behind. He also prayed Kenny was still asleep and that Mumphrey was able to suppress his cough.

Rather than worry about something he couldn't control, he focused on his own breathing. He inhaled slowly through his nose, held it for a count of three, and exhaled. Each time he completed a breath, he counted, adding one each time. He reached six hundred and fifty by the time his coffin rattled with the unmistakable grind and scrape of something set on top of it. Rick's breathing quickened but he worked hard to suppress it until he was sure the men had finished unloading the eight caskets.

"That'll do it," said one of the men. "You can grab a ride in the back of the truck and we'll take you back to camp, or you can walk. Up to you."

"We'll ride."

Less than a minute later the truck whined and rumbled when its engine started. It was loud at first, but soon enough the noise faded until Rick couldn't hear it anymore. Certain it was safe, he pressed lightly on the lid. It didn't move.

He pressed harder and raised his knees against the lid for additional leverage. Nothing. The wood was giving at the edges, but there was no moving it from the inset grooves at the top of the box. He was stuck. They *had* set another casket on top of him.

Rick's heart rate immediately quickened, thumping against his neck and in his temples. Sweat bloomed in the space between his chin and neck, under his arms, and in the small of his back. His breathing was irregular and impossible to regulate with short, controlled breaths. The casket instantly felt smaller, tighter, and as if it were shrinking.

Rick knocked on the lid with the top of his fists. He couldn't move his arms enough to gain the needed force for anything more than that. He kept knocking five, ten, fifteen times, before he stopped and listened for a response. There was nothing.

Was he the only one of the group they'd transported?

Had there been so many bodies that the rest of the group was still in building eight?

How many caskets were on top of him?

He'd been the first moved from the truck as far as he could tell. He could very well be at the bottom of one of the graves underneath several other pine boxes. While Rick wanted to scream, he couldn't be sure the wrong person wouldn't hear him. He called out loudly enough for anyone alive in the hole to hear him. The box swallowed his voice as he spoke.

"Hey," he said. "Anybody there?"

Nothing.

A little louder this time. "Hey! Kenny? Reggie? Mumphrey? Anyone there?"

All he heard in response was his own panicked breathing. "Anyone? I can't get out."

Rick turned his head as much as he could to one side. He still couldn't hear anything. He extended his legs and quickly pulled them back, banging his knees into the casket lid, accomplishing nothing but bruising his kneecaps.

"Help!" he yelled, no longer worried about whether or not soldiers heard his calls. He wanted out of the box. "Help!"

He was screaming for someone, anyone, to free him from the casket. His throat burned from the strain of yelling. He was drenched in sweat; his eyes stung; his clothes were constrictive. If he could have, he'd have ripped them off. He kept yelling for help, his calls increasingly laced with the warble of a man panicked and on the verge of a breakdown.

Just when he thought he might explode from the claustrophobia, he heard a noise. It was another voice.

It was Reggie. It sounded like Reggie. It was probably Reggie. Hopefully it was Reggie.

Please be Reggie, Rick thought.

"Rick?" he called. "I hear you down there. Hang on."

"Reggie?" he croaked hoarsely.

"Yeah, it's me. I'm coming for you. I think you're two or three boxes down."

"Kenny okay?"

"Yeah," Reggie said. "He's fine. He's standing up top. The women are good too."

Rick sighed with relief. Still, anxiety coursed through his body like an army of fire ants. His skin itched; his eyes burned; his throat ached.

He tried breathing in through his nose, out through his mouth. He was mimicking what he remembered from the Lamaze classes he and Karen had taken together when she was pregnant with Kenny.

Karen. He still couldn't reconcile her death. The woman who'd given herself unconditionally to him, only to suffer his infidelities and his diminishing interest in her love. He deserved to be buried alive, to die alone in the dark, thinking of her. She'd deserved so much better.

"Bang on the box, Rick," said Reggie. "I think I'm almost there."

Rick used the backs of his fists to pound on the underside of the lid. "You hear me?" he called out against the scratchy pain in his throat.

"Yep," said Reggie. "One more box."

Rick could hear him now. A loud scraping dragged across the outside of the lid. Reggie grunted and cursed, struggling to move the last of the boxes from atop Rick's would-be tomb. At last, a crack of dim, orange-hued light peeked from one side of the box.

Unable to wait for Reggie to lift the top, Rick asked him to move and he used his knees to bump the lid from its grooved resting place. It took three tries, but he dislodged it and the cool rush of outside air filled the box.

His eyes adjusted to the light and Rick saw Reggie standing above him, offering him a hand. Rick reached up and pulled himself out of the box with Reggie's help.

Rick ran his hand through his sweat-soaked hair. "Thanks. I panicked. I thought...I don't know what I thought."

"I'm not gonna lie," said Reggie, "you're down here. I had to move three coffins to get to you. We were all in the other hole."

Rick stepped out of his coffin and, standing on one next to his, he replaced the lid on his box. "Everybody's out?"

"Yeah," said Reggie, shoving one of the boxes back into place. "All accounted for."

Rick climbed over two boxes and stepped on a third to reach the edge of the hole. He reached up and grabbed the soft ground, pulling himself up and out of the hole. Then he reached down into the grave and helped Reggie to the surface.

He brushed the dirt from his shirt and pants and found Kenny standing on the other side of the graves, closest to the cluster of trees where they'd hidden hours earlier. Rick smiled at his son. It wasn't until he reached the trees that he realized Mumphrey wasn't there and that his son was crying. The women were crying too.

He spun around and looked at Reggie. "Where's Mumphrey?"

Reggie looked past Rick at the others, then bowed his head. "He didn't make it."

A thick lump swelled in Rick's already pained throat. "What do you mean? Where is he?"

Reggie nodded toward the graves. "He's in his casket. He must have passed while we were waiting."

Rick moved past Reggie to the edge of the twin holes. "Which one?" he asked without turning back. When nobody answered, he asked more forcefully. "Which. One?"

"Top box," he said. "Hole on the right. Next to Karen."

Rick spun around. "What?"

"Karen's body is there too. We accidentally found her. We were looking for you."

The sour taste of bile rose in Rick's throat. His stomach turned. His vision blurred and he dropped to his knees. It was too much.

"Dad?" Kenny said timidly. His hand touched Rick's shoulder. "You okay?"

Rick sank onto his heels. He dug his hands into the dirt, grabbing handfuls of it. He nodded, but he couldn't muster the words to reassure his son he was, indeed, okay.

"I said goodbye to her," Kenny said. "I said a prayer. I said one for Mr. Mumphrey too."

Rick reached up toward his own shoulder and put his hand on Kenny's. His son was so strong, stronger than he'd thought.

"You're a good son," Rick whispered through the choke in his throat. "Such a good son. Your mom loved you more than anything."

Kenny let go of his father and moved to his side. He squatted beside him and leaned on him. "I know. She loved you too."

Rick couldn't hold back the tears anymore. They streamed from his eyes, mixing with the sweat that still dripped from his brow. His body shuddered and he looked at his son.

"I loved her too," he managed.

"I don't mean to be a jerk," said Reggie, standing behind them at the edge of the graves, "but we should get going. If they're looking this way, they could probably see us. It's still an hour until dark."

Rick puffed his cheeks and exhaled loudly. He nodded. "You're right," he said. "There'll be time for mourning later. Plenty of time."

Kenny stood and offered his dad a hand. Rick took it and wrapped his arm around his son's shoulder. Together they led the somber group into the woods and relative freedom.

Once they'd cleared the trees and were farther south of the camp, they traveled east away from the setting sun. Nobody spoke as they walked. For Rick it was a silent eulogy for Mumphrey. The man he'd only known a week was as close a friend he had in this new world. They'd survived a fringe cult, criminal truckers, fake highway troopers, violent gas station attendants, and an assault on their new home. Now he was gone.

He'd taken the beating meant for someone else. Mumphrey hadn't decided to fight the power, hadn't carried a gun. He'd benevolently accompanied anyone who would have him join their party, a lonely man looking for acceptance and companionship. It wasn't his fault Gus had resisted with violence.

Rick had so many questions he'd never thought to ask as he trudged toward the ATV he and Kenny had left at Williamson County Gin.

What had happened to Mumphrey's family? Why had he lost his home? What was his vocation? Where was he born? How old was he? Rick hadn't bothered to find out those things and now it was too late. Memories of the old man's smile, his funny walk, and his familiar, repetitive language flashed in Rick's mind.

He thought Mumphrey might be better off in the ground. He'd gotten the better end of the deal. They were only a week into an apocalyptic series of events and society was already in a shambles, accelerated unnecessarily by a government intent on killing off people it believed were superfluous. Things would only get more difficult as the days and weeks became months and years. Mumphrey wouldn't have to worry about any of it. He was at peace.

"Rest well, friend," Rick mumbled as they turned north.

"What?" asked Kenny.

Rick looked over at his son. "Nothing," he said. "I was just thinking about Mumphrey."

"He was a nice man," said Kenny. "He made me laugh."

"He was funny, wasn't he?"

"Like I said," Kenny said, effecting his best Mumphrey impersonation, "he made me laugh."

Rick laughed. "Very funny."

"How close are we?" asked Candace. She was limping. "My blisters are asking."

Rick spun on his heel and walked backwards as he answered Candace. She and Lana were walking together, with Reggie bringing up the rear.

"A couple more blocks," said Rick. "Then we're at the ATV. From there, I can hop on and hurry back to the truck, or we can all walk to the truck."

"I'm good with waiting for you while you get the truck," said Candace.

"Why did you leave them in different places?" asked Reggie.

"Safety precaution," Rick answered. "We figured it was better to have more options. Leaving the ATV in a different place gave us flexibility. Just in case."

Reggie nodded. "Makes sense. By the way, Rick, I have to hand it to you."

"What?"

"That whole coffin thing was pretty brilliant," Reggie admitted. "I had my doubts, but it worked. I honestly thought we were stuck in that place. Thank you."

"No problem," Rick said. "I had my doubts too."

"You could have left us there. You didn't have to come back for us. You barely know us."

Rick shook his head. "I couldn't leave you. I have enough trouble living with myself. If I'd let you stay in the camp, it'd be even worse."

"You know, this whole thing is like an alternate universe," said Reggie. "The government imprisoning citizens and imposing martial law is straight out of a bad movie."

"I remember reading this book," said Rick. "It was called *The Perseid Collapse* by a guy named Konkoly. I don't want to give it away, but the power went out and society collapsed fast. Things got violent. I read the reviews on Amazon. I remember some people said the bad stuff happened too fast, that there was no way everything would go to hell in a handbasket within days. I thought they were wrong then. I *know* they're wrong now."

Reggie lowered his voice and turned his head toward Rick. "I overheard a couple of the soldiers talking about population control," he said. "One of them was saying he'd heard the whole idea of the camps was to induce the accelerated spread of disease. He said the faster people died off, the faster they could go to some underground bunker for protection."

Rick swallowed. It hurt to talk. "Bunker?" he asked. "Where?"

"I don't know; he didn't say. I wasn't supposed to hear any of it."

"I'll tell you what," Rick said, "I'm quickly learning that truth is stranger than fiction. If that Konkoly wrote a story like what's really happening now, nobody would believe it."

"I still don't believe it," said Reggie.

"I think we turn right here," Kenny called back to his dad.

"You're correct," said Rick. "One more block and we're there."

Five minutes later they were in the parking lot for Williamson County Gin and Rick and Kenny were on the ATV, heading for the truck. They promised the others they'd be back within ten to fifteen minutes.

The air had dipped from cool to cold. The chill was aggravated by the ATV's speed as Rick powered toward the truck. Soon enough, they'd be back at Gus's ranch. They'd be safe. They'd have food and water. And if they set up their security the right way, the group would be good to go for the long haul. At least those were the thoughts filling Rick's head until Nikki interrupted them.

Nikki.

Rick actively tried to push her from his mind, but she kept sneaking back inside. He still missed her. He'd promised her they'd be together again. That meant that as much as Rick would have preferred for Gus's ranch to be his final destination, he knew that likely wasn't the case. Sooner or later, and probably sooner rather than later, he'd have to go get her. Then, and only then, would he be good for the long haul.

CHAPTER 19

Clayton's shoulders were on fire. His fingers were cramped, his thighs thick with exhaustion. He shouldered sweat from his brow and pulled himself another rung higher. The higher he climbed, the more he could see his surroundings. The only available light was from what must have been a skylight at the surface.

"You still with me?" asked Bert. The Australian security expert was leading the trio up the narrow pit ladder that ran the length of the elevator's mechanical access shaft. Clayton was two rungs below Bert's feet. Chandra trailed them both.

"I'm hanging in there," said Clayton. "This would be a lot easier in microgravity."

Clayton tightened his hold on the rungs and looked down between the ladder and his body. Chandra was struggling.

"My hands are too sweaty," said Chandra. "They keep slipping."

"Use your arms," said Clayton. "Use the crook of your arms to give your hands a break. Loop them around the outside of the ladder like this."

Clayton demonstrated the move, letting go with one hand and wrapping his arm around the side rail. He shifted his weight to compensate for the maneuver and tucked his chin to watch Chandra imitate him.

"That helps," Chandra puffed. "Thanks."

Clayton looked skyward. Bert was moving steadily higher. To Clayton, he seemed indefatigable with no apparent dip in energy or pace. They'd started climbing ten minutes ago and had to be getting close to the top level. "How much more do we have to go?" Clayton asked. He was embarrassed by the question, asking it like a bored seven-year-old in the back of a station wagon on a road trip.

"A couple of minutes," Bert called down. "We passed level two just now."

There were stencils on the walls, indicating the relevant level. Clayton had noticed the marking for floors four and three. He'd missed two. That was good. As bad as Chandra looked, Clayton was certain he felt worse. In addition to the pulsing ache in his injured leg and the ambient headache that remained from dehydration, his lower back was sparking with jolts of pain. If he stopped to think about all of the things he'd put his body through since the power went out on the ISS, he'd collapse. It was too much to consider. It was better to focus on pushing through the various discomforts of the moment and power through to the top of the ladder, he figured.

He unlooped his arm from the side rail and reached for the next rung, pushing himself up using his good leg and then pulling with his opposite arm. Push with his leg; pull with his arm. Push. Pull. Push. Pull.

"There's no machine room at the top," said Bert, talking over his shoulder to the two men below him. "It's got an integrated machine plate structure at the top of this space."

Clayton climbed another narrow rung. "What does that mean for us?"

"It means the controller, the mechanism that actually controls the lift, has its own space off to the side of the access shaft," Bert said. "There's a door up there to the right. It'll give us entry into the controller space. There's a door on the other side of the space. That's how we get out of here."

Clayton held his position on the pit ladder and leaned back. Ten feet above Bert on a wall to the left of the ladder, there was a metal panel. It looked like an electrical access, but large enough to climb through. He drew himself flat against the ladder and restarted the climb. Push. Pull. Push. Pull.

Bert drew even with the panel and called down, "It's just a bit out of my reach. I'm gonna have to slide off here a bit and try to catch the latch."

Clayton kept moving until he was two rungs from Bert's feet. He looked through his armpit to the darkness below. Chandra was eight or ten rungs beneath him.

"C'mon, Vihaan," Clayton urged. "You're almost there. A few more and you've got it." He turned his head to look back toward Bert's progress when he caught a dark flash in his peripheral vision and felt a heavy slap against the side of his face. Stunned and dizzied, he lost his grip, slipping before falling from the ladder.

For Clayton it happened in slow motion, each instant drawn out as if he were watching the end of his life frame by frame. He didn't scream or grunt or call for help. He fell silently for that moment. Vihaan gasped. Bert yelled his name. Clayton considered the irony of gravity being his cause of death. His body fell to the left, twisting nearly perpendicular to the ladder until his right ankle hooked at the joint between the side rail and a rung. The side of his face and right shoulder scraped against the adjacent concrete wall of the shaft, slowing his fall long enough for him to instinctively reach out and grab for something, anything.

He was barely past perpendicular when his right hand caught and held a rounded conduit fixed to the wall. He reached with his left and planted it firmly on the concrete to brace himself. He was stuck for the moment, but he couldn't hold the position long. His shoulders couldn't support him for more than a minute. His sweaty hands were slipping.

"It was my boot. Hang on!" screamed Bert. "I'm coming down."

Clayton closed his eyes. He couldn't stare into the darkness, into the danger that threatened to kill him. It was the blackness of space without the beauty or endless possibilities. He twitched when he felt a hand around the ankle caught on the ladder.

"I'm right below you," said Chandra. "I've got this leg. Can you swing the other up and toward me?"

"No," Clayton said, his face half-pressed against the wall. If he shifted his weight at all, he was convinced he'd fall. He was teetering. He was screwed.

"What can I do?" asked Chandra, his voice echoing off the walls. "I've got your ankle, your leg. What do I do?"

Clayton had no advice. He couldn't engineer his way out of this. He couldn't do anything but acutely sense his hands losing their hold, the skin rippling against the concrete as they infinitesimally inched lower and lower. A muscle in the side of his neck seized. Sweat dripped into his shuttered eyes. His groin ached from the awkward split of his legs. He grunted and tried to firm his position but was stuck. Another hand gripped the back of his leg.

"Move lower, Vihaan," said Bert. "I've got his leg. Lower yourself."

There was a clanging behind him, the sound of Chandra clambering lower on the ladder and Bert repositioning himself. Clayton tried to count the number of times he'd been this close to death in the last week. He couldn't remember the number.

"All right, Clayton," said Bert, "I've got one leg. I've got it pretty tight here. I'm going to need you to push yourself free of the wall when I say so."

"That's not gonna work," Clayton said. "I'm too heavy. My momentum will be too much. You'll lose your grip."

"When you let go," said Bert, "your other leg will fall toward me. The rest of your body will run right into Vihaan. We'll catch you."

Vihaan's voice was barbed with fear. "Wait, what? He'll knock all of us off the ladder. The ladder is too small."

"This is the only way," said Bert. "We don't have time to think of something safer. If we all fall, we all fall."

Clayton started to argue, but a wave of calm washed over him. He was okay with falling. He couldn't ask two more people to risk their lives for his. He opened his eyes, staring into the beckoning blackness below.

"You can't do that," he said, the anxiety having left his voice. "Leave me. Let go. Get out of here. Don't risk yourself for me."

One, or both, of the men responded. Clayton wasn't listening. He was saying goodbye to Jackie, to Marie, to Chris. He was apologizing, thanking them, asking for forgiveness. He was praying for their safety in a new, uneven world.

While Bert and Chandra argued, Clayton took a deep breath. He pressed his fingertips onto the wall, released his hold on the conduit, and pushed himself free.

He kept his eyes open and watched the blackness rush toward him. He could feel the sudden breeze chill the sweat on his face as he swung downward. His heart leapt and he lost his breath. This was it. He was dying, offering himself to the heavens in exchange for the safety of two others.

And then he wasn't.

"Mother—" Bert grunted as he let go of one of Clayton's legs and grabbed onto the other, pulling it to his chest.

Clayton's momentum swung wildly in the instant before he crashed into Chandra. Chandra huffed and cried out from the impact but managed to hold onto Clayton's torso. The scientist slipped to one side, but held his balance, and the astronaut's journey came to a halting end.

"Sheesh," said Chandra. "You could have given us a warning."

Clayton's body was upside down, his back to the ladder. He reached to his side and grabbed a side rail with one hand. His other was wrapped around Chandra's torso. The blood rushed to his head and his temples throbbed.

"Hang on," said Bert. "I'm pulling you up. Relax your legs."

Taking Bert's direction, Clayton relaxed. His body surged upward and he clung to Chandra. There was pressure on the front of one foot and then the other. There was weight on his injured leg he hadn't previously felt.

Bert was huffing. "I've got your feet hooked under a rung," he said through heavy breaths. "I'm leaning on your legs. Can you do a sit-up?"

A sit-up? Clayton thought to himself. *What a weird question.*

He looked to his right. Chandra was holding him with one hand and the ladder's side rail with the other. One of his legs was wrapped around the rail and tucked underneath a rung.

"Can you do a sit-up?" Bert repeated. "If you can, with Chandra's help we can get you upright."

Clayton got it. "Yes," he said. With every ounce of energy left in his body, he tightened his abdomen, flexed his neck and lower back, and heaved himself free of Chandra's grasp.

Straining, he willed himself up and forward. He stretched his arms as far as he could, his fingers tensing until they found the rough metal of the rung even with Bert's shoulder. Bent in half, he held himself upright until Bert let go and maneuvered along the outside of the side rail to a position several rungs higher.

He carefully wiggled his feet free of the rungs and lowered them. Chandra clung to the edge of the ladder, giving Clayton enough space to center himself.

Bert sucked in a deep breath and exhaled loudly. "I don't know what you were doing there, but you almost killed all of us."

"I was trying to save you," Clayton responded. "I didn't want you to save me."

Bert smirked. "That wasn't going to happen." He climbed the remaining distance to where he'd been before Clayton's fall.

Clayton inched upward deliberately, moving hand by hand and foot by foot. There was a fiery stinging sensation along the right side of his face to go along with the other aches and pains. He couldn't account for all of the injuries he'd sustained. There were too many.

He stopped a rung short of where he'd been when Bert's boot had smacked him. He tightened his hold on the ladder and waited while the Australian stretched himself to open the access panel to the control space.

Bert shimmied to the edge of the ladder and somehow bridged the distance to the wall. He pulled himself inside the control space and then poked his head out. He waved his hand, motioning Clayton and Chandra to the top of the ladder.

"C'mon up," he said. "I'll help you across."

Clayton finished his climb and, with Bert's help, crossed from the edge of the ladder into the opening. Chandra followed him. The three of them were crowded in the dark space for no more than ten seconds when the lights came back on and blue light cast a dim glow in the six-by-six room.

"Where's your pad?" Chandra asked, still struggling to catch his breath. "Turn off the system. Hurry."

Bert reached around to his back to find his pad then searched the floor. His eyes widened. "I…I must have dropped it."

Clayton offered Bert his DiaTab, which had somehow not fallen from his back pocket. "Can you shut off the system with mine?"

Bert shook his head.

Chandra wiped his forehead and rubbed his hands on his shirt. "So they can see us?"

"No," Bert replied, "not at the moment. When we leave this space, they could see us. There are cameras in the supply room and the garage."

"Supply room?" Clayton asked. "I don't remember seeing a supply room on the schematics."

"It's technically part of the garage," said Bert. "They added it after they finished the electronic mapping."

Chandra tugged at his collar. "So what do we do?"

"We make a run for it," said Clayton. "There's nothing else we *can* do."

The men agreed and Bert led them out the opposite side of the controller space and into a corner of the garage. Colder air met Clayton as he emerged, sending a chill along his spine. He shivered.

"This is the garage?" he asked.

"It is," said Bert. "Stay here for a moment. We're out of their view in this spot. Once we leave, there are multiple wall- and ceiling-mounted cameras. This is a critical spot for them."

"So what's the plan?" asked Clayton.

"My suggestion is that we cross the garage to the supply room. They've got uniforms, jackets, helmets, that sort of thing. We can suit up and blend in."

"Good idea," said Chandra. "Then we run out of here?"

"We drive out of here," Clayton corrected.

"Oh, okay," said Chandra. "I guess that makes sense."

"Let's go," said Bert. "No time like the present."

The three men, sticking close to one another, scurried from the corner of the garage, crossing a wide, shiny expanse to the opposite side of the garage. They skirted past a half-dozen large military vehicles that looked similar to Humvees, but angrier. They had higher profiles, appeared larger than Humvees, and looked more like sleek tanks.

They crossed the space and found the secured door for the supply room. Bert closed his eyes and mumbled to himself. Then he slid open a wall-mounted keypad beside the door and punched in a series of numbers. The panel turned green and the door clicked open.

"Yes!" said Bert, holding open the door for Clayton and Chandra. "I was hoping I'd remember the code. I wasn't certain."

"Good thing," said Clayton. He smiled at Bert and then took in his surroundings. They were in what looked like a large military-themed walk-in closet. There were racks of hanging jackets, shelves full of uniforms and boots, all of it arranged by style and size.

"Get shopping," said Bert. "We need to hurry."

The men hurriedly disrobed and found the proper-sized clothing. The digital camouflage would help them blend in with both the outdoor surroundings and the people holding them hostage. It might, as Bert had suggested, make escaping a little less daunting. The only distinguishing absence on the uniforms was a lack of rank and name tapes. But with the field jackets on, hardly anyone would notice.

Clayton finished lacing his desert combat boots. Chandra was adjusting his pants. Bert was zipping up a field jacket. None of the men said anything as they readied themselves for the final leg of their escape mission.

"Once we're in one of those JLTVs out there," said Clayton,

"how do we open the bay door?"

Chandra tugged on the bottom of his shirt. "JLTV?"

"Joint Light Tactical Vehicle," said Clayton. "Replaced the unarmored Humvee a couple of years ago. Rode around in one during training for the ISS mission. It looked like all of the trucks out there were JLTVs."

Bert moved to the door. "Yeah, they are. There are pressure plates in the floor. When the truck moves forward, the plate activates and the bay door opens."

"That's it?" asked Clayton. "No additional security?"

"We didn't exactly consider the possibility someone would get into the garage unseen and steal a vehicle."

"All right then," said Clayton. "Let's go. The longer we stand here, the more time we give them to find us."

Bert grabbed the door handle, swung it inward, and motioned with his head. Clayton took a deep breath and led Chandra into the garage. Running as fast as he could, he skidded to a stop at the first JLTV he reached. He grabbed the handle of the passenger's side, pulled it, and climbed into the cab.

The cab was spacious with two tan fabric command seats set far apart. Clayton scooted across the passenger's side, squeezing between the seat and a large flat-panel display, and plopped into the driver's seat.

Chandra was right behind him. He ducked into a rear seat behind Clayton. Bert jumped in the front passenger's seat and slammed the door shut behind him.

The keys were already in the ignition. Clayton turned them to the start position then pressed the large START/STOP button to the right of the steering wheel. The engine coughed and rumbled to life. The gauges on the dash glowed. The battery and fuel gauges indicated they were full. Another light told him the gas pressure system had the vehicle in the low position and the tire management gauge showed the pressure was set to high.

Clayton's eyes danced across the different indicators and settled back on the fuel gauge. "We've got a problem," he said. "We're going to need more fuel than what's in the tank. And this is a diesel hybrid."

Chandra leaned forward between the two seats. "What do we do?"

"Get fuel," said Bert. "There are large diesel tanks on the edge of the property. They've got gravity pumps there."

"All right," said Clayton, shifting the vehicle into gear, "get me there."

He depressed the accelerator and the beast of a truck lurched forward. He pulled to within a couple of feet of the bay door. A circular green light on a post near the door flashed several times before becoming solid. A loud hum echoed in the garage and the door laboriously lifted.

Clayton reached above his head and pulled down a headset. "Put these on. If I remember correctly, this thing gets loud."

With his headset on, the ambient noise was deeply muted, as if he were underwater. He adjusted the cups around his ears and tapped the mic close to his mouth. The garage door was open enough to move past it. Clayton shifted gears, took his foot off the brake, and accelerated into the daylight. Blinded by the brightness of the sun off the white concrete, he couldn't see where he was headed at first. His eyes adjusted and he swung the wheel to the right, accelerating as fast as he could away from the bunker.

"Look," said Chandra, "the airport. We must have walked a pretty good distance."

Clayton glanced to his right. The airport was a couple of hundred yards from them. The paved surface ended and the truck bounced onto the frozen dirt. The ride, however, was smooth. The JLTV was designed with four independent wheels that each absorbed the shock of uneven terrain. Clayton pressed the accelerator and shifted into a higher gear.

"How fast will this go?" asked Chandra.

"I don't know," said Clayton. "We're going to find out."

Bert's voice filled Clayton's headset. "I don't get it. They're not coming after us."

"Could be they don't know we're gone," said Chandra. "Maybe

your trick with the Li-Fi worked."

"No way," said Bert. "There are too many alarms blaring right now."

Chandra leaned forward, his voice pitched with worry. "Do we have time to stop for gas?"

"We don't have a choice," said Bert. "We need extra fuel. The only place we know we can get it is here. They've got containers too. It's our only option."

The speedometer told Clayton he was traveling at seventy miles per hour. Not bad considering the size and weight of the truck. Ahead and to his left, peeking over a sloping grassy hill, was a collection of high-rise cylinders.

"Those the tanks?" Clayton asked.

Bert jabbed his finger toward the tanks, his head on a swivel. "Yes."

The JLTV rambled across the open field toward the miniature tank farm. Clayton kept his foot pressed hard on the accelerator as he hit what amounted to a mogul. The large wheels absorbed the shock, the truck whined, and it powered ahead.

"C'mon," urged Bert. "Get there, get there."

Clayton side-eyed the Aussie. "I'm going as fast as I can."

Clayton maneuvered to the left onto a dirt road that led to the tanks. He looked straight ahead at the large white structures. There were six of them rising into the sky, silver, unpainted pumper trucks reflecting the sunlight.

"Isn't all of this jet fuel?" Clayton asked as they drew closer. "This isn't going to work."

"Not all of it," said Bert. "Two of those tanks are diesel. They connect to twenty-eight miles of pipe that crisscross the property. The diesel can power the bunkers and the vehicles."

"Won't they run out?" asked Chandra. "I mean, depending on diesel? Once it's gone, it's gone."

"No," Bert replied. "There are collapsible solar arrays all over the place. They provide the primary source of power. Remember, everything down there is hydro-cooled and the lights are low-power

LEDs. Even the communication system is powered through solar. It's seriously efficient. The security grid is beyond state of the art. It's bleeding-edge technology. Each of those tanks holds nearly three million gallons of diesel," said Bert. "As a backup, it's more than enough."

Clayton cleared a rise and saw the dirt road ended at a chain-link fence that surrounded the perimeter of the tank farm. He looked over at Bert, who nodded. Clayton pressed the accelerator to the floorboard and wrapped his fingers tightly around the steering wheel. Without slowing down, he powered the truck through the fence, driving through it as if it weren't there at all, and then decelerated to a roll.

"Look for the tanks that are labeled 1-3-0," said Bert. "It's the low-sulphur highway diesel. The jet fuel will be 1-2-0."

They searched the tanks until Chandra pointed out a diesel tank at the far end of the farm. They navigated the narrow drive to the tank. Clayton kept the engine running.

"You said they had containers?" he asked. "Where are they?"

"Right next to the tanks in little sheds," said Bert. "We had to test the key panels on the sheds."

The men hopped out of the JLTV. Clayton's boots crunched on the gravel as he moved around the front of the monster of a truck. The front tire came up to his waist.

Bert had already unlocked the door and dragged out one of the large plastic fuel containers when Clayton reached the shed. Chandra emerged with a second.

"This thing has a range of three hundred miles if I remember correctly," said Clayton. "We're going to need enough to fill up at least twice."

Bert dragged another yellow five-gallon jerry can from the shed. "What's the capacity?"

"Hang on." Clayton found a fueling port and checked the stenciling on the truck. "There are two tanks. Each is about twenty-two gallons."

"Four-four divided by five…" said Bert.

"Eight point eight," said Chandra. "We'll need nine tanks."

"Are there nine in there?"

Bert ducked back into the shed. He carried out two empty cans and set them on the gravel. Clayton picked them up and carried them a short distance to a gravity pump adjacent to the large white tank. It looked almost exactly like the one he and Steve Kremer had used in Canada. He drew the pump handle, opened a valve on its side, the cap on the yellow jerry can, and started pumping the diesel.

Bert marched over to Clayton with a can in each hand and one under each arm. "This is going to take forever. We don't have forever."

"What do you want to do?" asked Clayton. "We can't leave without enough diesel."

"We can't leave if they stop us," said Bert. "I'm going to the other diesel tank. That'll double our pace."

Bert walked across the gravel to a pump catty-corner to the one from which Clayton was drawing diesel. He uncapped a can and started the gravity pump.

They'd both filled three cans each, with Chandra running the full cans from the pumps to the back of the JLTV, when the distant rumble of an engine and a cloud of dust caught Clayton's attention.

"Bert!" he called, pointing toward the dust.

Bert craned his neck. His eyes widened and he bit his lip. "We're done!" he yelled. "Let's go with what we've got!"

Clayton stopped the pump and capped the can. He reached the back of the JLTV and heaved the can next to the others.

"Somebody's coming," Clayton said at Chandra's look of concern. "We've gotta go."

Bert shoved his last can into the back, shut the rear door, and hustled into the passenger's seat. He then climbed back to the turret position between the rear seats and where they'd stored the diesel. Clayton shifted into gear, yanked the wheel, and sped toward the exit they'd created on their way onto the tank farm.

Parked outside the mess of warped chain-link fence and concertina wire was a pair of matching JLTVs. There was a woman standing in front of them. Her arms were folded across her chest. Her strawberry blond hair blew across her face. A uniformed guard stood beside her, an M4 pulled tight to his shoulder and leveled at her head.

Clayton slammed on the brake and the truck slid to a stop. Chandra poked his head between the seats. "Sally?"

"You know her?" asked Clayton.

"Yeah," said Chandra. Without saying anything else, he slid to the front passenger seat and exited the truck. He walked to the front of the JLTV, keeping his distance from Sally and the man threatening to kill her.

Clayton kept the engine running but set the emergency brake and hopped from his seat onto the gravel. He stepped around a fragment of chain link and stood in front of the open driver's door.

"Are you okay?" Chandra asked. "Did they hurt you?"

Sally swiped her hair from her eyes, revealing a bruised cheek and a cut under one eye. "I'm fine," she said. "But you need to come back."

"I don't understand," said Chandra. "What happened?"

Sally looked at her feet and rubbed the backs of her arms with her hands. "I…I didn't want to tell them what I knew, what you told me about leaving."

Chandra took a tentative step forward, reaching out for her. "I'm so sorry. I didn't—"

"We need you to step away from the vehicle," came a voice over a loudspeaker mounted to one of the JLTVs. "All three of you. Otherwise, things will get uncomfortable for all of you."

Clayton peered through the darkened windshield of the JLTV to Sally's left. It was Chip Treadgold.

"Vihaan," said Treadgold, his voice hollow over the electronic amplification, "I can't tell you how disappointed I am in you. I trusted you."

"Chip?" asked Chandra.

The passenger door swung open and Treadgold emerged. He stepped confidently toward the front of the vehicle, pointing his finger at Clayton. "And you, spaceman. You couldn't leave well enough alone, accept your destiny. You had to push and pull and create a problem for everyone. That's not the NASA way, is it? Asking too many questions? Disagreeing with authority? I think the good folks at Mission Control would be so disappointed in you if they knew."

Clayton's fists tightened. He glared at the New World Order-crat.

"I'm going to need all of you on your knees, hands behind your heads," said Treadgold. "I can't have you leaving here and letting people know how—"

The explosive percussion that interrupted Treadgold's Goldfinger-esque diatribe knocked everyone to the ground. Clayton's ears were ringing with a tone so loud he couldn't think. He tasted dirt in his mouth and felt it under his fingernails as he grabbed at the earth.

He rolled over onto his back and tried focusing when another pair of rapid blasts roared through his body. His world was blurred, the ringing was so deafening, but he could see the spin of a semicircle chain-feeder and the flash of muzzle fire from atop his JLTV. Bert was behind the thirty-millimeter cannon mounted on the truck, his hands gripping either side.

Clayton grabbed at his ears as his vision focused and he rolled back onto his stomach. A third shot from the tank-eating weapon tore over his head. He dragged himself forward, shakily drawing himself to his feet. He surveyed the apocalyptic scene in front of him, straggling toward Chandra, who was still on the ground. Sally was on her side, rolling around in apparent agony next to the M4.

There was no sign of Treadgold or the man who had his gun pointed at her. A red mist hung in the air, a darker splatter coating the open door of the truck. Its windshield was shattered, as was that of the mangled vehicle next to it.

Clayton staggered toward the opposing trucks. Both of them were awash with carnage. Either glass, shrapnel, or the thirty-millimeter hog of a round had obliterated all signs of life. He walked back toward Sally and Chandra, using the JLTVs to balance himself. He reached the spot where Treadgold had stood moments earlier. The ringing was still the only sensation of which he was aware until he felt a hand on his shoulder and jerked around ready to attack.

It was Bert. He had headphones around his neck and was saying something. Clayton tried to read his lips but couldn't.

"I can't hear you!" Clayton yelled. "I can't hear. The ringing. I'm deaf."

Bert nodded. He mouthed, "It. Will. Be. Okay." He pointed over Clayton's shoulder. "All dead. All dead."

Clayton dropped to his knees, covering his ears. More people had died so he could live. Ill-intended or not, people had died.

Bert squatted in front of him. "We need to go," he mouthed and pointed back at the truck. "Let's go."

With Bert's help, Clayton made it back to the JLTV. He sat in the front passenger seat. Chandra and Sally climbed into the back. All of them were dazed and obviously wounded from Bert's heroics.

Bert jumped behind the wheel, sped from the airport, and headed south.

Chapter 20

Rick watched his son from a distance. Kenny was standing alone where Karen had died at Gus's ranch. He'd been there for ten minutes. As far as Rick could tell, the boy hadn't moved. He was blankly staring at the ground, at the dark smudge that marked the spot.

The others were in the main house, cleaning themselves and getting resettled. Rick had parked the truck and ATV inside the garage. He was leaning against the door, his hands stuffed into his pockets. The painful swell crept back into his throat. He swallowed against the knot and took a deep breath. He needed to say something.

Crossing the short distance between the garage and the eastern edge of the main house, flashes of Karen's bloody death flickered in his mind. He could hear her final rattling breath, see the life drain from her sad, frightened eyes. Rick knew without anyone having to tell him he'd always live with the guilt of her death. He would shoulder the burden of what he'd done during her life.

"Kenny," Rick said, nearing his son, "you okay?"

Kenny's arms hung from slumped shoulders, his head down. It was only when Rick reached him that he noticed his son's swollen eyes and the tears that drained from them. His nose was running. The collar of his shirt was soaked, and the boy's chest fluttered as he cried quietly in place.

Rick stepped to his son and put his arm around his shoulder. Kenny flinched, stiffened, and shrugged off the embrace. Rick withdrew his arm and uncomfortably tucked his hand back into his pocket. He stood silently, waiting for Kenny to say something. It was several minutes before he did.

"I want to blame you," Kenny said, his voice raspy with phlegm. "I want it to be somebody's fault."

Rick didn't respond.

"You always think of yourself, Dad. You're selfish. Mom wasn't selfish. She always thought of everyone else."

"You're right," Rick said. "On both counts."

Kenny looked up from the ground and at his father. He blinked and sniffed. His nose crinkled and he wiped snot from his upper lip with the back of his hand. Rick started to reach out again, but Kenny stepped back.

"When you and Mom got divorced, I went to see somebody."

"I know," said Rick. "Your mom said it helped."

Kenny shrugged. "She talked about the five stages of grief. You know, the way you feel after something bad happens and how it changes over time."

"Yes."

"The first part is denial," said Kenny, "where you don't want to believe it's true. When you got divorced, I didn't believe it. I kept thinking you and Mom would get back together and we'd be a family again."

The aching knot in Rick's throat swelled.

"When that didn't happen, I got mad," said Kenny. "That's the second stage. Anger."

Rick swallowed past the ache. He withdrew his hands from his pockets and folded his arms across his chest.

"There are a whole bunch of stages after that," said Kenny, pulling his shoulders back and standing up straight. "It ends with acceptance. Finally, you just get okay with bad stuff. It doesn't make it better. You just live with it."

Rick realized in that moment he'd never asked Kenny about his feelings regarding the divorce, about his leaving them. He'd told Kenny it wasn't his fault, explained that he loved Kenny and he loved Karen, but it was better for everyone if they weren't married anymore. He'd even admitted he was to blame and that Karen had every right to be mad. He'd assured Kenny his mother was a good woman and he'd never said a bad word about her. But not once, as Rick thought back to the conversations they'd had as father and son, had he ever spent the time to listen to Kenny's feelings.

"Mom has been dead for a few hours," Kenny said flatly. "It doesn't seem real. Like, I expect to hear her voice and see her face. That's the denial part. It's the first phase. I've spent all day in the denial phase, acting like everything's okay. I mean, as okay as it can be."

Rick thought Kenny somehow seemed older. The way he stood, the words he used. He didn't sound like a little kid anymore. He was more like a young man.

"But I'm already at the anger phase too, Dad," he said, his eyes glaring. "I want to hit something or someone. I don't have a mom anymore. My mom is dead. The person who loved me most in the world is gone. I'm angry at you for that. I blame you. I don't want to blame you, but I do."

"I understand, son," said Rick. "I really do. You—"

Kenny's face curled with a sudden swell of anger. "I don't care whether you understand," he barked. "I'm going to feel how I want to feel whether you get it or not. You left me because you wanted to. You had a choice. Mom didn't have a choice. She didn't want to leave."

Rick's chin quivered. His eyes welled. He bit down on the inside of his cheek, trying to suppress his emotions. He took shallow breaths in and out of his nose, trying to calm himself. Kenny stepped toward him, his fists balled and shaking at his sides.

"I'm stuck with you now," he said. "And you're stuck with me. That would be okay, except I know you want to be with that Nikki woman. You want to go get her. I know you do."

Rick couldn't deny the thought had crossed his mind. He did miss Nikki. He did want to see her, hold her again. He needed her comfort. His son had him pegged.

"You're right," Rick said. "I do want to see her."

Kenny's eyes widened. His brow arched with surprise, his mouth hung open, and he blinked. Rick knew he'd caught his son off balance with honesty. As quickly as Kenny's guard was down, it returned. His jaw set.

"I knew it," he snarled. "I knew—"

"I'm not going anywhere, Kenny," Rick stated. "I'm not leaving."

Kenny huffed. "Why? Because you feel guilty? Because I'm mad at you and you know you're selfish and that everything I said was right?"

"Maybe that's part of it," Rick admitted. "But I'm not going for two other reasons."

"Yeah?"

"I love you. You're all I've got too. You're my son. You'll always be my son. I'll always be your dad, and my job is to protect you, to keep you safe. Plus, I owe it to your mom."

Kenny's features softened. His fists relaxed and he knuckled the tears from the corners of his eyes. "You're not going. Really?"

"Really," said Rick. "I'm staying here."

Kenny nodded. "I'm still blaming you," he said. "It's going to be a long time until I get to the acceptance stage. You staying here doesn't change that."

"I'll be here when you get there," said Rick. "And I know it doesn't help right now, but I blame myself too. I know I'm responsible for a lot of the bad in your mom's life. Remember though, Kenny, I am also responsible for the best thing that ever happened to her."

Kenny rolled his eyes.

"Are you hungry?" Rick asked. "There's food in the house. Later, if you want, we could have a service for your mom, say some prayers."

"Pray?"

"It never hurts."

Kenny started toward the house. "Okay."

Rick resisted the urge to put his arm around his son as they climbed the steps onto the front porch. He held the door open and Kenny walked inside. Rick watched the boy stride through the long hall to the kitchen. Kenny's shoulders were broader than he remembered, his walk somehow more purposeful, more confident. Rick took solace in that little victory. Kenny was maturing into a sensitive, articulate young man who could express himself without fear. Rick knew it was more than he could say for himself at that age or at thirty. Maybe in the midst of all he'd done wrong, he'd done Kenny right.

"I was wondering when you'd join us," said Reggie Buck. He was seated at the large farm table with his wife and Candace. They were eating peanut butter sandwiches. "Can I make you something to eat?"

Rick moved to the table and sat in an empty chair. "No, I'm not real hungry at the moment. I'm sure Kenny would like a sandwich."

Kenny was at the sink, elbow deep in a bag of white bread. "Is there jelly?"

"Marmalade," said Candace. "It's in the refrigerator."

"The fridge still works?" asked Rick. "They didn't shut it off?"

Reggie shook his head, his cheeks bulging with sandwich. "No, it's working. Pretty lucky."

"Luck is a funny word right now," said Lana. "Doesn't hold the same meaning it did a week ago."

"We should count every blessing," said Candace. "That's for sure."

"Thanks again for coming to get us," said Reggie. "You don't even know us and you risked a lot."

Rick nodded. "Sure thing. I'd like to think you'd have done the same."

"I wish I could say I would," said Reggie. "If I'm honest with myself, I don't know that I would. What you did was pretty selfless, Rick."

Kenny slid out the chair next to Rick and plopped a plated

sandwich on the table. It was cut diagonally, the way Karen used to do it, peanut butter and orange marmalade oozing from between the pieces of bread. Kenny gave Rick a glance and then stuffed most of one half of the sandwich in his mouth.

Reggie raised a glass of water to Rick but addressed Kenny. "I say we all toast your dad, Kenny. He was our hero today."

Rick tried to wave him off. "That's okay."

"Don't be shy about it," said Reggie. He lifted his glass higher. Candace and Lana did the same.

"I don't have a glass," Kenny said with a mouthful of sandwich. He stuffed another bite into his mouth without having finished the first and wiped his hands on his pants.

"Okay then," Reggie said, "you can toast him in spirit. Here's to Rick, a selfless hero who risked his life to save ours."

Rick blushed and lowered his head. He felt Kenny's eyes' burning intensity and couldn't look his son's way. He looked over at Reggie and forced a smile.

"Thanks," he said. "That's unnecessary, though. I think if anything, we should be toasting Kenny. He's a brave kid. He did everything I did and he's a third my age."

The group cheered Kenny. Rick still couldn't look at him.

Reggie's smile evaporated and his brow furrowed. "We are so sorry about Mumphrey. And your mother, Kenny. And your cousin, Candace."

"Thank you," said Candace.

Kenny shoved another bite of sandwich into his mouth. The room grew uncomfortably quiet until Lana cleared her throat and switched the topic.

"It's good you came when you did," said Lana. "If you'd waited much longer, I don't think you'd have made it."

"Why is that?" asked Rick.

"Security," said Lana. "We heard they're not letting anybody through their roadblocks except for military trucks. That starts tonight."

"And they're adding more of them," said Reggie. "Plus, no

weapons get through. If people show up at checkpoints, they're taking their weapons and making them give up their cars."

"They're offering them refuge," said Lana. "But they're actually taking them to camps like the one they took us to."

Rick leaned on his elbows. "How do you know this?"

"We overheard it," said Candace. "They called this phase three."

"Phase three?"

"Yeah," said Reggie after swallowing the last of his water. "Phase one was setting up the camps and the checkpoints. Phase two was rounding people up, actively seeking out people they deemed as long-term threats. Phase three is letting the people come to them."

"I don't get it," said Rick. "You'd think they'd be helping people, not imprisoning them."

"It's all about population control," said Lana.

"I heard that too," said Rick. "Still…"

"Makes sense to me," said Reggie. "Some natural disaster happens, you use it to advance some dark agenda. It's happened before."

Rick scoffed. "When?"

"9/11," said Reggie. "Our government used 9/11 to go to war, to implement the Patriot Act."

"You're saying 9/11 was an inside job?"

"No, of course not. I'm saying it was an opportunity for our government to have a willing populace. Same here. It's just more sinister."

"Sorry," said Rick. "I refuse to believe this whole New World Order conspiracy theory. It's too much. It's like you've been reading too many Steven Konkoly novels."

Reggie shrugged. "The facts are what the facts are, Rick. We're trapped here. We go anywhere and they're snatching us up, putting us in a camp, and waiting for us to die. They'll stick us in pine boxes and dump us in mass graves. All of those are facts."

Rick pushed himself from the table, his chair legs squealing on the linoleum floor as he slid backward. He walked to the other side of the kitchen. He didn't want to believe what they were telling him. He didn't want to face the facts. Yet Reggie was right; they were what they were.

He paused at the refrigerator and gripped the handle. Instead of opening it, he marched from the kitchen, down the hallway, and pushed his way out onto the front porch. His boots clunked on the wooden porch, the thin-framed storm door slapped shut, and the railing creaked when he leaned on it.

Rick had always been good at ignoring the truth, at refusing to swallow the difficulty life always seem to slop onto his plate. He grabbed the porch railing with his fingers and rocked back and forth, as if trying to pry the railing free. He couldn't ignore it this time. This wasn't something as temporary as an affair or lying to his wife about his whereabouts. It wasn't as minimal as promising to call a hookup and then deleting her number from his phone or intentionally giving a woman the number to Carrabba's Italian Grill instead of his own. This was permanent.

The storm door creaked behind him and Kenny slinked onto the porch. He held the door to close it gently and joined his father at the railing. He leaned on the rough-hewn cedar, mimicking his dad, and looked out onto the property, admiring the peaceful beauty of it.

"You were going to tell me about Eli Whitney," he said.

"What?"

"When we were at the gin, you said to remind you about Eli Whitney. I'm reminding you."

Rick smiled and faced his son. Kenny was getting taller. The top of the boy's head was even with his nose now. It wouldn't be long before the kid was taller than him.

"Well, for starters, he was your age when he began making nails in his father's workshop," Rick said. "He was a young entrepreneur."

"What did his dad do?"

"For a living?"

"Yeah."

"He was a farmer, I think."

"And his mom?"

"She—" Rick paused "—she died when he was ten or eleven. So

it was Eli and his dad for a while."

"How'd she die?"

"I don't remember," said Rick. "I do remember Eli went on to become a pretty amazing inventor."

"The cotton gin?"

"Yes," said Rick. "He went to school, traveled, worked on farms. He figured out what a pain it was to separate the cotton fiber from the seeds. It was a lot of manual labor. So he invented a machine that would do it."

Kenny leaned on the railing with his elbows. "Did he get rich?"

"He made some money from it, but other people copied it. He tried to sue them, but didn't have a lot of success. So he tried something else."

"What was that? The strawberry gin?"

Rick chuckled. "Clever. Can you imagine trying to pull all the seeds from a strawberry? If you could build a machine that would do that, you'd make a million dollars."

Kenny held up his index finger and thumb, a small gap between them. "That would be impossible, right? Dozens of those tiny seeds for every strawberry."

Rick laughed. He and Kenny smiled at each other for a brief moment before they again gazed out onto the property.

Kenny sighed. "You think we'll ever eat strawberries again?"

"Good question," Rick said. "I guess if we found some seeds, we could try it in Gus's garden. I'll have to check his garage. There's some gardening stuff in there."

Kenny ran his hand through his mop of hair. "What was the other invention?"

"Muskets," Rick replied. "He invented a machine that made musket parts, so he sort of invented mass production too. He was a smart guy."

Kenny stood there quietly for a few minutes, as did Rick. A cool breeze swirled across the porch and Rick shivered. It was getting later in what had been a ridiculously long day. It felt like a month. Rick scanned the property from the garden on the left, the chicken coop beyond it, to the greenhouse, and the row of pecan trees directly in front of the house. This was home now. For the foreseeable future, this place—with its five bedrooms, well water, and natural gas generator—was their home.

The longer he stood still, the heavier his legs became. They were cementing themselves in place, exhausted from the rigors of the past twenty-four hours. If he stood there any longer, he'd spend the night standing against the railing. He shifted his weight and looked at Kenny.

Without thinking about it, Rick put his hands on his son's shoulders and pulled him into his chest. He clung to Kenny with the fingers of one hand laced amongst the weighty strands of hair on his head and the other hand square in the middle of the boy's back. He held Kenny tightly, holding him close.

Kenny didn't resist. He lowered his head and wrapped his arms around his father. He didn't say anything, but Rick could feel his son's heart beating and his gentle sobs.

Rick worked to keep his composure. Perhaps Kenny was willing to reach that final stage of mourning, even if it would take the foreseeable future.

The foreseeable future.

In this world, Rick thought that term was oxymoronic. Kenny tightened his hold on Rick, spreading his fingers wide and gripping the fabric of his father's shirt. Behind them, the storm door creaked open and hit the siding with a vibrating crack.

"Sorry," Reggie said sheepishly, "I didn't mean to interrupt. I'll come back."

Rick patted his son on the back and pulled away. He kept his arm around Kenny's shoulder and faced Reggie. "No, it's okay. We're wrapping up here."

Reggie looked at Rick and then averted his eyes, clearly uncomfortable with the moment. "Sorry," he repeated. "It's—"

Kenny sniffled. "It's okay, Mr. Buck," he said, his words thick from the fluid in his nose. "I know there are things to do before it gets dark."

Reggie shuffled one of his feet. "True. We need to secure the fencing by the road and hide the entrance. The less it looks like anyone is here, the better."

"I don't disagree," said Rick. "We have a lot to do. If what you say is true, about the different phases of this operation, they'll leave us alone for a bit. That gives us time to prepare for the next time they come."

Reggie raised his eyes. "You're okay to help with the fence?"

"Sure thing," said Rick, "as long as Kenny can help us too."

Reggie grinned. "Of course. If we're gonna live here as a family, we all have to do our parts. The women are checking the stock of food, making sure the generator's working, and testing the well."

"Sounds good," said Rick. He followed Reggie and Kenny down the porch steps into the yard. There was a lot to do and, contrary to what he'd said aloud, there was no telling how much time they had to get it done.

Rick didn't have time to feel sorry for himself, to lament his ill deeds. He needed to be practical and clearheaded. Survival was the priority now. What might come next was far more important than what had already happened.

CHAPTER 21

WEDNESDAY, JANUARY 29, 2020, 4:45 PM CST
CLEAR LAKE, TEXAS

The faint odor of smoke hit Jackie first. That was what told her she was home. It was like the lingering scent of a bonfire clinging to a sweater in the hamper. It wasn't unpleasant or acrid. It was just there.

Jackie had rounded the corner onto her street, her heart fluttering with anticipation. It was replaced almost immediately with a sagging disappointment. Clayton wasn't home.

Not that she truly expected it, but there was that hope to which she'd been clinging that, for a moment, convinced her he'd be standing in the driveway with his arms open wide. They'd embrace in a Jane Austen-esque reunion.

Not to be. At least not yet, she told herself.

Although she'd only been away from her house for a day, it felt much longer than that. She trudged the final yards along her cul-de-sac, her eyes fixed on her property. The broken front windows, which they'd covered, were again exposed to the elements. The front door was open. Some of her clothing, including an expensive bathrobe Clayton had purchased for her at a Moscow hotel, was strewn on the hibernating St. Augustine lawn.

"That didn't take long," said Nikki. "Somebody watched us leave and then broke in."

Jackie sighed as she stepped onto the driveway and trudged up its gentle incline. "So much for Mr. Salt."

"How's that?" asked Nikki.

"He gave me hope in mankind," said Jackie. "Remember?"

Nikki nodded. She pulled the Glock from the small of her back. "We should make sure there aren't any squatters. Might be best if you wait outside."

Jackie huffed and drew her Glock from her waistband. "Please, woman. I can handle myself."

Chris rubbed his thumbs along his pack straps. He was stopped at the intersection of the driveway and the narrow cement walkway that led to the front porch, his back to the house.

"What about us, Mom? You want us to come inside too? Or you want us to wait outside while you and Deep Six Nikki put a sleeper hold on whoever's in the house?"

Marie, who'd pulled her pack from her shoulders and was sitting on a large landscaping stone that framed a flower bed near the driveway, huffed. "Or you could put three bullets in him. That works too."

Jackie gasped. "Marie! Apologize to Nikki. That was rude."

Marie rolled her eyes. "Sorry."

"It's fine," Nikki said. "I get it."

"It's not fine," said Jackie.

"Mom!" Chris pressed with a hint of a whine. "What do you want us to do?"

Jackie hesitated. The violence of the afternoon still raw, she wasn't sure her children should be out of her grasp, let alone her sight. Nikki was right though. Who knew what awaited them inside the house?

"Stay out here," said Jackie. "Keep your sister company."

Jackie shrugged her pack to the ground and gripped the Glock with both hands. She followed Nikki into the house, leaving the front door open when they entered the foyer.

"I should have invited Salt to come here for a day or two," Jackie whispered. "It would've been smart to have a man around."

Nikki raised an eyebrow. "That hurts."

"You know what I mean," Jackie whispered.

Nikki smirked. "I do. That's why it hurts."

The women moved through the foyer toward the kitchen. The refrigerator was open and empty. Only the foul smell of what food had been in there remained. It wasn't overwhelming, but it did force both women to crinkle their noses and hold their breath. Jackie closed both doors and Nikki checked the pantry.

It too was empty except for two bottles of olive oil and a jar of Mateo's Hatch Chile Salsa. A roll of paper towels was unraveled on the floor. Nikki kicked it and it rolled into the corner underneath the bottom shelf.

"They got everything," Nikki said. "It's bare."

Jackie took a deep breath. "Let's check the garage."

The women moved through the laundry room and into the garage. It was dark inside, the only light the dim ambient daylight filtering through from the kitchen. Jackie reached into the side of her pack and pulled out a small LED flashlight. She punched on the lamp and scanned the garage.

The car was still there, though its doors and trunk were open. Not a good sign, but she panned left toward the freezer then maneuvered her way toward it. Once there she propped open the lid and shone the light inside.

"Fudge."

Standing at the threshold and keeping watch, Nikki chuckled. "Fudge?"

Jackie sighed. "That's the mom in me. I worked hard to stop cussing once I had the kids. Now I can't seem to find the filth, even when it's called for."

"I'm guessing fudge means the freezer is just like the pantry."

"I'm afraid so. Only empty plastic ice bags left." She slapped the freezer shut and used the light to find her way around the clutter and back to the laundry room.

"So we've got the food in our packs and nothing else," said Nikki.

"Awesome. Now I'm extra glad we didn't bring along Salt. He would have eaten too much."

They walked back to the kitchen. "We never should have left," said Jackie. "That was a huge mistake. If we'd stayed, we'd still have our food. We'd have more people to defend ourselves, more weapons. I acted rashly and emotionally. I can't do that. Not now."

"You did what you thought was best," said Nikki. "Don't beat yourself up."

Jackie was looking across the room and up toward the catwalk that connected one half of the second-floor living space to the other.

"Jack—"

Jackie put her finger to her lips. "Shhhh."

Nikki's eyes narrowed and she followed Jackie's eyes upstairs. She shrugged and shook her head.

Jackie pointed to her ear and then upstairs. Nikki closed her eyes until a rustling noise drew her attention upstairs toward the media room.

There was someone in the house.

Jackie's pulse pounded against her neck and chest. Sweat bloomed on the back of her neck. She was momentarily frozen in place.

Nikki nudged Jackie and the two of them moved toward the stairs. Jackie looked back toward the front door as she passed it. The kids were sitting next to one another outside. Marie had her head on Chris's shoulder. They were oblivious to what was happening inside the house. That was good.

Jackie stopped Nikki at the bottom step. She pointed to herself and then up the stairs before leading Nikki toward the second floor. Both women had their hands on their Glocks.

Cautiously, Jackie climbed the stairs one step at a time. She moved upward quietly, careful to cushion each step in the carpet, inching higher until she reached the top step. She pressed her back against the wall and waited for Nikki to move beside her one step below.

When she reached the second floor, she could tell the media room was well lit. Whoever had invaded her home must have raised the blackout shades that typically covered the windows and kept out any external light.

She tried listening for the noise again, but her pulse was thumping in her ears. She licked her dry lips, her tongue dragging along the cracks, and exhaled. She looked down at the carpet in front of her. It was soiled with a dark amorphous stain of dried blood.

The noise repeated itself. It was a rattling sound. Somebody was definitely in the room. Jackie sucked in a deep breath and nodded at Nikki, then bounded toward the media room, the weapon leveled at what she imagined would be center mass for anyone who confronted her.

Nikki was right behind her as she entered the room, both women quickly positioning themselves at either side of the wide door. Jackie scanned the room with the weapon, her hands trembling. The space was empty.

Jackie spun around. Nikki did too. They were alone in the room. Then Nikki thumped Jackie on the shoulder and pointed at the window.

An open window was pulled unevenly and one edge was sliding against the frame and sill. As the slight breeze blew into the room, the shade moved with it and created the rattling sound.

Jackie lowered her weapon and crossed the room to the sectional pressed against the back wall of the room. She leaned on the cushion and fixed the curtain.

Nikki chuckled. "That was intense."

Jackie pushed herself from the cushion. She was about to respond when, from the corner of her eye, she saw a flash of movement. She turned to see a woman jump onto Nikki's back, grabbing for the Glock. Nikki tumbled forward into the room, the feral woman still on her back.

Jackie immediately leveled her handgun at the woman's back but, worried her shot might go through the target and hit Nikki, she tossed her gun onto the sectional. She leapt on top of the woman, grabbing clumps of her long greasy hair and trying to pull her from Nikki.

The woman screamed and cursed and let go of Nikki. She reached behind her, grabbing Jackie's wrist. In a deft move, she leveraged her weight and spun onto Jackie. A waft of sour chicken soup accompanied the woman as Jackie fell onto her back and the crazed attacker pressed against her, managing to get one hand on Jackie's throat. She squeezed.

Jackie's airway constricted and she gagged. The woman's sunken eyes were wild. Her face was gaunt. There were bleeding scabs on her cheeks and around her whitish lips. Her broad, flared nose was red at its tip. She cackled and mumbled unintelligibly as she pushed harder onto Jackie, who flailed, trying to pull the woman's hand from her throat.

Jackie was trying to muster another burst of strength when the pressure around her neck released. She opened her eyes and saw Nikki grabbing the woman from behind.

She had one arm around the woman's neck, her elbow pointing directly at Jackie. With the other arm, she applied pressure to the back of the woman's head with her hand. As Jackie rolled away from the woman and out from underneath her weight, Nikki dragged her back and lowered herself to the floor behind the attacker.

She wrapped her legs around the struggling, bug-eyed woman, putting her insteps on the inside of the woman's thighs. She extended one of her arms over the woman's neck and toward her chest and reached the other under her arm. Nikki's face reddened and strained as she clasped her hands over the woman's heaving chest. The woman tried kicking and grabbing. She was ineffective. The woman's throat was in the crook of Nikki's elbow and her wild eyes struggled to focus as the noose tightened.

With her free hand, Nikki grabbed the bicep of her choking arm. Maintaining her leverage, she leaned back and flexed her choking arm repeatedly. Her sinewy muscles strained and relaxed, tightened and loosened.

The woman's eyes fluttered and rolled back in her head before she went limp. She was out.

Nikki slugged the woman to one side and rolled away from her. She pushed on the carpet with her fists and stood up with the help of the sectional's wide arm. She cursed the woman on the floor and kicked at her with her boot.

"Meth head," she said and crossed the room, extending a hand to Jackie. "Crazy drug addict."

Jackie took Nikki's help and pulled herself to her feet. "You okay?"

"I was going to ask you that," Nikki said. She tugged on her shirt and pulled up her pants. "That woman was in beast mode."

Jackie ran her hand through her hair and exhaled. "I was going to shoot her, but I thought I might miss and hit you."

"You did the right thing," Nikki stated firmly. "No need to have Marie and Chris come running in here if they heard the shot. That would've only made things worse."

"What do we do with her?"

"From experience," said Nikki, "we've got less than five minutes and she'll be crazed again. We need to tie her up."

"And get her out of the house," said Jackie. "I've got some bungees in my pack."

"You go get them and I'll keep watch. If I need to, I'll knock her out again."

Jackie moved to the door and stopped. She motioned toward the unconscious meth addict on the floor. "Was that the shutdown thingy?"

Nikki smirked. "Yes. The shutoff valve."

"I gotta say," said Jackie, "that was kinda badass."

Nikki's smirk blossomed into a cheeky smile. "Thanks. Now go get the bungees. She won't be out long, and she stinks like skunk in a blue cheese factory."

Five minutes later they had the woman bound and at the bottom of the stairs. She was struggling against them, calling them foul names, and arguing about her condition. When they reached the front door, Marie appeared on the porch.

Her jaw dropped. "What is that?"

"A meth head," said Nikki, huffing as she dragged the woman by her underarms. "Give us room."

Marie stepped to the side. "What are you going to do with her?"

"I don't know," said Jackie. "We haven't figured that out exactly."

Marie leaned on the brick wall adjacent to the door. "You gonna shoot her?"

Nikki dropped the woman into the grass. She squirmed, her muted calls dampened by the duct tape Nikki had strapped across her meth-addled face.

Nikki planted her hands on her hips. "If I was going to shoot her, I would have already."

Jackie stepped toward the woman, keeping enough distance to avoid getting hit by her barefooted donkey kicks. Chris joined her and she put her hand on the boy's head while she watched the creature in front of her writhe in agony. The drugs had clearly aged the woman, digging deep lines into her forehead and around her eyes. Her hair was stringy and greasy, verging on the appearance of mange. Veins popped in her arms and hands against skin the color of a manila folder. The drugs had robbed her of her youth. To glance at her, Jackie might have figured her for fifty years old or older. However, her eyes betrayed that notion. She was probably in her twenties or early thirties.

"I've got an idea," Jackie said. Nikki and Marie joined her, looking at the dung beetle of a human struggling to right herself onto her legs. "It's up to you whether or not you live or die," Jackie said.

The woman stopped struggling and lay there in the grass. She nodded. Her body trembled and her chest surged up and down as she tried to calm herself. Her pupils were dilated. Chances were the woman was still high on methamphetamines.

"All right," Jackie said, "we're going to let you go."

"Wait," said Nikki, "I'm not good with that."

"Me neither," said Marie. "I'm with Deep Six Shooter."

Nikki scowled at Marie. "Not funny."

"Listen to me," said Jackie. "We're going to let this woman go. And she is going to run as fast as she can away from this house and this neighborhood. If she doesn't, she faces more than getting choked unconscious."

Chris's eyes widened with excitement. "You did the shutoff valve?"

Nikki shrugged.

"Ooh," said Chris. "Wish I'd seen that."

The woman on the ground was nodding her head, as if she was agreeing to the conditions. She was trying to talk.

"I don't think that's a good idea," said Nikki. "She'll come back. She'll attack us when we aren't looking."

The woman on the ground shook her head vigorously, greasy strands of hair slapping her face.

"We don't have another option," said Jackie. "We can't keep her here. We can't kill her."

Marie huffed. "We couldn't, but Annie Get Your Gun could."

Nikki finally snapped. "I saved your life, Marie. I didn't *want* to kill him. I didn't have time to think through a list of nonlethal options."

Marie rolled her eyes and walked away, into the house, shutting the door behind her with an angry bang.

Nikki turned back and caught Jackie's stare. She looked at the ground. "Sorry, she's your daughter. I shouldn't have talked to her like that."

"We have more important things on our plate right now. Are you good with this?"

Nikki looked down at the druggie and sighed. "Yeah, I guess."

"All right then," said Jackie. "I'm going to take the tape off your mouth and the binds from your legs. Then you're going to run. You'll have to figure out how to untie your hands."

Nikki bent down over the woman. "Let me get the tape." With a single instantaneous rip, she tore the wide strip of silver tape from the woman's face.

The woman squealed and gritted what was left of her yellow teeth. She cursed and shook her head wildly. The tape left a red streak across her face and took with it the scabs on her cheeks and around her lips. Specks of blood bloomed across her face.

"That felt good," Nikki said. She stepped back while Jackie worked the bungee around the woman's thighs and ankles.

Once Jackie was finished, the woman sat up and scooted back across the grass. She struggled to find her balance and rolled onto her side.

Jackie pulled out her Glock and aimed it at the woman. The empathy was gone from her voice. "You can go now. Don't come back here. If you do, I'll kill you."

The woman grumbled something, inched her way into the mulch, and used a rotting tree stump to right herself. She stood and stared blankly at Jackie for a moment, cackled, and ran toward the driveway. Jackie kept the gun trained on her until she disappeared down the cul-de-sac and her squealing laughter was no longer audible.

"What now?" asked Chris.

"We shore up the house, block the windows and doors, and make this place a home again," Jackie replied. "Everybody sleeps in my room."

The three of them stepped toward the door as Marie swung it open. The moody teenager stood at the threshold. "Mom, have you been in your bedroom?"

"No," said Jackie, walking into the house. "Why?"

Marie stepped back and then led her mother toward the master bedroom. "You have to see it. I can't really explain it."

Jackie quickened her steps across the travertine to her bedroom. She gasped when she saw it and then nearly retched at the overwhelming stench.

The room looked as if wild animals had ravaged it. The mattress was half off the bed. The sheets were piled on the floor. The television was pulled from the wall and hanging by a couple of cords. One of the walls was smeared with a wide brown streak.

"It smells like an abandoned port-a-potty in the middle of the jungle," said Marie, the back of her hand covering her nose. "And that's not fair to jungle port-a-potties."

Jackie pulled her shirt up over her nose and tried breathing through her mouth, surveying the damage. Next to the bed on the floor was a syringe and a wad of tinfoil. There were prescription bottles strewn across the room.

"We haven't even been gone two days," Jackie said in disbelief. She wandered into the bathroom, watching her step. She opened the door to the toilet and immediately closed it. Bile stung her throat and she tried to keep from vomiting.

The water she'd left in the bathtub was a murky greenish color and there was a thin film dotting the surface. It resembled pond scum. She pushed past the bathroom and into her master closet. She reached into her pack and pulled out the light. She thumbed it on, expecting the worst. At least there was some good news there.

Piled into a corner of the closet, partially obscured by clothing, was much of the food missing from the pantry. There was also some of the freezer meat, still packed in sealed plastic bags. It was likely no good, but at least now they had days more supplies of canned and boxed goods. If the gas was still working, she could boil water from the pool and cook with that.

Jackie called to the others, who reluctantly joined her in the closet. Each of them grabbed handfuls of what they could and carried it back to the kitchen. It took three trips.

Standing at the kitchen island, Jackie wiped her sweaty forehead with the back of her hand. She leaned on the granite, letting its cool seep into her palms.

"What do we do about the bedroom, Mom?" Marie asked.

Jackie shrugged. "We let your father deal with it when he gets home. Chris, go close the bedroom door. We'll have to find somewhere to sleep."

"I'll get to work on the windows and doors," Nikki said. "Once I'm finished, we should be okay for a while."

"For a while," Jackie said with a hint of sarcasm. "For a while."

CHAPTER 22

MISSION ELAPSED TIME
76 DAYS, 03 HOURS, 01 MINUTE, 43 SECONDS
OKLAHOMA PANHANDLE

Through the ringing that resonated like white noise, Clayton could finally hear the hum of the engine above the annoying high-pitched din. Chandra and Sally were asleep in the backseats. As far as he knew, Sally hadn't awoken since Bert's surprise attack.

They'd stopped once to refuel and still had plenty of diesel in the back. The truck had moved at a comfortable clip, easily maneuvering off the highway shoulder to avoid abandoned vehicles. Since the sun had dropped beneath the horizon, Bert had slowed down. They were traveling at forty miles an hour, careful not to move at a speed too fast for the conditions.

Clayton reached up and pulled on his headset, adjusting the mic. "I dozed off for a second. Where are we?"

"Close to Boise City, Oklahoma." Bert replied, thumping a rhythm atop the wheel as he drove. "We're a few hours to Amarillo. I'm hoping to find some food there."

"Yeah," said Clayton, "we didn't think this whole thing through, did we?"

Bert glanced at Clayton, his face aglow from the dashboard instruments. "Not really. No worries though. We'll be fine."

Clayton tugged on the seatbelt shoulder harness and sat up in his seat. Ahead, in the distance, were flashing red lights. He rubbed his eyes and leaned forward, putting his hands on the dash above the flat-panel monitor in front of his seat. The lights were still there, strobing varying degrees of red.

"You see that?" he asked Bert. "Those lights up there?"

"I see them. Guessing it's a checkpoint."

Clayton scratched his head. "In the middle of nowhere?"

"Certainly seems as though everywhere is the middle of nowhere right now."

"Good point," said Clayton. "What are you going to do?"

Bert shrugged. "I'll stop. As far as they know, we're soldiers. We're headed to Amarillo."

"That's good," said Clayton. "Tell them we're headed to Rick Husband Airport. Part of it is a former Air Force base. Say we've got business there."

"All right," said Bert.

"What if they ask for ID?"

"We've got some."

"What?"

Bert cleared his throat. "I took them from the…the bodies of the soldiers at the tank farm. I also took this."

Bert reached under the seat and pulled out a nine-millimeter handgun. He pulled back the slide to chamber a round, then he put the pistol back. He glanced at Clayton.

"There's one strapped under your seat too."

Clayton looked over his shoulder at Sally. She was out. Her mouth was agape, her head leaning against the window, shaking with the vibration of the truck on the highway. He shifted the subject, breaking the uncomfortable silence.

"We should tell them Sally is our prisoner," he said. "She's the reason we're headed to Amarillo. Delivering her there?"

Bert nodded. They were approaching the checkpoint. An armed soldier stood in front of a pair of concrete Jersey barriers that blocked half of the highway. Another set of barriers was set back several feet, creating a serpentine path through the checkpoint.

The soldier raised his hand, palm out, ordering Bert to stop the JLTV. Bert downshifted and set the emergency brake. He rolled down his window and the soldier approached.

"Good evening," said the soldier, both hands on his M4, which was aimed at the ground. "Where are you headed?"

"Amarillo," Bert said. "We have a delivery at the airport."

The soldier peeked into the window, eyeing the cab and all four people inside. He grunted and stepped back. "Where are you coming from?"

"Denver."

"What's the delivery?"

"The drugged woman in the back."

The soldier's stone face twitched. One eyebrow arched higher than the other. He took another step back and surveyed the JLTV's exterior.

He stepped back to the window. "You have transport papers?"

Bert hesitated. He looked at the checkpoint and back at the guard at the window. He dropped his right hand from the wheel, easing to the spot where he'd hidden the pistol.

"We don't need transport papers," said Clayton, his voice laced with false offense. "Are you kidding me, soldier?"

The soldier's eyes widened with surprise and he adjusted his grip on the M4. "Excuse me?"

"We're in a state of emergency," said Clayton. "We've got serious business in Amarillo. Strategic Command needs us there yesterday and you're asking us for papers? What is this? Who is your commanding officer? I need to see someone with authority."

The soldier leaned in, apparently unfazed. "I need to see some identification."

Clayton reached between the seats to the stack of rectangular plastic Army identification cards. He leaned across Bert and offered them to the guard. When the guard reached for them, Clayton pulled them back.

"I need to see yours, soldier."

The guard flashed his badge, holding it in front of Bert for a

220

second, then motioned for Clayton to hand over his. Clayton obliged. The guard thumbed through them, studying each one. He'd given up his situational awareness to check the cards. Clayton reached under his seat, pried the pistol free of its Velcro binding, and silently chambered a round.

Holding the weapon at his side, hidden between his seat and the passenger-side door, he slid his finger inside the trigger guard and felt a slight protrusion that ran along the center of the trigger. It was the embedded trigger safety.

It was a Glock, like he had at home. He'd never used the weapon except for target practice. He didn't want to use it now. He didn't want to open fire on the kid doing his job. He hesitated but slid it back under the seat. Bert, however, had his in his hand. He was apparently ready, again, to do whatever needed doing.

The guard handed back the identifications. "Hard to tell who's who now when you've got beards. But you're good," he said. "Be safe. Thanks for your patience. We're not letting anyone through without cause."

The guard stepped back and raised his arm above his head. He waved his hand in a circle, signaling the other soldiers to let the JLTV pass. Then he motioned for Bert to put the truck in drive.

Bert laid his Glock on the floorboard and accelerated, maneuvering to the right and then left, carefully working the truck through the serpentine barriers. When they moved past the last of them, Bert pressed on the gas and gunned the engine away from the checkpoint.

"That was close." He exhaled. "I was ready for another firefight."

Clayton sank back into his seat, releasing the uncomfortable tension in his neck and shoulders. He tugged on the seatbelt, adjusting it against his chest and hips, watching the headlights illuminate the white lane lines in the center of the highway.

"Speaking of firefight," he said, "what happened back at the tank farm?"

Bert reached down for the Glock and slid it into his strap. "What do you mean?"

"You went all Rambo," said Clayton. "How did you even know how to operate that cannon on top of the truck?"

"It isn't a cannon," Bert said. "It's a thirty-millimeter chain gun."

"A chain gun."

Bert chuckled. "Actually, I guess it is a cannon. I know how to use it because I fired something similar before. I'm former Australian military, Tactical Assault Group. We hunted terrorists. That's where I got my security training."

Clayton was speechless. He'd met plenty of ex and former military. The astronaut corps was riddled with them. Bert had never struck Clayton as military. That wasn't a good or bad thing, it just *was*.

Bert rubbed the week-old beard on his neck. "I haven't had this much hair on my face since Afghanistan."

"I didn't know," Clayton mustered.

"I don't talk about it much. It seems like a long time ago, even longer since the world went to hell."

"I didn't mean to judge," Clayton tried to apologize, "or seem flippant."

"No worries," said Bert. "If I'm honest, it wasn't my finest moment back there. I didn't have anything smaller. That thirty cal was a bit of an overkill. It tore people apart."

Bert stared into the V-shaped path of light ahead of them on the highway. The ex-Special Forces operator chuckled to himself nervously. He wiped his forehead and then ran his hands along the steering wheel. "What about you?" asked Bert. "You're an astronaut, right?"

Clayton's eyes drifted to the horizon and then up to the black sky. The milky red aurora was gone. "I was," he said. "Until I crashed back to Earth."

"What happened up there?"

Clayton sucked in a deep breath and exhaled through puffed cheeks. He shifted in his seat and leaned his elbow against the door. "That's a short question with a really long answer," he replied.

"We've got time," said Bert. "If we're going all the way to Houston, the odometer tells me we have another seven hundred miles at least."

Clayton leaned back and closed his eyes. Seven hundred miles was nothing. It was easy. ten hours under normal driving conditions, not more than fifteen or sixteen hours as things stood. Soon enough he'd be home. He'd start the next chapter of his life, the one where his family was the focus and the center of everything he did. Their survival and happiness would trump his own. He was about to speak when his seat jerked forward and something hit him from behind. There was pressure at his throat, something sharp rubbing against his skin. A voice snarling at his ear threatened to kill him, her hot breath uncomfortable on his neck. Sally was awake.

"Stop the truck," she growled. "Pull over now and stop the truck."

Clayton struggled against the hold, but her leverage was just so that as he moved, she tightened her suffocating wrap and pressed her pocketknife forcefully against his neck. Instead of fighting her, he dropped his hands to his sides, his right one finding the Glock. When he tried to grab it, she jerked him to one side and he lost his grip. He was struggling to breathe. It was all happening so fast.

Bert momentarily took his hand off the wheel in surrender and decelerated quickly. "All right," he said. "I'm pulling over."

The truck slowed and Bert applied the brake, turning the engine off. He was parked straddling the line that separated the shoulder from the slow lane. Clayton tried reaching for the gun, his right arm twisting to reach it. He couldn't find it.

"Leave the keys in the ignition and get out," Sally demanded.

Bert hesitated. He shifted his body to look at her. She kicked the back of his seat with her left foot.

"Get out!" she screamed.

Bert fumbled for the door handle, tumbled out of the truck, and slid clumsily onto the highway. He backed away from the truck, his right hand in front of his face, begging Sally to stay calm. He'd left the door open, the window still down from the checkpoint. When he was clear of the truck, Sally loosened her grip on Clayton.

"You," she said, "spaceman. You get out too." She shoved the back of his head and freed him from her hold.

Clayton fell forward onto the floorboard. He reached up and grabbed the door handle, swung it open, and climbed out onto the shoulder. He stumbled back on the uneven edge of asphalt but kept his balance enough not to fall into the grassy embankment aside the highway.

Less than a minute later, Vihaan tumbled from the truck onto the ground next to Clayton. He was conscious but lethargic, and seemingly confused. He moaned and then called up to Sally. "Where are you going, Sally?" he asked. "What happened? Why are you—"

"Idiots!" Sally spat, and unleashed a profanity-laced diatribe, ending with, "Selfish *idiots*." She hung out the side of the truck, spitting as she yelled. "You think I really befriended you, Vihaan? Really? Me? You? *Please*. My job was to keep you inside and occupied. Spaceman here destroyed that. Now I can't go back. Hell if I'm staying with you. You wanted out. You got it."

Vihaan lay on the ground, seemingly stunned by the nasty revelation. He pulled his hands to his face.

Sally slammed shut the passenger's side door and scrambled to the driver's seat, reaching for the ignition. Her face reddened and her features tightened with anger. "Where are they keys?" she snapped. "Give me the keys!"

Bert reached into his pocket and dangled the keys from his finger. "You didn't think this through, did you? And what's worse, you brought a knife to a gunfight." He pulled his left hand from behind his back, revealing the nine millimeter, and leveled it at her.

The red hue drained from Sally's face. She instantly paled, her eyes bulging with the recognition she'd misplaced her hand.

"Get out of the truck," Bert said. "I don't want to kill a woman, but I have before under far less irritating circumstances."

Sally cursed and spat at Bert, but climbed from the truck. She stood at the open door, her feet planted shoulder-wide in a weak show of defiance.

Chandra struggled to his feet and walked around the front of the truck, leaning on the front grille for support. His balance was clearly off-center. "You were lying the whole time?" he asked. "What about the bruises?"

"Part of the plan," she hissed. "All of it was an act. That moron Treadgold never should have brought you to the bunker. I told him that when he assigned me to you."

Chandra lowered his head and leaned his full weight against the truck. Clayton could see the scientist was processing the data, trying to calculate how he hadn't forecasted this outcome.

Bert waved the gun at Sally. "Move away from the truck. We have places to be."

Sally laughed. "What, you're going to leave me here in the middle of nowhere?"

Bert looked at their surroundings, curling his lip into a sneer. "Yes."

Sally looked back at Chandra and then at Clayton. She ran a hand through her strawberry blond hair and stepped toward the center of the road. She was halfway between Bert and the truck, her eyes darting around, her chin trembling.

"Vihaan, Clayton," said Bert, "you two go ahead and hop back in. I'll be there in a second."

Clayton moved to Chandra and put his hand on the scientist's shoulder. He ushered him around to the passenger's side of the JLTV and helped him into the cab. He reached under the seat and found the Glock, pulled it free of its strap, checked it, and held it in his hand.

Bert pointed in the direction they'd traveled from. "Take fifty steps that way," he said to Sally. "Count out loud. You stop before you get to fifty and I'll kill you."

Sally cursed at all three men and started counting. She moved deliberately north, away from Bert and the truck. When she'd hit twenty-five, Bert crossed the street and climbed back into the truck. He started the engine, released the brake, shifted into gear, and accelerated south.

***

MISSION ELAPSED TIME
76 DAYS, 11 HOURS, 07 MINUTES, 01 SECONDS
BOWIE, TEXAS

Bert eased the truck into a parking space in front of Bowie City Hall. It was early morning and they needed to refuel. It had taken eight hours to travel four hundred miles from Kerrick, Texas, at the Oklahoma border to the small town northwest of Dallas. They'd managed to avoid any additional checkpoints.

"I'll fill it up," said Clayton. He shouldered open his door and jumped to the street. His legs were heavy, his joints stiff from the long, silent overnight ride. Clayton had tried to sleep, but Chandra's whimpers from the backseat had kept him awake.

He eased to the back of the JLTV and opened up the tailgate, pulled a couple of the jerry cans to the ground, then heaved one of them to the fuel access. Bert appeared from the other side of the truck.

"Bowie, Texas," he said, employing his best Southern twang. "Have you ever been here before?"

Clayton plopped the can's spout into the tank. The can vibrated as diesel glugged into the tanks. "No, never have. Though I saw a sign that suggested this is where the world's largest Bowie knife is displayed."

"How large?"

"Twenty feet."

Dust swirled around the men as a soft breeze chilled the air around them. Bert crossed his arms over his chest and tucked his hands under his armpits. He looked at the cream-colored brick building in front of the truck. Its quartet of windows were adorned with metal green awnings, as was the front door. Above it was a green placard embossed with gold lettering. BOWIE CITY HALL.

"You think Vihaan's going to be okay?" he asked.

Clayton shrugged. "I don't know. I don't know if any of us are going to be okay."

Bert frowned. "That's a downer."

"This is a different world, Bert. People have turned into aliens. Their basest instinct seems to rule. We have limited food, little water, and almost no fuel. Once we go through the cans, we're stuck wherever the needle pegs empty."

"You might be right on the people, the food, and the water," Bert smirked, "but we might be just fine on the fuel."

"How so?"

Bert motioned past Clayton. "That truck over there has likely got more diesel in it than we can carry."

Clayton looked over his shoulder and saw a white bobtail fuel truck. Along the side of the truck was black and gold labeling that read "Kelly Propane and Fuel, LLC." On the bottom right of the fuel tank on the back of the truck was a red diamond that warned of flammable diesel fuel on board.

Forty-five minutes later all six of their cans were full. Clayton lugged the last of the jerry cans to the back of the JLTV. He walked to the driver's side and climbed behind the wheel.

"My turn," he said. "You catch some sleep, Bert."

Chandra was already asleep. He was lying awkwardly splayed on the backseats, snoring.

Clayton was driving southeast on State Highway 287. If the road signs were right, it would take him through Fort Worth and Waxahachie. He knew from experience he could find Interstate 45 from Waxahachie. He'd driven through there before on a camping trip to Dinosaur Valley State Park with Chris.

He accelerated, unconsciously pushing the truck faster and faster, willing himself toward home. What had been a week seemed so much farther in the distance. Hours earlier, before Sally had put a knife to his throat, he'd been about to tell Bert what had happened in orbit.

What *had* happened?

He remembered that moment the radio went dead on the ISS and how he'd gripped the sides of the laptop display directly in front of him. The screen had been black. He'd thumped the spacebar with his thumb. He'd hit the power button as if he were trying to score on a video game. Nothing had worked, not even the joystick that controlled the Canadarm2. He'd jockeyed it back and forth and slapped at it out of frustration. Nothing.

In his mind, a movie played as if he were watching it happen to someone else. Boris Voin was stuck, tangled in the tether that connected him to the ISS. Ben Greenwood was floating with his hands up in surrender.

At the time, he'd not seen them move. They had not indicated they were alive. As he drove the JLTV toward Fort Worth, his mind replaying that seminal moment in his life, he could see Boris's gloved hand curl. Ben Greenwood's arms twitched. They'd been alive.

Clayton couldn't be sure that his memory wasn't playing tricks on him. It was possible he was rewriting his own history to justify his ill-advised spacewalk. However, something told him that wasn't the case, that in the confusion of the moment, he hadn't processed their movements. His eyes had missed them, but his subconscious hadn't. That was why he'd felt so compelled to try to rescue them. That was why he'd clung to the belief they might be saved. That was why he'd risked his own life for theirs. It wasn't selfishness, as he'd told himself. It was heroism. It was what any righteous human would do for another.

It might also have been something else that drove him to the gargantuan, futile effort that defied every bit of his training. Clayton didn't want to admit to himself that was it. But it was more plausible than the notion he'd not seen either of his crewmates exhibit signs of life in the seconds after the coronal mass ejection blasted through the ISS.

The "something else" was his twin sister. As a rational adult, he knew that her death hadn't been his fault. As an eighth grader at the time, only fourteen years old, he'd not been rational.

As the ambulance took him from the mangled wreckage of their car, leaving his sister behind, Clayton had wailed. He'd reached for her, called her name, and cried for the medics not to take him.

He and his twin had an unbreakable bond as children. They'd promised each other they would always be together. They would never leave the other behind. They'd promised each other with a blood oath that no matter what happened in their lives, one would always be there to help the other. The oath, the promise, was his idea. She'd eagerly agreed.

When Carrie died in the crash, he'd left her behind. He'd failed to be there to help her. As a fourteen-year-old, he'd carried that weight, knowing he'd not kept his promise. At her funeral, he'd laid a white glove on her small casket and whispered to her so that only her spirit could hear him.

Driving Highway 287, weaving around stalled trucks and cars, zipping past backpack-clad loners hiking and thumbing for rides, Clayton remembered for the first time in years what he'd said to her.

"I'll never leave anyone behind," he'd said, his hand resting on the polished mahogany. *"I'll never break my promise again, and I'll do everything I can to get as close to you in Heaven as I can."*

Clayton's sore throat tightened and his eyes welled. Had he really done all of that? Go to space, attempt to rescue two dead men, and drag their bodies from outer space back to Earth, across a glacier, all because of an adolescent promise he'd made to his dead twin?

In so doing, Clayton had left behind the only people who really mattered. He'd left Jackie, Marie, and Chris to fend for themselves in the worst possible environment. He took a deep, ragged breath, and cleared his mind.

How in the world did I ever pass the psych evaluation?

Bert was asleep in the front passenger's seat, his head bouncing against the headrest as the truck rumbled along the highway. Chandra hadn't moved from his awkward recline.

Clayton checked the fuel gauge and smiled. It wasn't a worry now. In some magical deux ex machina moment, the gods had provided a truck three-quarters full of diesel. Now there was no question they'd reach Clear Lake.

No question at all…

CHAPTER 23

THURSDAY, JANUARY 30, 2020, 6:02 PM CST
CLEAR LAKE, TEXAS

Chris heard the rumble first. He bounded down the stairs and into the kitchen. Jackie was boiling water from the swimming pool in a pot. She had a large handful of uncooked spaghetti noodles in her hand. She looked up from the pot when Chris called her name.

"What is it?" she said. "You seem excited."

"There's somebody coming. Like the Army or something."

Jackie snapped the noodles in half and dumped them into the pot. "How do you know?"

"I heard something loud, like a tank, and went to the back window upstairs," Chris said. "There's some big truck with a gun on it rolling up the main loop."

"I think I heard that too. Where's Nikki?"

"She's upstairs," said Chris. "I think she's reading one of your books."

Jackie wiped her hands on her shirt and edged around the island toward her son. "*Grapes of Wrath*," she said. "I told her it would make our plight seem more palatable. Let's go check on this tank."

She crossed the kitchen to the family room. Before she reached the front door, she drew the Glock from her waistband, pulled the slide, and aimed the weapon at the ground. At the door she stopped.

"Hey, Nikki!" she called upstairs, one hand cupped at her mouth. "C'mon out front. Bring your gun."

Jackie admired Nikki's handiwork at the front windows. They were boarded up with plastic and large pieces of undamaged wood from the fire across the street.

Jackie unlocked the front door, unlatching the new hotel bar she'd installed. She'd taken it from the Bucks' place across the street. They didn't need it.

The sun was low in the sky, offering an orange glow across the neighborhood. The tall pines in her front yard cast long shadows across the driveway. Jackie stood on the front porch, waiting for Nikki.

"What's going on?" said the fighter, stepping outside, her Glock in her hand. "I was just reading about the government-run camp and the plot to stage a riot so they can shut it down."

Jackie nodded toward the main loop. "Hear that rumble?"

"Yeah," said Nikki. "It's getting louder."

The women stepped from the porch onto the driveway. At the end of the cul-de-sac, the front end of a high-rise sand-colored truck eased right and turned onto their street. It was rolling slowly, but the engine whined and whirred in the lower gear.

Jackie tightened her grip on her weapon and stepped closer to the street. Behind her, the front door opened and closed. Chris and Marie were standing on the porch. Although she considered telling them to go inside, something stopped her. She walked out into the street and straight toward the oncoming armored truck. Her deliberate steps quickened and she instinctively started jogging, then running, at the truck as it slowed to a stop halfway down the street. It squealed when the driver set its brakes.

"Jackie," Nikki called, "what are you doing? Jackie!"

Jackie didn't listen. She ran straight for the truck, covering the final feet in a full sprint. She knew. She *knew* her husband was home. It came as no surprise to her when astronaut Clayton Shepard emerged from the right side of the truck and leapt toward her.

Jackie wrapped her arms around a man she almost didn't

recognize and buried her face in his chest. He was rank with odor, his hands calloused and rough on her face and neck. She hadn't even looked him in the eyes, but it was him. Clayton was home.

Both of them sobbed, holding up each other's weight as they embraced. Moments later, two more bodies joined theirs. Chris and Marie bowled into their parents, almost knocking them to the ground. The family stood there in the street for what at once felt like an instant and forever.

"I knew you would come home," Jackie said, pulling her face from Clayton's uniform. "I knew, against every rational bone in my body, that you'd find your way back."

Clayton stared into her eyes and she saw a sadness, a deep pain looking back at her that hadn't been there seventy-seven days earlier. She couldn't imagine, she didn't *want* to imagine, what he'd done to make it home to her. She touched his ragged, spotty beard. His face was pale, his cheekbones more pronounced than she remembered. Jackie stepped back, her arms still around him, and looked at the digital camouflage uniform. She patted his chest and motioned toward the JLTV.

"So you enlisted?" she joked. "Is that what took you so long?"

Clayton hadn't said anything yet. He'd been crying and laughing and holding his family. His chin quivered and he inhaled a shallow breath. "I'm sorry," he said. "I'm so sorry."

Jackie sniffed back her own tears. "You can be sorry later. We need to get you cleaned up. You stink."

When she turned to lead her husband to the house, two other men emerged from the truck. They cautiously stepped forward but kept a comfortable distance. Clayton must have sensed she'd seen them. He turned around.

"This is Bert Martin and Vihaan Chandra," said Clayton. "I wouldn't be here if it weren't for them."

Jackie tucked the gun in her waistband and walked toward the men. She offered her hand. "Thank you," she said, first to Bert and then to Chandra. "Thank you so much. Of course you're welcome in our home. I'm cooking noodles right now."

The men thanked her and followed her back to the house. Jackie stopped when she reached Nikki.

"This is Nikki," said Jackie. "*We* wouldn't be here if it weren't for *her*."

Clayton shook her hand, as did Vihaan. Bert held the grip a beat past comfortable.

"Do I know you?" he asked. "You look familiar."

Nikki glanced at Jackie and then responded, "I get that a lot."

The group walked back into the house, where Jackie guided them upstairs to find clothing and wash clothes they could soak in the bathtubs. She steered Clayton clear of the master bedroom.

He stood on the foot of the stairs, looking at her. She held his hand and rubbed the back of it with her thumb.

"I'd tell you I owe you a trip to St. Lucia," he said. "But we don't have a boat."

"It would probably take more than a boat," she said. "You go clean up and come right back. We have a lot to discuss over dinner."

Clayton gave Jackie another hug before climbing the stairs. He used the handrail to move up one step at a time.

"You're limping," she said.

Clayton looked back at Jackie. "We have a lot to discuss over dinner."

***

Clayton leaned on the granite kitchen island, as he'd done so many times before. It felt different this time. Not only because they were eating by candlelight, or that there were three people who were virtual strangers standing around the island, eating with him, but because his world was irreparably changed.

Chris was noticeably older than the last time he'd seen him. He was taller, his facial structure more mature. The baby fat that had filled his dimpled cheeks was gone.

Marie was more of a woman, the spitting image of her mother. There was a wisdom in her eyes he hadn't seen before. She moved gracefully; the awkwardness of her early teenage years had disappeared.

Jackie was as beautiful as she'd been the day he'd met her, let alone the day he'd left for Star City, Russia, and his trip to the ISS, but there was an edge to her. She was hardened in some intangible way. She'd seen or experienced things that had altered her vision of the world, he was certain. There were things he assumed he didn't want to know, but needed to know.

He'd noticed the burned pile of debris where homes once stood across from his, seen the boarded windows, and the bloodstain on the floor. He was afraid of what he'd find in the forbidden master suite. There was time to learn about all of it.

They were a family again. That was the comforting thing. They were, however, a different family than they'd been before, and there was no going back.

Clayton finished the last of the pasta, sipping the final noodle into his mouth like a straw. Chris laughed at him and he smiled.

"I wish the spaghetti had gone further," said Jackie. "I wasn't expecting company."

"We apologize for the intrusion," said Chandra. "We won't be staying long."

Jackie chuckled. "I was joking. Our house is your house; our food is your food. You brought my husband back to me."

Chandra blushed and looked at his empty plate. "Thank you."

"How much food do we have?" asked Clayton. "I mean, how long can we go with seven people here?"

Jackie shrugged. "A week."

"What about JSC?" asked Clayton. "Could they help?"

"Been there, done that. It's a long story," said Jackie. "Probably not. They'd take us in, but not Nikki or Bert and Chandra. And their accommodations aren't good for the long term. They have food and power, that's about it."

"There's the ranch near Austin," Marie said. "We could go there. I bet Nikki would like to see Rick. We know they're self-sustaining from what Candace said."

Clayton shook his head in confusion. "Who's Candace?" he asked. "And Rick? Rick Walsh? Kenny's dad?"

"Yes," said Jackie. "He was camping with the boys and met Nikki when the power went out. They all made it back here. Nikki stayed with us when Rick took a group of people to a prepper's ranch near Austin."

"Candace's ranch?"

"Her cousin's."

"Who's Candace again?"

Jackie dabbed the corner of her mouth with a paper towel. "She lived in the other cul-de-sac. She came to stay with us when the power went out."

Clayton scratched his beard and ran his hands through his hair. "Where exactly is this place?" he asked. "And we know they've got plenty of food?"

"We don't know anything, really," Nikki answered. "We were told it's got a farm and well water and natural gas power. It's in Coupland, east of Austin."

"And you're Rick's latest—"

"Clayton Shepard!" Jackie gasped.

Nikki smirked. "I'm nobody's anything."

Clayton waved his hands in front of his face. "No, no, I didn't mean it like that."

"Yeah, you did," said Nikki. "It's fine."

"Well," said Clayton, "from the look of the neighborhood and the house, I'm not sure staying here is any more of a viable long-term option than JSC. As much as I want to stay here, I think we're better off trying the ranch."

"It's a risk," said Jackie.

"With all due respect," said Bert, "everything's a risk now. How far is Coupland?"

"Less than two hundred miles," Clayton responded.

Bert shrugged. "We've got enough fuel to get us there. We could all pile into the JLTV out there, though not everyone would have a seatbelt."

"What about checkpoints?" asked Nikki. "At NASA, they talked about the government shutting things down."

"We're in a military vehicle," said Bert. "We've got military uniforms upstairs. We'll be fine. Plus, we avoided most of the checkpoints on the way here. We can figure it out heading to Coupland."

Jackie looked at Clayton. She eased closer to him and nudged him with her hip. "So it looks like you're not done traveling," she said. "You're not home just yet."

"Home is wherever you are," said Clayton.

Marie rolled her eyes. "Give me a break. I missed you, Dad, but I didn't miss your corniness."

"I did," said Jackie. "I missed it."

"I missed a lot," said Clayton. "And I want to hear about it all, good and bad. But let's get to Coupland first."

"We'll leave in the morning," said Bert. "We could be there by midday, nightfall at the latest."

"After what we've done," said Clayton. "That's easy."

***

Clayton stood in the driveway, the faint odor of smoke hanging in the cold air. He inhaled and tightened his grip around Jackie's waist. She stood in front of him, her back pressed against him, and together they looked skyward. She held his wrists with her hands.

"I looked up at the sky every night," she said. "I talked to you. I prayed for you. I cursed you. I searched for you."

Clayton kissed the top of her head and inhaled her scent. He felt her lungs expand and contract with her breaths.

"No matter how far away I knew you were," she said, "I always believed you'd come back to us. It didn't make sense. I'm too smart to think you could navigate whatever it was you had to navigate to get here, but I believed."

"Did you really?"

"I did," she said. "I knew it was you in that truck today. I don't know how, but I could see you in the truck behind the wheel. That's why I ran to you."

Clayton replayed the moment in his mind: her running to him, grabbing him, clinging to him.

She pulled his arms from around her waist and turned to face him. "I never stopped believing," she said. "Never. I knew you wouldn't leave us behind."

Clayton looked into his wife's eyes. She was a good woman, a strong woman. She should have been the astronaut. *She* was the hero. He couldn't tell her there were moments when he thought about giving up. He couldn't admit he'd been ready to fall to his death. He kept telling himself there was plenty of time for that. There'd be time once they reached the ranch. There'd be time days or weeks from now. Or there wouldn't be time. In this nightmarish world, nothing was certain anymore. Everywhere was the middle of nowhere.

Still, they had each other now. He'd somehow bridged the gap between his family and a powerless, floating RV two hundred and forty-nine miles above the planet's surface. He'd crash-landed, fought off wolves, buried friends, stolen a plane, escaped from an underground bunker, and somehow made it back to the woman who believed he would do all of it and come back to her alive.

And he had.

CHECK OUT THE AMAZON INTERNATIONAL BEST SELLING TRAVELER SERIES

ACKNOWLEDGMENTS

Endless thanks to Courtney, Sam, and Luke. Your love and support is empowering. A huge thank you to my editor, Felicia A. Sullivan, who worked on this during an incredibly busy time in her life. I'm grateful. Thanks also to both Pauline Nolet and Patricia Wilson for their proofreading expertise and to Stef McDaid for making the books look out-of-this-world.

And to artist Hristo Kovatliev. You're genius.

Thanks also to Steve Kremer for his insight and expertise. He is a modern day Renaissance man with boundless knowledge.

Thanks also to Mark Bowman for his help with the science of the Soyuz and to former NASA Astronaut and author of The Ordinary Spaceman, Clayton Anderson for his guidance and friendship.

Thanks to my parents, Sanders and Jeanne, my siblings, Penny and Steven, and my mother-in-law, Linda Eaker, for their support. Also, thanks to Jane Daroff, my aunt who has faithfully read all of my books. I think she might know the characters better than I do.

And thanks to the readers who keep enjoying the nonsense I concoct in my brain. I'm indebted.

Made in the USA
Lexington, KY
09 July 2017